I0617692

# candy kisses and Bullet Holes

# Fill Her Up

## Christopher Wright & evan shelley

ROBOROTIQ
R.P.
PUBLISHING
v. 7.2

Lafayette, CA

# CANDY KISSES AND BULLET HOLES FILL HER UP

Copyright © 2010 by Christopher Wright & Evan Shelley
Cover Art & Design © 2010 by Evan Shelley & Christopher Wright
Interior Art © 2010 by Evan Shelley

## ALL RIGHTS RESERVED

This is usually a space for some legal speak about not reprinting stuff, but instead I want to tell you an erotic story. Once upon a time there was an attractive lady who enjoyed sex, and her only turn on was copyright infringement. She constantly had suitors presenting her with bootlegged copies of all the newly released entertainment. And her favorite thing to do was troll the library and lift full chapters from random books so that she could sell them on the street to the local school children. It was hot. Then she went to jail. Which was very sexy. But TRAGEDY! She was shanked with a shiv in the clink. Also she was stabbed. Luckily the medical staff was top notch and they stitched her right up. Her new sexy scar made her even more attractive and everyone wanted to touch her awesome body. One day in the prison yard, with everyone admiring her banging physique, a squirrel came up to her. And it bit off her fucking face because she was a filthy thief. Oh, and she probably died too. So please don't infringe on copyrights. Get the expressed written consent of the copyright holder before reproducing this in any form. Offer the right price and we'll sell out. Hard. It's the American Dream! For more information—or more erotic stories—please contact **Roborotiq@gmail.com**

## Library of Congress Control Number: 2010907994

## ISBN: 978-0-9827930-0-8

## Printed in the United States of America

## This book is a work of fiction

Any resemblance to actual persons or places is, quite frankly, pretty awesome and I'd love to meet/visit those people/places because this book is so fictional it even makes up its own grammatical rules and then breaks them just so people think it's cool. Sadly, the one thing it can't make up is self-esteem.

*This book is dedicated to the following: Superman's cape, bottled and Italian soda, the original Nintendo, hidden treasure that's easy to find, the many times Marty McFly says heavy in Back to the Future, secret passageways, Supercool, never crossing the streams...or maybe crossing them, the green side of Rubik's Cubes, that scene in Transformers when Megan Fox leans over the engine of Bumblebee, and the Monster Squad. Keeping the world safe from monsters since 1987.*

# previously

The world went completely bat-shit insane.

It was awesome.

## Characters you should know:

**Victor** – When the world went crazy so did he. Occasionally he talks to himself out loud without realizing it. (this is what it looks like when he does.) He's trying to work on quitting. Also, he's the narrator so you're stuck with him.

**Emma** – She's Victor's main squeeze. She claimed to be a compulsive liar, but that was probably a lie since she never seems to lie all that much. Also, Emma is not her real name. But Victor calls her that anyway. She doesn't seem to mind.

**Jimmy** – He was a good kid until he died and came back sort of evil. But then he decided to be nice again. He only has half a face due to some unhealthy habits he picked up after death. Also he can build cool shit. He's kind of lame...

### ...NOW LET THE STORY BEGIN!

# Act I, Scene 1

My name is Victor and I'm a slave. (and here we go again.) Don't interrupt! (…)

Now as I was saying, it wasn't always like this.

But then along came a girl.

Emma.

I met her when people's nightmares started to come to life. Or at least that's what I thought was happening. But I was wrong. Dead wrong. In reality, the Triple-verse had begun to bleed into one and I was confronted with two other versions of me. But zero other Emmas. So I burned it all down. Everything seemed perfect for awhile, yet it only solved two things. Jack and shit. And Jack just got jettisoned. (very original.) I'm 100% original, baby. (yeah right.) Groovy!

For the last sixteen weeks I've found myself in a dire circumstance. Lost in space and, um, enslaved. But that's neither here nor there. This ship I'm on, the Adventure Galley they call it, is searching the galaxy for some sort of space whale. I don't know what they call it. (fliperisakiss.) I also don't care.

There's talk of slave death matches at the next port, and most of the slaves are preparing. I'm not. I have a foolproof plan. See I'm going to bide my time. Relax. Wait until the last minute. And then, when it seems like all hope is lost, I'll get rescued by Emma.

It's flawless.

I hear a latch slide behind the walls, unlocking the heavy door to the holding cells on the Adventure Galley. The captain has apparently also decided this place isn't crowded enough with all us slaves so all other space-found booty gets crammed in too.

Green blood oozes from one large fliperisakiss they have freshly killed while roaming the outskirts of mapped spacelane 47. The

7

stench is unbearable. I mean, if you're a pussy. I can bear anything.

"..ℏ⬜ℏ_↕ ⬜ℏ_⬜⬜ _⬜ℏ ℏ ⬜_⬜," an alien pirate slurs as his hand slips from the slimy fliperisakiss' ear lobe. "↕↕⬜⬜_⬤!"

I turn to my neighboring cage, "Well, looks like old Grease Mitts is having his usual meat-handling problems!"

Grease Mitts knocks my cage bars with a stun baton, breaking my self-congratulating inflections of once again coming up with an innuendo for the circumstance. He speaks galactic basic in a broken tongue, "Air lock out with you! I have no worry!" (galactic basic? It's just English.) But galactic basic sounds more sci-fi. (you mean it sounds more Star Wars.)

"↕↕⬜⬜_⬤ !" I yell back at him in his language. I have no idea what I just said but it pisses him off and he lunges the baton through the bars, trying to jab me. I deftly shift away and knock the stick from his greasy hand. He moves away from the cage too fast for me to hit him with the charged baton. But that's fine, he isn't my target. I drive the baton into the locking mechanism of the cell and the door springs open. Without a full charge on the baton it's basically worthless, but I've taken this into account. I toss the recharging baton into the cell of the gladiatorial slave champion and throw myself at the two alien pirates charging me. I scream my war cry.

They pin me to the floor but, as anticipated, don't call for back-up. Out of the corner of my eye I see a swiftly moving appendage crush the back of Grease Mitts' head. He'll definitely have to sit the rest of this one out. The other alien releases his grip on me and begins backing away from the newly freed slave champion. I slowly get to my feet, half expecting the gladiator to turn on me. But thankfully the slavers were total dicks so he focuses on one of them instead. who is currently reaching behind his back to pull out a wicked looking blade.

The slaver promptly reaches behind his back, whips out a

wicked blade and severs both the champion's arms. Proud of himself he begins to laugh, joyful at the sight. Of course there's a reason why this particular slave is gladiatorial champion. He can regenerate his limbs quite rapidly. The slaver really should know this. I mean, I know all about it and I've never even seen it, but these guys aren't too bright. His stupidity makes his reaction all the more laughable as the slave's arms surge out of his elbows and crush the slaver's face.

I give some congratulations and offer up a high five, but my former neighbor just looks at me silently. So rude. (most of the other slaves don't speak English, you know.) Nevertheless, some acknowledgement would be polite. It's just simple courtesy.

We stare at each other awkwardly for awhile before I finally say, "Mutiny?" which I take he understands because he's smiling now. Or at least I think it's a smile. His face is very disgusting.

It takes a few minutes, but we free the rest of the slaves and burst out of the slave quarters screaming war cries. (you're the only one screaming anything.) It's called enthusiasm. The rest of the slaves are busy brutalizing anything that gets in their way. (I think that one is humping the bulkhead.) Ha! I, however, have no time for that. I'm headed straight for the bridge and this so called "Captain Valiant".

I get lost a couple times. It's a big ship. (but we're here now so what are we waiting for?) Oh, well I have to think of something brilliant to say as I burst through the door. I'm thinking "Hey Captain Valiant! Meet General Mutiny. He's about to court marshal your ass!" (that's awful.) No, I think it'll work. I'm going for it.

I burst onto the bridge, "Hey Captain Valiant! Meet... Emma?"

"Hey Vic," What. The. Fuck?

"Ah, a pleasure to meet you," says an unbelievably handsome man sitting next to Emma. "I'm Captain Valiant. And you, clearly, are Victor." He gets up and shakes my hand with all the suaveness of body soap. (nice.) "Victor, now that...*that* is a *valiant* name." And with a smile that's just dashing I...why am I here again? (mutiny.) That's just out of the question. I could never stay mad at this man. "Please, have a seat. Emma and I were just discussing the terms of your release."

"So when you say discussing the terms of my release you mean?"

"Oh please," says Emma, "get your mind out of the gutter. We were just trying to figure out which slave quarters you were in."

"But now you've fortuitously found your way to us," says the captain. "Problem solved. Although I must tell you that you slaves do great work and you will be missed."

"Actually, I didn't work at all," I say.

"Oh. Well then it'll be good to be rid of you," there's that smile again. (phenomenal.) But that's unimportant! Emma's here!

"So," I turn to her, "how exactly did you find me?"

"We pieced together a few clues from the Roboracle before he disappeared and Jimmy built a space ship. He's down in the engine room talking to some cute engine girl or something. We really need to get going though."

"Why?" (why? Why are you asking why? I thought we wanted off here) Yeah, but Captain Valiant is so cool!

"Candy Island," she says, "we have to get to Candy Island."

"Candy Island?" asks Valiant. "That sounds exciting and dangerous—two of the key ingredients of *adventure*—and here on The Adventure Galley we're always looking for *adventure*."

"Yes! Captain Valiant comes with us!" I'm so excited! (too excited really.)

"That's fine," starts Emma. She's so pretty when she's determined. "I don't care who comes, but let's go. The fate of the universe rests on Candy Island!"

(maybe we should tell them about the mutiny outside?) Nah, I'm sure it'll work itself out.

Anyway, the Adventure Galley…it's pretty sweet. And trust me I've seen enough sci-fi movies to know what I'm talking about.

Emma, Valiant, his manservant droid and I, the mighty Victor, survey the infinity of space.

"Captain Valiant," I start, "I have just one question for you; how do I become as magnificent as you?"

"That's an excellent question," says Valiant. "And let me tell you that the first step is procuring a space ship."

"That's pretty logical. So where do I get a space ship and how much do they cost?"

"I wouldn't know about that, for I came by the Adventure Galley through *adventuring*."

"That's fantastic news! I'm kind of known for adventuring. Emma, tell him how I'm known for adventuring."

Emma rolls her eyes, "We did this thing once."

"Exactly! And that thing was adventuring and—"

"But Vic, didn't you say something about a mut—"

"Please Em, no interruptions. I'm working on self improvement," Emma looks at me, bemused. "And I know what you're thinking, how can I be even better than I am right now? The answer is I don't know! Which is why this conversation is of utmost importance. So Captain, what comes after spaceship acquisition?"

"Hmm," ponders Valiant. "I'd say that proper dental hygiene is critical, for several reasons. But I'll detail this all to you later. First I'd like to know about this mutiny you mentioned because squashing a mutiny is the 5th most important thing a captain must be capable of doing. In fact, you should probably be writing this down—wait no! Scratch that. I'll dictate all you need to know to my trusty Manbot. A

11

bold, blistering manifesto.  <u>The Valiance of Valiant</u>. Its praises will be sung across the ages.  I'll have your copy delivered upon completion.  Now, back to this mutiny."

"I mentioned a mutiny?" I ask.

"Yes," Emma says with a hint of frustration, "when you were talking to yourself."

"Huh…well yeah, I sort of started a slave mutiny on my way here."

Emma shakes her head, "Oh Vic, you didn't."

"Look," I say, "some people may love the slave life.  I mean, steady work and free housing.  It's great.  But I took a long look at my life.  Really evaluated things.  And, well, it just wasn't for me."  Emma is still shaking her head.  "Hey, don't give me that attitude!  I need adventure, something I'm sure the Captain here understands."

"It's true, a man needs *adventure* to survive," states Valiant. "As for this little slave uprising, not a problem," he pushes a hidden button on the wall of the ship and a sexless voice comes on.

"SLAVE CATASTROPHE AVERTED.  SLAVE QUA-RTERS SECURE."

Captain Valiant's smile never falters and he tells me to go with Emma to my own personal quarters to clean up and dress for dinner in the Captain's private dining hall.  He turns and strides briskly back towards the bridge.  His Manbot escorts us through the main corridor, over a few humming thresholds and through a door.  Manbot withdraws, leaving us alone, as the door closes behind us in a whoosh. It's the same sound the slave cells make when they close.

But this is no prison.

Before us is a grand suite of feathers, fluff and fixtures I have never encountered in my terrestrial life.  Pleasures of a thousand galaxies fill every niche of the room.  A bar stands with colored liquids

12

as diverse as a supernova in each bottle.  A large bed of cilia wave millions of long slender tendrils with the currents of air traveling through the room, waiting for someone to cling to and caress.

Even with this splendiferousness before me, all I can think of is one thing.  The one thing that kept me going through the weeks of imprisonment.  Emma!  And now she is here beside me.  We have little time to make up for what has been lost.

"So?" I ask.

"Yeah," she replies, a slinking smile envelopes her lips.

"I was thinking now would be a good time to—"

"mmm hmm."

"—talk about what you've been up to these last few months."

"Later."

"Later we'll be having dinner with Captain Valiant," I protest. She reaches out, caresses my cheek, "heehee, it tickles," I say, because it tickles.

"Look, we have enough time before dinner to—"

"Talk, I know.  So what have you been up to?"

"Really, Vic?  I haven't seen you in months."

"Right, and I'm curious to know how you've been."

"It's just, I was hoping we could spend this time a little more *intimately*."

I stare at her blankly.  She stares back, her smile gone.  So it's a staring contest she wants? (I kind of doubt it.)  Fantastic!  I can do this all day.

"SEX, Victor! I'm talking about sex!"

"Oh. OHHHHHHH! Christ! Is that all you ever think about? We have Captain Valiant waiting for us so we can eat dinner.  *Captain Valiant*, Emma!  He is universally renowned for his amazing exploits."

"Really? Name one."

13

"He saved me from a life of slavery!"

"After he enslaved you."

"And there's two. Face it Em, the man is a champion...and my god those eyes..."

She sighs, "Should I be worried here?"

"Only if you make me late for dinner. You see, Captain Valiant and I share a bond. A special fraternal bond, if you will. It's the bond of two men who have seen war and fought monsters. A bond of men who have faced the void of space, turned around and said 'that was kind of boring'. And the key to any sacred bond is punctuality so—"

"Fine! Fine, just...just go fawn over Mr. Triumph while I change."

"It's *Valiant* Emma, and he's a captain."

"Just go."

I never knew Emma was such a sore loser. (what?) The staring contest. She's clearly upset over losing so handily.

"There was no staring contest!" Emma shouts from what I can only assume to be the bathroom. Typical loser talk. (if you say so.) Now if only I could remember which way the dining hall is. (don't ask me, I was paying less attention than anyone.) "Right! And stop talking to yourself!"

# Act I, Scene 2

It takes longer than desired to reach the dinning hall due to a homonymic misunderstanding that lead me to go left, the direction I presumed correct, instead of right. Fuck the English language.

I finally enter the hall. It's much larger than I expected and at the far end I notice a speck that I can only presume to be Captain Valiant, already seated at the head of a rather substantial table. "Ah, Victor!" Valiant's voice boasts forcefully, somehow in surround sound. "Welcome!"

"I'm not late am I?" My voice feels meek.

"What was that?" Valiant bellows yet again, confirming my feelings.

"I was just asking—"

"Victor, I'm sorry, but you'll simply have to use the intercom. There are buttons at every seat."

I approach the first seat, lean over and press the button, making sure to speak in all directions while looking for invisible microphones, "Oh, I was just wondering if I was late." I let go of the button briefly before amending my statement. "You can hear me, right?"

"Of course I can and you are, in fact, the first to arrive."

YES!!

"Now take your seat and prepare yourself, for I guarantee you are about to sup as you've never supped before."

I press the button, "I don't think I've *ever* supped before."

"Well then," he exhales with a hint of laughter, "my guarantee has been fulfilled. As if there was ever a doubt! Manbot, clap Victor on the back for me would you." Valiant's robo-manservant emerges from the wall and slaps me on the back as I seat myself. It hurts. A lot. The pain of glorious friendship! Then a voice erupts from behind me.

"Victor! You're okay!"

Jimmy.

Jimmy and his metal half mask covering up his bone face. I told him the Skeletor thing made him look badass, but apparently he'd rather look like a half-assed Casey Jones rip-off. As gigantic as this room is, he had to spawn on my end. Damn it.

And knowing Jimmy I better cull his enthusiasm before it manifests itself in the form of hugs.

"Don't touch me." I see out of the corner my eye Jimmy rear up, pull back his outstretched arms. That was too close.

"Yeah, I wasn't—er I mean I was just—it's nice to see you Vic."

"I know," that's when I notice the petite girl with luminescent red hair walking up behind Jimmy, "and who's that?"

"Oh, that's um—" he stutters

But Valiant interrupts, "Ah, I see you are being introduced to our chief engineer and my most trusted ally, Lieutenant T.S. Cole."

"Hey," she says with a nonchalance that can only mean she thinks I'm incredibly cool.

"Nice to meet you Lieutenant Cole, I like your hair."

"Thanks, I guess. I was just feeling red today."

"Um," I say.

"And you can just call me Sera. I'm not big on formalities," That must mean we are best friends now. Excellent, one step closer to being Captain Valiant's number one. (good luck with that.) Shush.

"Did you say something?" Valiant asks.

Button depressed, I try to halt a similar fate for myself: "Me? I, um, well you see…"

"Don't worry about it," Jimmy interrupts, making himself useful for the first time ever, "Vic just does that sometimes. You can

16

pretty much ignore it."

"Ah, the freedom to ignore whatever I please is truly the greatest freedom of all," says Valiant.

As I'm trying to listen to more of Valiant's rousing diatribe, Jimmy, sitting down next to me, starts up. "So Vic, I was just thinking about that thing you were saying last time I saw you and—"

"Oh," button pressed, "what's that Jimmy? I can't hear."

"I was saying that I was—"

"Jimmy, the intercom Jimmy!"

"But I'm right next to you?"

"What?!"

He presses his button, "I said I'm sitting right next to you!"

"I have eyes, Jimmy! Christ, it's not like—" but another, more welcome interruption enters the fold.

"Um," Emma's voice floats to me as I turn to face her, "I think I'm way overdressed." My deadly little butterfly glides across the hall towards me, her gown flowing delicately over her like a chocolate fountain. Of course the dress is stark black so the analogy is less than apt, but the thought of her covered in chocolate was too good to pass up. She sparkles; glitters as she walks. A thousand stars ignite and extinguish with every step. I see an entire universe before me and I just want to fall inside her until I feel my eyes freeze and my lungs burst in a delectable cacophony of pure awesome. I have no idea how much of that is a metaphor.

"Don't be absurd," Valiant disrupts my sci-fi suicide fantasy. In my naked excitement I didn't realize I've been holding the intercom button this whole time, "it is we who are all horribly underdressed. Please be seated, the feast is about to begin."

With a wave of his hand, our meals materialize in front of us. Simply amazing this space tech, I guess the computers can read my mind or something. Because in front of me, now materialized is my all time favorite dinner, a McDonald's Big Mac value meal with a nice refreshing Coca-Cola. I hesitate to ask where Captain Valiant was able to procure this earth staple when we are so obviously in space. Before I can even open my mouth to ask, Sera interjects: "Your food, you like it? It's your favorite, right?"

Curious. I don't think I'm thinking aloud again. Or am I...? No. Odd. Wait, I've got it: "WITCH!"

Sera laughs. Or should I say cackles! (WITCH!) "It's got nothing to do with magic," a likely story from a witch, "it's just that I can—I mean, the ship can do these things."

"Things," I say, "things intrigue me. Continue!"

"Well it's just that I have this, or rather the ship sort of does this scanning thing and it can sort of devise what you eat the most."

I remain skeptical, "I haven't had a Big Mac in months."

"You'd be surprised how much you become what you eat, plus there's this whole brainwave thing involved," she looks for understanding, but I will give her none! "Anyway," she continues, "then there's all this transmutation stuff that happens on an atomic and subatomic level. Complex energy manipulations and, well it's hard to explain."

"Simplify it then," I demand.

"I, um—well I guess I...the ship is a witch."

"Of course! No one would ever suspect the ship. Incredible!" Note to self: consider burning ship.

The intercom blares to life once again, "The Lieutenant is being far too modest. None of this would be possible without her. She is by far the most *valiant* engineer I've ever encountered."

"Oh it's—it's nothing really," Sera stammers a bit, her hair seems an even brighter red than before, "I just, you know, I made it so

18

the ship knows the needs of its crew, and then poof! Fixed."

"That's pretty amazing," Emma chimes in, "where'd you learn how to do all this?"

"Oh, I don't...it's just the genes, I guess."

"Yes, she is quite simply a goddess," says Valiant in his valiant voice. Only that voice could command a goddess. (yeah, it's like hearing a Martin Luthor King speech read by Jesus as played by Steve McQueen). So cool.

Everyone's looking at me.

"Vic, chill, everyone heard that," Emma assuages me.

"But I wasn't pressing the intercom button."

"Dude, we're sitting right next to you," Jimmy, my good friend is keen to point out.

Valiant again takes control of the conversation. He stands and walks down the table to where the rest of us are seated. "Well, if no one is going to use the intercom I might as well move to the conversation."

"Damn it, Jimmy! Look what you made the Captain do!"

Jimmy apologizes meekly.

"Not to worry," reassures Valiant, "anger is such a petty emotion. Hardly worthy of me, Captain Valiant."

He goes to seat himself next to Sera when she nearly jumps from her chair, "Actually sir, you can have my seat. I just...I realized there's something I forgot to do."

"Can it wait Lieutenant?"

"No, sir. Not really."

"Aren't you going to eat?" asks Jimmy.

"Oh, of course—I mean I'll take care of that, but yeah. I've got to go."

"Well, hurry back Lieutenant. We've much to discuss."

"Yes sir. Absolutely," Sera scampers off looking a bit pale. I

19

think her hair even lost some of its luster. Oh well.

Valiant takes his seat next to Jimmy and I am in no way jealous. Not even a little, "Now Jimmy, Lieutenant Cole was telling me a few stories about you. Exciting and *adventurous* tales. I must know can you really do all those things?"

Jimmy's face lights up, though he is modest, he thrives on praise. Succinct as always. "Yeah, I guess I'm pretty good with mechanical stuff."

"Jimmy old pal, I think our new friends are inquiring about your other special ability, you know, the one that you've most recently acquired." He stares at me with his one eye blankly for a few moments.

Emma shines her smile on him to provide the necessary encouragement for him to open up. "Go ahead and tell him, Jimmy. It's not much of a secret with you wearing that mask and all."

"Oh that, yeah I can also bring back dead things, but they're not really themselves. More like walking dead things that do what I tell them. I have to cut a little piece of my own skin off and put it on a dead guy. That usually does the trick."

I notice Jimmy chowing down on a platter of assorted sushi. I never would have pinned him as a sushi person. Squirrel maybe. The guy is into some freaky shit.

Emma, being the cultured lady that she is, dines on a plate of orange glazed duck. Suddenly, and strangely, I am very aroused by the sight of her eating.

Valiant again begins one of his stirring addresses to us, his new friends. I tingle at the thought that my ragtag band of killers is now befriended by such a cool outfit as the Adventure Galley crew. "My friends, I'm honored to be your host tonight. Honored that I have been entrusted to accompany you on your quest to save the universe. When

20

I was a young boy I embarked for the first time to save the universe from the forces of evil. My friends, I did succeed. And I did so with only some toothpaste, a scooter and a cat named Lollipop.

"So as we sit here on the eve of our journey's commencement let us toast to excellence. To excitement. Vigilance. And most of all, to *valiance*."

God, he is so cool.

"Oh my, where is my head!" The Captain exclaims, "I've forgotten the wine. Manbot! The wine please." Moments later our glasses are filled to the brim with wine with the most aromatic bouquet I've ever inhaled, and Valiant is raising his high. We follow suit. "To Lollipop. The bravest cat the universe has ever known."

"To Lollipop," we say in unison. And we drink.

"My god," Emma says, "what is this wine? It's delicious."

"Why it's the wine of the fliperisakiss, the most sensual of all wines."

"What's a fliperisakiss?"

I know this one!

"It's some weird space creature we hunt!" I explain.

"Oh," Emma looks disappointed, "is this its blood we're drinking?"

"My dear girl," says Valiant with a smile, "I wouldn't have the slightest clue. After all, I make *adventure*, not wine. But enough talk. Eat, drink, enjoy. And save room for dessert."

# Interlude:

## An insatiable appetite

So hungry.

Sometimes when it's bad the Thing can't remember a time without hunger.

The cages are full. They're always full.

The Thing approaches the nearest and the animal within speaks

"Please," it says.

"I just want to go home," it says.

The Thing opens the cage and the animal is grateful.

And then the Thing starts to eat.

And the man screams.

They taste so much sweeter when they scream. Still the sound can grow tedious quickly. The Thing tries to mask the man's cries by crunching his bones. It doesn't work so the Thing begins to hum.

The hunger is almost gone, but the man is not. Unfortunately leftovers never hold. Time to stop playing with the food. The Thing rips at the man's throat.

The screaming stops, but the Thing keeps humming

*Twinkle, twinkle little star.*

And eating.

*How I wonder what you are.*

It's almost time…

# Act I, Scene 3

"**. . .** for dessert! Who wants some?" asks Valiant.

I'm stuffed so of course I say, "I do!"

"Excellent, you won't be disappointed."

Yet I can't help but be disappointed when dessert is placed in front of me: "It's ice cream."

"Not just ice cream. Go on, taste."

I wonder what kind of fantastic treat this could be; I bet it'll be something amazing like— "vanilla?"

"Delicious, yes?"

"So," Emma says, "is vanilla scarce out here?"

"Oh no," says the Captain, "it's just my favorite. Ah! The Lieutenant is back." Sure enough, Sera has silently reentered the hall looking much more peppy than when she left. "I presume everything is taken care of?" Valiant inquires.

"Sure thing, sir. Just a...there was a little problem down in the slave quarters. No big deal really. Problem's gone." Sera sits down across from Valiant, next to Emma.

"Dessert?" asks Emma.

"Oh god no! I couldn't even."

"But you had to miss dinner, you must be a little hungry?"

"Um, well it's just that—I was, um," Sera seems nervous. Even her hair looks nervous. Holy crap! I think she's probably got a thing for Emma. Good for her. "Well, what's for dessert?" she finally manages to spit out.

"Ice cream," I say.

"Vanilla?" she asks.

"Yep," says Emma and Sera relaxes.

"Oh, no thanks then."

23

"Alright," says Valiant, "enough with these frivolities. Manbot, clear the table. We have business to discuss." Within a minute the table is as if unused and the Captain gets to the point, "Candy Island?"

"Yes," says Emma.

"And the fate of the universe is there?"

"That's what we were told."

"By?"

"A prophetic robot."

"Hmm, yes. Robots are the most accurate prophets," and after a pensive pause, "it's settled then, we'll go to Candy Island and the universe will be saved. Manbot, make sure this moment is recorded and stored so that you may write an epic poem about it later."

"There's just one problem though," says Emma, "we don't know where Candy Island is."

"A problem, my dear, is being held captive in the Brothel of Infinite Sadness without a box of tissues. This merely requires a detour. Manbot inform all hands to set a course for The Eyes of the Universe."

Sera lets out an audible groan

"Something wrong, Lieutenant?"

"No, sir," Sera says, "it's just, well The Eyes, sir? That place is so boring."

"Yet from there we can see the path to *adventure*," says Valiant, "Now everyone go and rest up, we'll arrive at The Eyes by tomorrow afternoon. Good night." Then almost as an afterthought, "and keep your toothpaste nearby."

# Act 1, Scene 4

I wake from my precious few hours of sleep to the morning alarm blaring louder than imaginable and a sneaking suspicion that I did not set it for 3:00am. Emma stirs next to me in an agitated semi-conscious state and questions my ability to program an alarm clock. "Didn't you set it for 8? ...is so loud," she slurs

I reach over and push the power button. The alarm continues. I hit the reset button, but still nothing happens. Emma provides encouragement, "Shut the damn thing off!"

The alarm must be wired for surround sound and it's definitely not helping to clear my still groggy mind. I pull the power cable to the alarm. "EEEEEEEEEEEEEEEEEEEEEEEEE!" the alarm keeps blasting. Emma buries her head under a pillow.

"Damn thing must be battery operated," I murmur to myself. Flipping it over and opening the case reveals that no batteries are currently installed. The alarm continues to aggravate my morning condition. I smother the alarm with my pillow. The alarm is still going! Not even a slight dulling of the noise! I punch the reset button again. The alarm continues. I put the clock on the floor and smash it with my heel. The alarm continues.

"It's not stopping! We're going to wake up the entire ship! SHIT!" I'm yelling over the piercing sound. I stamp down on the already broken alarm clock three more times with no effect.

"Did you unplug it?!" yells Emma. "Turn it off!"

I begin to rip the electronic components from each other when suddenly there's a pounding on our door. Emma hops out of the bed, runs to the door and opens it. Jimmy stands there silhouetted by the lights from the corridor. The large white globes of his eyes glare fearfully from the shadow on his face, "We're under attack!"

25

I look at him dumbfounded.

"Can't you hear the alarms?!" he shrieks.

Suddenly everything becomes clear. I don't know whether its the panic in Jimmy's voice which brings me out of my sleep induced stupor, or the happy fact that it wasn't my demolished alarm clock which woke up the entire ship. Whichever the case, I'm into my clothes and strapped with weapons faster than a space junkie could suck the wine from a fliperisakiss.

"Jimmy, anything else you know about this attack?" I ask.

"The alarms just went off and I saw a flash of laser-fire outside my window. One of the beasts had the branding of the Dread Space-Pirate Robots!"

I pull my salvation, a nickel plated pearl handle .45 automatic from its holster and head with Emma and Jimmy toward the deck and Captain Valiant. Surely he will have this situation under control.

I turn into the last hallway before the bridge when a beam of white flame cuts through the ship's hull. Two robotic hands penetrate the slit which has just appeared and pull the hot metal open to birth the robot pirate through. I open fire on the robot as it drops into the ship, but bullets merely ricochet off of its metal frame. I push Emma and Jimmy back behind the turn, and duck out to throw more bullets at the pirate robot. With a slow mechanical whir of motors the slim robot realigns' itself to my direction and hails down laser fire with two Gatling guns. Chunks of the ship's walls are peppered away as the robot seems to have no worry of wasting ammo. The robot bears down on my hiding spot with lasers humming. I've gotta think of something fast or else we're gonna be perforated meat. Nothing comes to mind.

"Okay," I turn to my companions, "Any ideas to destroy this thing or should we start getting it on in our final moments of life?" They look blankly back at me and won't even provide a peep of inspiration how to defeat this metal monster. "Well then," I start, "guess this was a good run. Time to get freaky," I begin to unzip my pants in preparation for my final moments of life.

Jimmy and Emma both look at me as if I'm insane.

"What?!" I yell at them. "We have less than a minute left!! Hurry it up!" I've finally got my pants off when the robot turns the corner and levels its guns at us. Damn! Not even as much as a pre-death hand job!

The robot's guns start spinning in preparation to end us when a red blade of light strikes the robot; its head erupts in a shower of sparks and wires. The robot crumples to the ground.

"Did I catch you at a bad time?" asks Captain Valiant, quizzically eyeing my pants around my ankles. "I could use some help on the bridge if you don't mind," he valiantly states while switching off the red blade of light and slipping the device back into his pocket.

I stand and pull my pants up, "Uh. Okay. Let's go."

I'm completely unprepared for what we see before us. Looking out the bridge's 360 degree panoramic viewport, I understand the panic with which Jimmy colored his morning warning. Dozens of space beasties with transparently thin and iridescently glowing wings drift impossibly through the dead of space surrounding the ship, robot pirates guiding each on kamikaze runs.♥ However impressive the sight, what first catches my eye is Sera lying immobile and blue blood issuing from the pockets of her eyes and out her nose.

I'm frantic, "What happened to her?!"

"Not now, Victor," Valiant valiantly keeps a valiant calmness. "I assume it would be too much to hope that one of you has ever piloted a vessel of this size?"

I stare blankly at Valiant, looking as dapper and valiant as ever,

---

♥ Flash! Ahhhahhhh!

and then at my friends. Jimmy with the same blank stare as me, and Emma who is already in motion. She seizes a lever at the control helm and pulls back. The ship lurches back and the nose dips forward into a spiral. The robot pirates easily follow on their space beasts. Laser fire flashes overhead but Emma's sloppy flying keeps the ship from absorbing the majority of damages.

Valiant addresses his manbot servant, "Take her down to medical. See what you can do." Manbot lifts Sera, and leaves the bridge. Valiant then turns to Emma. "Impressive flying," he tells her with a suave calmness which makes me more than a little jealous. I decide to change the subject.

"What the hell happened to Sera?!" I demand from Valiant.

"This isn't the time for discussion," he chides, and I slam against the wall as Emma takes a sharp turn. "The Lieutenant is stronger than she looks. She'll be fine. That is assuming we don't die presently." Valiant switches on a communications relay, "On my mark, fire all guns at the small planet on approach 45 degrees portside." He flips the switch off and addresses Emma once again, "Keep this heading. When I say so, burn the landing jets at full power and keep the thruster's to the max. We've only got one shot at this before we're tapped out."

"But won't that tear the ship in half?" Emma looks more than a little confused.

Valiant just smiles, "MARK!" He steadies himself against the wall and I lose all sense of up and down as the ship spins uncontrollably end over end. The sheer g-forces push me to the floor and hold me there. Jimmy is similarly paralyzed. I can hear the ship's guns blazing but only catch brief dizzying glimpses of the chaos outside. A web-like pattern of laser fire sprays unavoidably in all directions. Jimmy's vomit flies across the cabin onto the 360 view-port

28

and suddenly I can't keep my Big Mac down. I gloriously release my value meal and slip into an endless black oblivion.

Emma slaps my face and begins shaking my shoulders to awaken me. The ship has stopped spinning and it seems odd that the space outside is now grey instead of pitch black. Uncertain, I can only ask, "What happened?"

"We've crashed," Emma responds curtly. "Hurry, get up. This isn't over yet."

"Where's Jimmy?" I ask, searching the small space and seeing no sign of him.

"Valiant took Jimmy along with him. Most of the crew is warding off a boarder who's trying to complete the destruction of the ship," as a side note she adds, "oh, and Valiant wanted me to give this to you." Emma pulls an antique looking Colt revolver from her waistband. The thing looks like one of Clint's classic gunslinger pistols but with some other-worldly modifications. Emma stuffs it into my hand and pulls me to my feet. "He said that it would work better than your 'ancient projectile gun'."

"So what are *we* doing?"

"Just gonna grab some gear and be proactive," Emma pulls me down the hall, away from the bridge. "Valiant believes there's a traitor in the crew."

"Really, why?"

"Something about pirates being barred from this sector, and Sera being hard to catch off guard. Not to mention they knew our exact position. I didn't really follow, but he's asked us to interrogate a pirate."

"Oh?" I ask bemused. "And how the hell are we supposed to interrogate a robot?"

"Don't know yet, but we'll worry about that once we've

29

captured one. Come on, it's not a large planet, but we'll still have some walking to do. I can't imagine that any pirates who landed are too far from here."

"Well, if they aren't far can't we just wait for them to come to us?"

"Carry this," Emma shoves a bag filled with god knows what into my hands, "and let's go." She takes off down the corridor, seemingly knowing where she's going so I've nothing better to do but follow her. "Okay, this is it. Get in here."

I join Emma in a smallish, bare room and the door closes behind us. The lights throb dully while a base hum keeps the rhythm. "BIO AND ATMOSPHERIC SCANS COMMENCING," utters a soft, artificial voice. Everything tingles.

I lean into Emma, "I thought we lost power?"

"Well, I know the ship can't fly…but I guess it would be pretty stupid to not have reserves for life support and all that. Hey don't look at me like that! I don't know how space ships work!"

"SCANNING COMPLETE. ATMOSPHERE SUITABLE FOR HUMAN LIFE. ENJOY YOUR DAY AND ENJOY YOUR STAY." There's a whooshing sounds as the ships exterior doors open revealing a rather disappointing sight.

"This planet sucks!" I say, and I mean it.

"Aww, it's not so bad," Emma chirps from just behind me, clearly excited.

"Whatever, it's just a rock."

"At least that should make it easier to find robots. But come on!" I can hear the smile on her voice, "It's a new planet, how cool is that? Besides, there could be tons of stuff to see once we get to exploring."

I start walking, "Fine, but this better not take long. I hate walking and—OW! FUCK!—and I hate rocks!" Without looking I give the rock I nearly tripped over a swift kick. And then I get surprised.

"Excuse me!" says the rock, "but I'm not a rock!"

I remain skeptical, "Hey shut up, alright! Rocks aren't supposed to talk."

"Vic, it's not a rock. It's a robot."

I look down, "Huh, a robot."

"Nice eyes," says the robot.

"Oh man, I'm so going to enjoy torturing you," I say back.

"Torture? What's this about torture?"

I ignore him in favor of Emma, "Come on, let's get these rocks off his legs and get him back to the ship." She gives a longing glance back to the boring rock planet and sighs before helping me move our new found captor.

As we busily remove the rocks from his lower torso, it occurs to me that we won't have any way of controlling this pirate robot once we've freed him. I stop Emma, "Hold up a second. Let me see what you've got in that bag." I fumble around for a little while before finding what I'm after.

"Why have you stopped removing these rocks?" The robot asks innocently.

This robot is good! Play us up! Thinking we're fools!

"What are you doing, Victor?" Emma asks with some urgency.

"Oh, you know," I pull a rotary laser saw from the bag, "Precautionary measures." I flip the switch and get the laser cycling really fast before I cut off the robot's right arm.

"Is this necessary? I'm very attached to that," explains the robot as I begin working on his other arm. "Oh well, I suppose you can't be talked out of this. Did I say you had nice eyes? I meant to say they are gorgeous."

31

"You won't get any sympathy from me," I tell the robot. I get to work removing the rocks from his legs, one at a time, so I can cut those off too.

The robot's head spins to face Emma. "My, it must take hours to get your hair to look so amazingly straight and elegant. What kind of conditioner do you use?"

I cut through the first leg.

The robot continues, "Do you have an assistant on the ship who washes it for you? I simply must know how you keep it so perfectly adorable."

I hastily cut through the robots last leg. "I'm gonna cut his head off after this."

"Oh relax, Vic," Emma smiles. "He's just a nice, charming robot!" Then she addresses it, "Thank you for the compliment! No, I don't have an assistant, but I do use a series of various conditioners."

"Incredible," the robot yet continues, "I hadn't noticed before, but your smile could melt the entire ice planet Thoth. I even feel my own heart warming."

I pull my 45 auto and shoot point-blank into the robot's face. The suddeness of my rage startles Emma, "VICTOR!" She warns disapprovingly.

The bullets have done nothing but add a few dents to the robots otherwise smooth exterior. I twist some of the exposed wiring in his leg together and see one of his glowing eyes go dim, but then relight.

"VICTOR!!" Emma screams again.

"WHAT?!" I yell back at her. "It's not hurting him anyway!"

"Just," Emma pauses, "just get him back into the ship."

We pull the last few rocks off the pirate robot and lift him off the ground. The robot gives Emma another compliment and I can tell it'll be a long haul back to med-bay.

# Act 1, Scene 5

As we enter Med Bay, Manbot is busy tinkering with Sera. Noticing us he, or it, scampers back through an alcove in the wall. Sera is okay, I guess, albeit unconscious. At least I can see she is breathing. Our newly acquired POW has been engaged in conversation with Emma the entire way here. Luckily I'm getting pretty good at blocking out unwanted voices.

We lay the robot's torso on the bed next to Sera's and Emma gives me a look indicating she has no idea what to do next. Fortunately I have an idea or two, "We need to find a tub or whatever to put this guy in, something that can hold water."

"Um," Emma says.

"And salt too. Lots of salt," Emma just looks at me, more confused than ever. "Trust me. I know what I'm doing."

There's an awkward moment where it appears that Emma doesn't trust me despite how cool I think I sounded when I told her to trust me. Thankfully it passes.

"Well," she says, "we could probably fit him in the sink over there." She's right, the robot fits comfortably, "Now, any ideas on where we can find some salt?"

"None whatsoever, but that's your job. You're the torture nurse, after all."

"Torture nurse?"

"Or torture side-kick. Whatever. Just find some salt!" Emma grumbles something but still starts to search. I turn on the faucet. Things are about to heat up!

"A bath!" screams the robot. Ha! Thus the torture begins. "Oh I've never had a bath before. How delightful!" Not exactly the response I was anticipating, but no matter. Let the bastard think he's getting the royal treatment and then BAM! Torture! "Ah, and the water is warm too. I've heard warm baths are the best kind."

I let out an exasperated sigh, hoping to cull my robot rage. Emma only makes matters worse by engaging the thing, "You can feel the warmth?" she asks, as if it's more important than looking for salt.

"Not exactly," the robot replies, "but I do have a sophisticated temperature gage that is telling me that this water is quite warm and presumably pleasant."

I can't keep quite any longer, "You won't think it's so pleasant when I add the salt!" I suppose this is as good a time as any to enact my foolproof torture plan. Step 1: Explain to the prisoner every minute detail of what you plan to do to them. Exaggerate if necessary. It'll freak them the fuck out. "What I'm going to do, robot, is dump salt in your little bath. Lots of salt. And do you know why? Because salt water erodes metal. And what, pray tell, are you made of?"

"Why metal of course!" the robot chimes in cheerily. "And what a sound deduction you've made. After a month or so I'll be looking a bit disheveled won't I?"

"A month, huh? That's, uh, that's a bit longer than I antici-pated."

"Vic, we don't have a month," says Emma.

"I know we don't have a month! Just let me think…okay, plan B. Forget the salt and get me a paper and something to write with. Bath time is over, buddy!" I attempt to move the robot back to a bed, but he seems even heavier than I remember, "On second thought, you stay here. Torture will work just fine right where you are." Emma startles me slightly when she shoves a pen and some paper in my face. I start to write. It only takes a second. I hold the paper up to the robot, "Now read this."

"Of course," says the robot, "but first you should know there is

34

an error in what you've written and I wouldn't want to cause you any embarrassment in front your lady friend so maybe—"

"Just read it!"

"2+2=5"

"Ha! Explain that one!"

"Well, as I was saying earlier, you made a simple mathematical error in that 2+2=4 not 5. An easy way to remember this is to take two fingers on your left and two on your right and—"

"I don't need a math lesson from you!"

Emma leans in, mouth close to my ear, "Please tell me this isn't your plan."

"Relax," I say, "I'm just getting warmed up." I turn my attention back to the robot, "So maybe you're a math wiz, but let's see how you like this! 01110000011000010110111001110100001110011001000000111000001101011101110000."

"Haha! Good show, man!"

"What did you say?" Emma asks.

"I don't know, I'm just trying to confuse him. I'm pretty sure it's working, but I probably need to hit him with a more concentrated burst. I can't speak it fast enough," so I get to writing again. This is what I come up with: 0110011001110101011000110110101100100000011100100110010010111101100010011011101101101000010000001100011011101010101101110011101000001000000011100110110100000110100101110100000100000011000100110111101101101010110001000100000011100000111010101100110111001101110010010000001100011011101010110111001110100000100000010010010010000001101100011010100010101101011011001010010010000001110011011011001010101111000. It should fuck him up good. "Now what do you think of this?!"

The robot gasps. Yes! Finally things are working out. "You would dare even to write this kind of language in front of a lady?"

"Damn it!" I yell. Deflated I go sit on the bed next to Sera's. Emma joins me.

"What now?" she asks.

"I don't know. Find something sharp to poke his wires with?"

Just then Manbot re-enters the room, "Oh, you're all still here. *Fantastic*."

His robotic sarcasm grates me, but more importantly, "You can talk?"

"Of course I can talk. Such a typical human mindset to believe the servant droid is mute. Just call me when you're done so I can attend to Lieutenant Cole before she regains consciousness."

"What happens if she wakes up first?" asks Emma.

"I," Manbot starts, but there's an audible click before he continues, "you clearly wouldn't understand."

"Well, you don't have to wait for us to leave," says Emma.

"You'd only get in my way," says Manbot. He turns to leave, but abruptly stops, "Although if you are really looking to torture that pathetic thing over there, perhaps you should consider magnets."

"He's right," says our captive robot, "we robots don't much like magnets. Although I don't think they are best for extracting information."

"Don't tell me how to torture you," I say. "But where am I supposed to find magnets?"

"This machine I'm next to is practically one giant magnet," says Manbot. The machine he's talking about looks like a small CAT scan machine, just more spacey. "Don't worry, I'll operate it for you," Manbot starts again, "I'm sure you'd only break it if you tried."

"Won't you get hurt too, Manbot?" asks Emma.

"Only if I'm inside the machine, which I won't be. *Obviously*. Just get that thing on the conveyor belt and I'll do the rest. Then I can

36

get back to my real work."

I grab the robot pirate and Emma helps me lift him, "I don't know about this, Victor."

"What's to know about? Manbot is a robot so he should know robot torture better than us." Emma gives a reluctant "I guess" before dropping our prisoner on the conveyor.

"Pardon me," interrupts the robot, "but might I inquire as to what all this torture is about?"

I have no intention of answering, but Emma, as always, is a different story, "You know the Dread Space Pirate Robots?"

"That is where my affiliation lies, yes. Although I must say I wasn't too pleased with the way I was jettisoned and abandoned under rocks only to be found for purposes of torture. Of course I never imagined that torture would be such fun. Oh but I digress. Now what about the Pirate Robots would you like to know?"

"We wanted to know," Emma says as Manbot begins switching switches, "exactly how the pirate robots knew where to find us and what exactly the pirates want?"

The conveyor belt glides into action, gracefully leading our prisoner into a transparent tube, "Is that all you want to know? Why the bath alone was worth that information. Your ship has a mole."

"Yes, yes! We know," Emma jumps with excitement, "but we don't know who it is. Do you?"

"Of course I do. It's—" a gentle hum is emanating from the machine now, "—oh well that tickles...but the mole is—the mole is—is—izzzzzzzzzzzzzzzzzzzzzzzzzz*!!" The robots eyes go dark.

"What the fuck just happened?!" I'm almost screaming, but Emma, in her rage, puts me to shame.

"Why'd you start the machine, Manbot?! NO ONE TOLD YOU TO START THE MACHINE! COULDN'T YOU HEAR HE

WAS ABOUT TO TELL US EVERYTHING!"

"Sure," says Manbot, "blame the robot who was only doing exactly what he said he was going to do. Standard human fare."

Emma shoots Manbot a look that would castrate anything with testicles. Manbot doesn't have testicles. She gets quiet; whispers sharply, "Get out of here," her punctuation a snake's hiss. "Now."

"As you wish," Manbot retreats into the wall while Emma holds back tears. Be they of rage or sorrow I'm not sure. She always gets too attached to obnoxious robots.

# Act 1, Scene 6

With Sera still out and the ship currently grounded Valiant summons Jimmy and me to assist him in repairs. He wants us to round up all the slaves and make them do the work. I tell Valiant that I'm probably the wrong guy for the job since I hate anything that resembles work. However, he seems to think that my Spartician type slave revolt has given me some slave-cred, and I just can't say no to that man. Besides, I can't help but reminisce about all the good times I had back in my slave days:

That sunny day when I got captured on my way back from the grocery store. All that space travel. The time away from Jimmy and The Roboracle. No longer having to hear that robot's bullshit prophecies of doom about how I'll soon by captured and enslaved. Telling the slavers they could fliperisikiss my ass as I slacked off everyday. And then there was that time I escaped and met Captain Valiant. Sometimes I wonder why I ever left. I can't wait to see the old gang again and talk about the good old days.

"Well," says Valiant as he emerges from the slave quarters, "they're all dead."

"Who?" I ask. "The slaves?"

"Yes, and the slave handlers as well."

"Are you sure? They could just be faking it to avoid work. I used to do it all the time."

"No, no. I tested that. I said at your feet slaves and they did nothing so I said that's an order by the way and still nothing so then I said maybe I wasn't clear but this is your captain, Captain Valiant, speaking and I'm ordering you to attention. Still nothing. No one disobeys a Valiant order unless dead. Also, several were in pieces."

Dead, huh? Disappointing, but that's still no reason for anyone

39

to disobey Captain Valiant.  If I were dead I'd still do what he said.  That settles it, "Jimmy!  Do your thing?"

"Uh, w-what thing?"

"What thing?!  The thing, Jimmy.  The thing!  What with all the cutting and the skeleton face and the bad music.  That thing!"

"Are you sure?  Emma doesn't like me doing that and—"

"And Emma's not here so just do it already!"

"Yes!  This is gonna be great.  Can you just hold this for a minute," Jimmy hands me his mask, revealing his awesome face.  "Okay guys, just wait here.  This'll only take a few minutes."  Jimmy enters the slave quarters and closes the door behind him.  Moments later a wailing buzz pounds through my head signifying Jimmy is in full crazy mode.  I notice Valiant give a slight cringe as the humming begins, making me pretty pissed at Jimmy.

"Sorry for the noise, Captain.  It's just part of his whole deal."

"No need to apologize.  The music of the dead is a powerful thing.  I remember the first time I ever heard it.  In the Brothel of Infinite Sadness.  Just days after the death of my dear Lollipop.  It's lingered with me since," Valiant shakes his head and sighs before putting his Valiant smile back on, "but never mind all that."

We stand there listening to the music for awhile longer.  Finally it tapers off; dies completely.  Jimmy comes back out, saving Valiant and me from an awkward silence.  "Okay, done," he says, pale and slightly out of breath.  Valiant and I peak into the former slave quarters to see a whole lot of mangled, walking corpses.

"And they follow your orders?" Valiant asks.

"Yeah," Jimmy responds with boyish glee.

"Excellent, then let's put them to work.  We should have the ship running in no time."

Curious, I ask what we might want to do with these things once

40

the ship is fixed. "Should we just have them bury themselves somewhere so we don't have to worry about them eating our brains?"

"They aren't going to eat your brains, Vic. They only do what I want them to."

"So what, Jimmy? I'm supposed to entrust the safety of my brain to a guy with half a face? Please!"

Valiant lets out a hearty laugh, "Now Victor, have a little faith in your friend's gifts. Besides, unadulterated loyalty is a valuable commodity no matter where you go. And you'll have to remind me to have Manbot record that last bit. Very important to heroism and whatnot. Where is Manbot by the way?"

"With Sera," I say.

"Ah yes, the Lieutenant. Very well then."

"I wonder how she's doing," I think out loud.

"We'll go check up on her momentarily. In fact, you go on ahead, Victor. I just need to help Jimmy get these slaves working in the right areas."

Back in the med bay Emma seems to be attending to Sera. She's still unconscious. Someone has washed the blood from her face and placed her inside a shallow bath of blue liquid. I think she's naked. I fully approve of this method of medicine. I watch as Emma dips her finger in the bath. She shudders; goes flush with a smile. A look I find faintly familiar. No one seems to have noticed my re-entry and I'm about to ask what that blue goo is when Manbot makes it redundant. At least somewhat.

"Please refrain from contaminating the Phoenix Bath," Manbot says in a way that makes me wish he had balls that I could kick him in. Emma looks to be taking the admonishment better than I.

Still unnoticed, I speak. "So what's a Phoenix Bath?"

Manbot turns his head in my direction, lets out a mechanical

41

sigh. "Oh, it's *you*," he says, ignoring my question.

"Hey, Vic," Emma starts with a smile, "how are things with the ship?"

"Fine, I guess. Not much I could do though, Jimmy's doing most of the heavy lifting."

"Jimmy? Really?"

"Yeah, most of the slaves died so he did his creepy Jimmy thing."

"Oh," Emma looks upset, "I really wish he wouldn't. He's hurting himself."

"Whatever, it got me out of work. As far as I'm concerned it's the most useful he's ever been," Emma looks down; shakes her head, hoping to show her disappointment with my comments. Yet I notice she's still smiling underneath it all. "Anyway, someone tell me what a Phoenix Bath is."

Manbot once again turns to me, "You do know what a Phoenix is, don't you?"

"Of course I do! It's the capital of Arizona."

"Ugh, humans. The Phoenix is a great bird that—"

"He knows what a Phoenix is, Manbot. It was a joke."

"Oh my. How *hilarious*."

Ignoring Manbot, Emma continues. "So does this Phoenix Bath bring people back to life?"

"Sera's wounds are not life threatening," and then, "this is medicine, not magic."

"Well, then Phoenix Bath is a stupid name for it," I mutter. Albeit audibly. But before Manbot can make some snarky, condescending comeback Emma interrupts.

"So it's just some sort of basic healing solution?" She asks and I take advantage of this reprieve from Manbot to go poke, prod and

42

occasionally shake the brain-dead torso of our former captive robot.

"I'd hardly call it *basic,* but yes," retorts Manbot.

"What does it do exactly?" Her voice sings with curiosity

"It heals."

"God Manbot, you are such an ass!" A strident motorized click emanates from within Manbot as he turns away, skulking back into the wall and leaving us alone. All the while I'm shaking this dead-bot more and more violently, my robot-rage at maximum capacity. Suddenly the dead torso sounds off softly.

"SYSTEM REBOOT IMMINENT."

Excitedly I turn to Emma, "Hey, I fixed it!"

Emma, reflexively stroking Sera's forehead, looks at me. "What?"

"The dead robot isn't dead anymore! It's like I'm Jesus. But for robots!" Emma starts to respond when Sera shoots up, practically jumping out of her bath.

"We're under attack," a breathless and extraordinarily naked Sera says.

Emma stares at me, bewildered before turning back to Sera. "Well, um—I mean we *were* attacked by pirates or robots or something…but we won!"

"The Captain?" Asks Sera, still naked and becoming even more so by the second as the Phoenix Bath drips off her. I sort of try to overt my gaze, but find that too impossible. She seems to be glowing a bit. Probably from the blue goo.

"He's fine," says Emma.

"And the ship too?"

"Actually, the ship crashed. Sorry."

Sera manages to relax a bit and even smiles. "No worries, I'll have the ship ready to take off in no time. Can you help me out please?" Emma reaches out taking Sera's hand, still wet with goo. Emma's eyes roll back into her head as she lets out a small giggle. Then she drops to the floor, twitching slightly.

Holy crap I think Sera just gave Emma a seizure! (what should we do?) We might have to kill her.

Sera snaps around to face me. "What? Don't try and kill—wait who are y—are you talking to yourself?"

"Probably!" I'm panicking now. "What did you do to her?!"

"I, um—nothing! I mean, I-I guess my tolerance for this stuff is pretty high…but she's fine. She just feels…really good. Let me help her up." Sera steps out of the bath and stands over Emma, still writhing on the floor.

"Ah! You're dripping more on to her!" Am I scared or turned on? (I don't know!)

"Oh no! I'm sorry I didn't mean—turned on? I—" Sera stops to take in the situation as the med bay doors swoosh open revealing Valiant and Jimmy.

"Lieutenant Cole, what is going on here?" Valiant asks, totally breaking the terrifying, yet erotic tension.

"Sorry sir, she took my hand when I was still in the tank, I guess she's never been exposed to the Phoenix solution."

"Lieutenant."

"Yes sir?"

"Why aren't you saluting?"

Sera pauses. "It's just considering the situation and my current state—do I have to?"

"I am your captain."

"Y-yes sir," Sera stiffens, hand to her head. Looking slightly in Jimmy's direction as she does, her hair flashes a blinding pink.

"At ease, Lieutenant. And do get dressed. We have uniforms

for a reason you know, and the hull breach should be nearly repaired so it's time to get the engines back online."

"Yes Sir!" Then turning to Jimmy, meekly. "Hi Jimmy." Jimmy is speechless. And that's the story of how Jimmy saw his first naked woman. (we should high five him later). Oh we will!

"Hey!" Jimmy yells. "I've seen naked women before!"

"Oh Jimmy," I laugh, "no you haven't."

"I have to!" and once again in Sera's direction, "I totally have." Sera doesn't seem to be paying too much attention as she's grabbing a towel next to me.

Emma seems to have taken this time to snap out of whatever she was snapped into, "Wow, that's even better than an ice cold Coke in August." Clearly she's delusional. But otherwise okay.

"My apologies Emma, I'm afraid Lieutenant Cole accidentally exposed you to a very powerful drug. It's not harmful, but it can be overwhelming."

"No problem," she smirks

Captain Valiant strolls over to the once lifeless, now miraculously rebooted, robot pirate, "Did we find anything useful?"

Emma shakes the last bit of fog out of her head and answers, "No, we almost had the information but your Manbot, who is extremely rude by the way, magnetized him. Though he does appear to be coming back online."

"Wait, how could my Manbot be rude?" The Captain has a genuinely incredulous look on his face.

"You mean to tell me that you have never thought the way he speaks to people is, um, dickish?"

"Well, I seldom entertain these days, but that's not what puzzles me. What I find troubling is that the Manbot is mute."

"Um, Captain," Emma looks worried, "do you think Manbot

45

could be the spy?"

Sera answers instead. "What? Manbot? I don't—well he does have access to the entire ship through the walls, which would explain how I was snuck up on…but I don't know."

"But he also used magnets on the pirate," Emma says, "and he must have known what would happen."

"And," Valiant interjects, "he's been deceiving me as a mute all this time."

Okay, I just have to interrupt now. "Look, no one hates robots more than me and I can't stand to be the voice of reason…but this just doesn't make sense. Why would he knock Sera out just to revive her later? And why would he talk to us knowing that Captain Valiant thinks he's mute? It's stupid even for a robot."

"Those are valid points you make," says Valiant, "although Manbot always showed an affinity for the Lieutenant and it may be that he just needed the engines offline. As for the other, I haven't the slightest idea why he would reveal himself so clearly unless—Sera access the ships computer." Sera, now disappointingly wrapped in towel, rushes over to the med bay doors and starts doing something technical. "Locate Manbot," orders Valiant.

A moment later Sera says, "Nothing sir. Manbot isn't on the ship."

"Well, that answers the question then," says Valiant.

"It does?" I say and Valiant nods. And he's never wrong. "Well, I still don't get it. I guess we have to go after him."

"Not at all. Our destination is still The Eyes for that is the way to *adventure*."

"But if Manbot tells them where we are headed," Jimmy chimes in finally, "others could be waiting for us."

Valiant smirks, "Only if we're lucky."

# Act I, Scene 7

They're waiting alright, but it isn't the Dread Space Pirate Robots. An ancient scientific outpost floats perilously close to the entry vectors outlined in the Universal Travel Log and immediately hails all of the commonly known space frequencies with an SOS upon our arrival.

Our communication panel lights up like Emma dipping her hand in the Pheonix Solution, "STATION ORBIT UNSYN-CHRONIZED. WARNING. IMMEDIATELY ALTER ENTRY VECTOR. WARNING. COLLISION IMMINENT. WARNING."

Since the Eyes are a boring place anyway, as Sera so colorfully revealed, I recommend to Valiant that we not alter course but instead dock with the drifting station and see if we can't make some excitement! He thinks it's a good idea, since we also don't have any clue of where to start searching for Candy Island anyway. So Sera guides the ship into a parallel docking pattern with the station.

We draw close and see an asteroid-peppered hulk with markings that identify it as the Colossus Unity. It's an impressive mass of metal which outsizes our vessel by ten. Looking to the Captain for some answers, I find a completely bewildered, unblinking Valiant and Sera gaping out the viewport.

"Captain?" He turns, startled.

"I...I'm sorry. I just can't believe what I'm seeing," The Captain pauses in thought before beginning to answer my unasked questions. "This ship has been lost for millennia. We're told stories in our youth of this, but...no one ever would believe it. Spinners of myth would tell you that its purpose was to join the very fabric of alternate realities. Further that the ship itself was lost into nothingness upon its christening voyage. Yet here, drawing closer to us by our docking claws, is a fully realized space station damn close to how I imagined it

47

from the stories."

"If the stories are true," Sera interrupts, "then its reappearance now only confirms it. They found their way back from another dimension!"

"What the fuck is this bullshit?! Lets get the hell away from it!!" I contest. "Who knows what kinds of scary is on that ship?! I survived hell once♦[♦] and AM NOT GOING BACK!!!"

"CALM THE FLIPERIPIKISS DOWN!" Emma orders.

"Only the scientists would have known how to operate the ship and bend it through the fabric of a universe. It should be safe to say that we may even be welcome aboard!" Valiant chuckles to himself, "We'll be famous! 'Fantastic discovery made by the Adventure Galley led by her captain, Captain Valiant!'"

Valiant bustles over to a communication channel, spits orders at a skeleton crew, and swiftly departs the helm to prepare for boarding. Our airlock has, meanwhile, sealed to the Colossus Unity and work is already underway on opening the vacuum door. I place my hand on the grip of my holstered pistol and squeeze down reassuringly.

"If they're are aching for a fight...then lets be ready."

Emma acknowledges with a pump of ~~her~~ a♠[♠] shotgun and turns to lead the way.

As we approach the vacuum door, one last battering punches the torch-melted door neatly out. "Excellent timing!" exclaims Valiant who acts as if he's been waiting for hours. "Come be the first to see the marvels and treasures unimaginable!" I draw my pistol and follow Valiant into the station.

---

♦ DVD the Novelization - Thanks, ES
[♦] Of course the hell in question is metaphorical, not the actual Hell. That has a capital H – CW
♠ She uses whatever the fuck shotgun she wants - ES
[♠] It was a pointless edit, just like all of these footnotes - CW

48

I'm not all that impressed.

Sure it's big, but it's also empty and quiet. Too quiet. The kind of quiet that can't help but be accompanied by ghosts. And not just any ghosts, I'm talking space ghosts! I don't know how to fight ghosts at all. Guns and fire, my two greatest weapons, are probably useless against them.

We walk down a spooky corridor. Once the lights even flicker. The atmosphere is perfect for it to happen. I know a ghost is going to pop out around the next corner. OR MAYBE IT'S BEHIND US! I jump around, a tiger-like panther ready to pounce. No ghost is catching me off gua—

"Hello," says a voice behind me. I don't recognize it. Oh God, no. Slowly I turn, pistol at the ready. A pale figure stands before me. (GHOST!!!!) RUN!!!!!!!

But before I can make another move, Emma pins me to the wall. She's much stronger than she looks. Meanwhile the ghost is curled up on the floor blabbering. "Ghosts! Nonononononono! Not again, no more ghost not this time—" and so on. I can't say I'm much impressed with his terror inspiring abilities.

As the ghost makes a mockery of his kind, Valiant whispers something to Sera and she crouches down in front of him or it. "Hey, relax," she says. "There aren't any ghosts here. Our companion is just a little, um, overzealous. He thought *you* were a ghost."

Still curled up and staring at his feet the maybe-not-a-ghost blabbers on, "Me a ghost? Oh no, not now not yet. A scientist. And science knows that ghosts don't exist so my existence means I can't be a ghost. Of course knowledge and reality don't always mesh which is something you learn here on the CU. But if you aren't ghosts then—" he finally looks up, catches Sera's eye, "well, what are you first one I see this night. So pretty, so bright," Sera shifts uncomfortably, embarrassed I guess. "No, certainly not a ghost…very well!" He pops upright, extending his hand to Captain Valiant, "Welcome, visitors, to the Colossus Unity. The station that goes where it's needed or is needed where it goes, be it by chance, fate or force. So the question is what do you need, or what can we make you need there must be—Not now! Yes I'm asking. That's just what I was doing!"

I have no idea what this guy is going on about, but Emma is clearly bothered by his behavior and I just sort of want to shoot him to see if ghosts actually exist or not. Valiant, on the other hand, is in no way phased by it at all. "You know this station is very famous Mr…?"

"Ickby. Dr. Ickby. Not Mr. I'm a scientist, remember? Not a ghost, not a mister."

"A pleasure to meet you doctor. I'm Captain Valiant. I grew up hearing tales of the Colossus Unity; it's a great honor to be here."

"Makes sense. It does. Yes. Very famous and fabled, all one would have to do is look at it to know. Have you seen it? Of course you haven't! You just got here so—yes yes! I concur. We must tour. How else can you know what you know without a tour? Come. Follow. Now.

"First let me show you this corridor. It's one of many and its purpose is to connect one place to another. A brilliant design and…" It's time to zone out.

We walk around for awhile as Ickby says things I don't pay attention to. Valiant is enthralled, however. Jimmy shows about as much interest as me because he's too busy staring at Sera, who is currently swapping whispers with Emma and giggling a bit. I try not to look at Sera too much as I can't stop picturing her naked. And since I've declared her my current best friend it would just be wrong for me to think of her trim, Phoenix soaked nakedness dripping blue onto Emma. Just so fantastically wrong.

50

"Excuse me, Dr. Ickby," Emma's silky voice brings an end to my inattentiveness, "but where's the rest of the crew?"

"Oh you won't be seeing more crew," Ickby replies.

"You're the only one here?"

"That's absurd! No, it's just that they," he comes to a halt and motions us all to gather around. Lowering his voice to a whisper, "they've all turned invisible and—" he pops his head up and shifts it from side to side checking for something, "—and I think possibly imaginary." His voice returns to normal and he begins to walk again, "but don't tell them that. They'd only complain and MY GOD! They never stop complaining. Speaking of which, did I tell you about the time we met God?"

"You met God?!" Jimmy asks.

"Absolutely! Except not met, but spoke to. He spoke to us. He said 'I AM GOD! BRING ME MORE DORITOS!' and not one of us knew what that meant so naturally it terrified us and we fled. Haven't been the same since. Not in the slightest."

"How do you know it was actually God?" I can't resist asking.

"Weren't you listening? He said 'I AM GOD!'" Hmm, can't argue with that logic.

"And where," asks Valiant, "have your other *adventures* lead you?"

"Everywhere. Nowhere. Somewhere, I don't know. What? Fine I'll tell them. I said fine! There was the Brothel of Infinite Sadness. I got dehydrated. A few parties with too much dancing, the 3$^{rd}$ Age of Vicious Enlightenment, that really old star, Seraphim, and Texas. Lots of places, no time to tell. So let's get on with it, you need something whether you know it or not. What is it? And if you don't know take a guess, that's just as good as knowing."

"We have set out to save the Universe," declares the Captain.

51

"Ah, overachievers! Personally I'd just concentrate on one place or maybe eleven since eleven is one twice not like two which features not a single one at all when written."

"As it so happens, we do have a place of specific interest."

"Lowering your expectations already, a shame to have the universe in such unsure hands. Quite a shame. Sad really. And what is this place that is more important than the universe I wonder?"

"Candy Island," says Emma.

"Candy Island is it? Yes, yes die Insel des Süßigkeit. The delectable, mythic land of sweets. Marvelous! We went there twice, maybe five times."

"So you can help us get there?" asks Emma, trying not to sound too excited.

"Get there? Oh you don't want to get there. Awful place. Dreadful, really."

"Well, we sort of need to."

"Need to? Why didn't you say so! You'll love it there. A kingdom of fantasies made flesh; dreams come true. Although plenty of us died there…but if you have to die somewhere, and as I understand it most people do, then Candy Island is where you want to end up. Yes indeed, if wonderful, wonderful death is what you seek, then you are in luck!"

"It's really that dangerous?" ask Jimmy.

"Dangerous? Why heavens no! Haven't you been listening? Paradise! And look! Just in time. We've arrived at a destination." All I see is a dead end, but Ickby says something I don't understand and the wall opens into a sprawling room of clutter. "This is the Command Center. It's where commands get centered. I've heard that a few have achieved Nirvana, but if you're a scientist you would realize that is the stupidest thing you've ever heard. Unfortunately, none of you look like

52

scientists and are thus trapped in your ignorance. I'd cry for you if I cared. But I don't so let's get going, we can be there soon."

"Wait," interrupts Valiant, "go now? We can't just leave The Adventure Galley behind. We have space pirates after us and they love to loot almost as much as everyone loves me."

"Right, sure. Park it in the hanger bay. We have one, it's open. I'll open it. Do it. Or don't, but hurry. I've got things to work on that I'm not working on now—" Ickby yaps on, following as we make our way back to the Galley.

# Act 1, Scene 8

It's taking longer than expected to move the Adventure Galley to the hanger bay, mostly due to having to fix the door we busted down in order to board the CU. So instead of waiting around, everyone went off to do their own thing. Jimmy and Valiant are overseeing the repairs while Emma followed Sera somewhere. I think they were gathering clothes or weapons or unbearable sexual tension. I decided to go back to the Med Bay because medical supplies are important. Also it's the only place I remember how to get to and from.

The floor is still stained blue from my previous visit and the pirate robot is still declaring that his resurrection is imminent. Imminent apparently means something different in space.

I rifle through the cabinets that I can figure out how to open, finding medicines with all sorts of crazy names: Andromidoxin, Galacticotin, Reduxidon, Penicillin...how am I supposed to know what the hell these things do? On second thought, medicine is for pussies. I'm outta here.

"Um, excuse me."

What the fuck was that?

"Is anybody there at all?"

I guess I better turn around and, "oh, it's the robot."

"Is that what I am?" asks the robot. "I can't seem to recall."

"Well, you did die."

"Did I? That sounds dreadful."

"Probably. So wait, you don't remember anything?"

"It certainly seems that way."

"Hmm, interesting."

"Yes, I would agree that it is quite interesting."

"Don't interrupt me."

"Oh, terribly sorry."

"As you should be! After all I did resurrect you. Thus you owe your life to me and possibly your worship."

"I can see certain logic in that."

"You better!"

"But might I ask what my primary function is?"

"You are a …a, um…a kill-bot? Yeah that's it, a kill-bot."

"Does that mean I should start killing you?"

"No! You kill who I tell you to kill."

"Very well then, and do I have a name?"

"No, no name. You are too cool for names."

"How splendid!"

"Yeah, sure. I'm going to drag you out to meet my friends now."

"We have friends?!"

"*I* have friends. *You* have masters."

"Oh my! Friends and masters? Such fun!"

"You're really going to have to work on your attitude problem."

After a brief search I find a tarp and I shove the robot down on to it, dragging it in the direction of the airlock. It takes a lot of energy, something that I don't like. When did they start making robots so heavy? Fortunately I see Jimmy and Valiant up ahead, "Hey guys! Check out the robot that I brought back to life." The two make their way over to see for themselves. "He's my own personal kill-bot now and I figure he could double as the Captain's new Manbot."

Valiant looks him over, "He won't be much of a Manbot without arms and legs."

"Jimmy's going to fix that."

"I am?" questions Jimmy.

55

"Yes," I say, "you are going to give him some awesome tank treads and, like, some hands with retractable claws."

"Why?"

"Why? WHY?! Why not, Jimmy?! How about that! It's because he's a badass, that's why!"

Jimmy hunkers down beside the robot, "So you're a badass, huh?"

"I'm just happy to be here with you all," says the robot. So chipper, so disgusting. I don't even like my own kill-bot.

"Some badass he is," says Jimmy.

"Listen, he needs to look the part before he can immerse himself in it," I say.

"Fine, I'll see what I can do," says Jimmy before turning his attention to the robot. "So what's your name?"

"I don't have one!"

"I guess we'll have to give you one then."

"Absolutely not!" I doth protest, "He can't have a name, he is the Robot With No Name. With only his marvelous stoicism and a fistful of dollars he wanders the land killing the good, the bad, and the ugly. Mostly the ugly. And he does it all for whatever the other movie was called. He smokes cigars and wears a serape and a cool hat. So you'll need to get him those too."

"Where am I supposed to get that stuff?"

"Not my problem, Jimmy."

"I'll figure something out, I guess. The Robot With No Name, huh? I think I'll call you RW2N."

"Oh fuck you, Jimmy! If you even dare, I swear that I will kick your ass."

"Jeez, calm down Vic. It's just a name."

I'm done talking to Jimmy so I turn to Valiant, "How close are we to being finished here?"

"Repairs are just now done," says Valiant. "We'll be back on the Colossus in a few moments. Now robot, have you ever composed an epic poem, or perhaps a sonnet? Poetry of any kind?"

"Why I haven't the slightest clue," says the Robot With No Name, "but I'd certainly love to try." I can't believe I brought him back to life.

# Act 1, Scene FINAL

We finally managed to get the Galley into the Colossus's hanger bay and now we're back at Command Center listening to Ickby and his craziness. I can't take it anymore, "When are we going to Candy Island?"

"Candy Island?" Ponders Ickby. "Who said we are going there?"

"Everyone said we were going there," this guy is almost as crazy as me and there isn't enough room for that much crazy.

"Of course we *were* going there, but we aren't any more. We are there. Have been since we closed the hanger bay. Very fast ship. Didn't you notice? Of course you didn't. Tragically stupid. Well, let's go have a look!"

Ickby leads us all to some elaborate viewing area. And goddamnit! "That's not Candy Island, it's Earth," my disappointment has no appropriate metaphor.

"Earth is where Candy Island is, everyone knows that. Except all of you. Which is why I pity you in my free time. Not that I have any. Very busy alwa—yes I know it's time! Okay then, time to get you to the surface. Follow me." Ickby practically sprints down the maze of corridors while we struggle to keep up. Racing around a corner, I almost run into him, having come to an abrupt stop. "This is the teleportation room."

"Like in Star Trek," I say.

"No, not like in Star Trek. Why would you say that, don't say that. What's Star Trek? You," he points to me, "you go first."

"Um."

"Don't worry about it. It's just like Star Trek."

"Oh...awesome! Let's do this!"

"Right, now stand here," Ickby motions to a fancy looking platform, "and take this." He shoves something into my pocket, violating my personal space. "It's a tracking and communication device. Very important. Now stand still and don't sneeze. And don't worry. This is going to hurt a lot."

"Wait wha—" but before I can finish my body explodes. Every cell vibrates excruciatingly. I can't find my hands, I can't see. The explosion implodes as I slam back into myself and…and…

Bleargggg.

Oh jesus

Bleargggg.

Fuck me

Bleargggg.

Like Star Trek my ass.

(welcome to Candy Island?) Let's not talk about candy…


BLEARGGGG!

# Interlude

The Thing knows it draws near.

It's been so long.

Often the tide of hunger being all there was to measure time.

But now it's close.

The bitterness of recent failure accentuated by the phantom sweetness

of its last meal stung profusely.

Yet none of that matters.

The hunger is gone for now.

And all the rest is falling into place.

What a happy day.

**Characters you should know**:

**Victor** – He's crazy.

**Emma** – She's awesome.

**Jimmy** – He's still sort of lame.

**Captain Valiant** – He's a valiant motherfucker

**Sera** – She's Victor's new best friend (according to Victor) who can change her hair color and looks great naked.

**Dr. Ickby** – He's ancillary. Kind of like the red shirts on Star Trek... so he'll probably die.

**The Thing** – Is a 1982 John Carpenter movie starring Kurt Russell that teaches a valuable lesson about how isolation in the arctic coupled with aliens leads to massive freak outs...

**. . . LET THE STORY CONTINUE!**

# Act II, Scene 1

I have no idea how much time passes before I feel the relentless drip-drop of rain spattering every inch of me. It's coming down hard. Kneeling in the mud, the retching complete, I start to sink so I force myself to my feet. Other sensations and senses migrate back to me slowly, but my body's still numb. It's cold and dark and a faint candy shop smell surrounds me. The ringing in my ears subsides as a familiar voice rushes towards me.

"—ctor? Vic can you hear me," I try to speak, but bile blocks my voice. I gag, spit. The voice comes to me again, "If you can hear me just say anything."

I find my voice, "Emma?"

"Yes! Oh thank Christ. We thought you were dead."

"Where are you? I can't see you."

"We're all still on the ship. Ickby didn't check the weather patterns and the storm really fucked with the teleportation."

"I hadn't noticed."

"Look, we can't come down there until after the storm passes and it's causing a lot of interference with the com system. I don't know if we…so it's…meet you…"

"Em? Emma, you're breaking up. Hello? HELLO!" Fuck. (I guess it's just us.) Double fuck.

(so now what?) Now, I get my bearings and check this place out. Okay, so I'm on a pretty big wet, muddy hill and it's pouring. Oh hey, check that out! (a castle!) A freakin' sweet looking castle! (it doesn't look too far away, although getting down the hill might prove difficult. It's pretty steep.) Well, what's behind us? Ah, a terrifying jungle. So we've got a horrible jungle of death or a castle where it's probably not raining. It's a toss up, but I think I'll take the cas—(hey!

Did you see that?) Don't interrupt me. (but there was something moving in the jungle.) I don't have time to pay attention to movements! I have a castle to get to. (do you remember what happened the last time you decided to ignore something I pointed out?) No. (well, it's back when you failed to save the world.) And yet you can't say "failed to save the world" without "save the world". Therefore I win an—

Something tugs at my pant leg.

What the hell is it? (looking down might help.) But what if it's something groteseque and freaky? (like a giant spider.) AW MAN! That's way worse than what I was thinking! (well, I'm looking.) Damn you—oh hey a giant candy heart!  With arms and legs. (is that freaky?) I—I don't know.

I take a few moments to evaluate the little guy.  It's white—one of the better flavors of candy heart—and it comes up to about my knee. Its limbs don't appear to have joints, but they seem to bend just fine. Like Gumby or Stretch Armstrong.  Its hands are cartoony, very Micky Mouse-esque.  It's looking up at me, or . . . well it doesn't have eyes or a mouth, but its face is tilted up towards mine.  Pink letters lay against its white face.  They read WHO R U

"Um," I say.  But before I can continue, the heart does a little jump and slides down the hill towards the castle.

"Well, that was rude," I whisper to no one.  Unfortunately someone hears me.

"I've been expecting you," an extremely scary voice whispers from the jungle behind.  Oh crap! (what is it?!) I'm not sticking around to find out!

I take a cue from the heart and dive head first down the hill in the direction of the castle.

(are you crazy!) Hell yeah, WHOOOOOO! (um, rock!) Yeah, rock on! (no, we're headed for a rock!) A candy rock? (I don't know but it looks—

CRACK

Ow.

My head goes some such and I can't things. There's blackness creeping around and I think maybe feet. Consciousness is going away and I can't woo her back. This day suc—*

# Act II, Scene 2

I don't know where I am and my eyes don't want to cooperate yet, but it's warm and soft so that's an improvement. I shift slightly and a cotton candy voice caresses me, all fluff and sugar. "Wakey, wakey sleepyhead."

"The fuck?" is all I can manage.

"Now now," the voice hardens. "That's no way for a handsome man to speak to a Princess," a licorice whip to my heart. "But," the cotton candy returns, "that bump you have certainly took away your better sensibilities. Don't worry. I won't hold it against you." She leans to whisper that last part and I catch the sweetness of her. Freshly baked cookies and vanilla fill me.

My eyes, and other parts, can't help but obey. And when the world comes into focus, "Wow." She's a creamy frosting angel atop an ice cream cake of unbridled sexiness. She melts and I melt with her…whatever that means.

"Wow, what?" She speaks in caramel notes so rich I can almost taste them.

"Wow, you," I say

"You are *so* sweet," she giggles.

I try to pull myself together and forget all the candy metaphors in my head, "You said you were a princess?"

"That's right, I'm Candy Princess."

"Oh, you're the Candy Princess of Candy Island," I say in an attempt to get a handle of this situation.

"Yes, but it's just Candy Princess. There's no the."

"Your name is Candy?"

"Candy Princess, silly!" She laughs and the world is nothing but gumdrops and rainbows as the candy metaphors return. "But now that you know me I'd sure love to get to know you," and with a bat of the eyelashes, how can I refuse?

"I'm Victor."

"Such a princely name!"

"Yeah, I get that a lot," I proceed to tell her my whole story. Never once does she look less than enthralled. I'm a fantastic storyteller, clearly. "And now I'm here because apparently the fate of the universe is on Candy Island and my friends are stuck in space until the storm passes."

"That so exciting. You must be very brave."

"Oh I am. So do you think you might know what this fate of the universe thing is?"

"Mercy, no!" She pauses for a moment and for the first time I see her face without a smile. "But It might know."

"It?"

"There's," she stops, leans in close enough to make my mouth water, "there's a monster on Candy Island."

"Really?"

"Yes, it's somewhere in the Candy Jungles."

"I saw something in the jungle earlier."

"Oh dear! Was it the monster?"

"I didn't really see it, but it sounded like a monster."

"And it attacked you? That's how you hurt your head!"

"I, um...yeah. It caught me off guard and knocked me down the hill."

"You poor, poor thing. Thank goodness one of my Candy Citizens alerted the guards. The horrible things that could have befallen you left alone against that beast."

"Yeah, lucky me. So what kind of horrible things is this monster known to do?"

"Well, it's been slowly brainwashing all of my candy citizens and, the rumor is, it's been teaching them cannibalism."

"Why would anyone eat people when they have an island of candy?"

"Oh you silly goose, people on Candy Island *are* candy!"

"Then what do they eat?"

"All sorts of things."

"I see…wait!  Are you candy?"

Never losing an ounce of cheer from her voice, "Well I guess you'd just have to eat me and find out."

I, um…

For the first time in as long as I can remember, I'm speechless.

"Now come on, get up and follow me.  There's so much for me to show you and storms here tend to be a tad lengthy, so we've got all the time in the world!"

As I stand up, I feel the dull throb of my skull from where I was cracked on the head and cringe.  Candy Princess glides slowly out of my humble convalescence room, which by the way is a splendid abode of colorful smells and total kick-assery.  The fog departs my eyes and reveals that the smells are actually licorice and peppermint pillars, their pinnacles stretching to a gigantic dome of marshmallow goodness filled between with butterscotch glass.  A mural of bright colored delectability adorns the walls.  Depicted in this mural is a woman riding on white clouds of liquid chocolate and raining sugar down upon a grateful worshipping audience.  Upon closer inspection, I find it is my host upon the white chocolate cloud, merely gesturing with her hand to transform the landscape from thick choking jungles to a candy cane stripped paradise.  Candy Princess follows my glance to the mural.

"The candy citizens have written such pretty songs all about me and the wondrous things I'll someday do!  This mural is fashioned after my most favorite."

"I'd like to hear it," I tell her.

"But there's no one here to sing it for you," she says sincerely.

"You could sing it."

"Oh I *couldn't!*" She blushes.

"Please," I say.

"Well…maybe with a pretty please."

"Pretty please," and then to put the icing on the cake, "with sugar on top."

"No girl could ever say no to that," she laughs. Softly she starts her song. Her voice is a nightingale soda pop laced with grenadine glazing the fabric of my sugar-free soul, dying each note a shirley temple red and just as sweet. As much as Jimmy's is the music of the dead this is the music of pure joy. A carousel of midnight candy kisses and forgotten fairy tales. Well, except for the lyrics. They suck, but she can even make sucking extraordinary:

> *A princess will rise in the heavens one night*
> *A moment of joining; a celestial sight*
> *A Twinkle in her eye*
> *And a lemon meringue pie*
> *Hence a starburst of light*
> *Rains smore's delight*
> *Chocolate, marshmallow, and candy across the land*
> *Candy Princess' gift at last at hand.*

She ends abruptly as lightning from the raging storm flashes orange through the butterscotch dome. The rainfall, so terribly loud on the outside, is made a gentle pop rocks patter that surrounds me, a candy comfort, while orbs of soft edible light illuminate and coat the room in pleasant tangerine. I can't imagine for the life of me how the candy doesn't melt. I don't mention the song, nor does she.

Gesturing towards a large chocolate door, Candy Princess tells me to change into something clean and meet her outside. She has a feast planned for me, her honored guest.

After leaving me to get ready, I reach for the chocolate door handle. It breaks off into my hand. (crap!) I know!

"Is everything alright?" Candy Princess asks from somewhere outside.

"Fine! Everything's fine!" (okay, what now?) Simple, I eat the evidence. And, oh god, it tastes so good. Some of it melted in my hand so naturally I lick it off. (you could have tried to find a bathroom.) Didn't want to look, plus did I tell you how delicious it is? Besides, I can just wipe the rest off on these crappy clothes I'm wearing. Everyone wins! Hmm, maybe I should just eat the whole door. Leave no evidence. (no one could eat that whole thing.) Oh *really*! (anyway, we have to meet Candy Princess for dinner) Ah, good call. Later then.

The chocolate knob situation taken care of I pull open the door to reveal an enormous closet of brightly colored outfits. Now I don't know jack all about clothes, but I've always wanted to dress like James Bond.

Candy Princess guides me down a maze of different hallways before we come upon an ornately decorated candy dining room with short yellow candy people scouring about in mad preparation for the aforementioned feast. From my brief tasting of the door knob earlier, I can't stop my mouth from growing heavy with saliva in anticipation of the joygasm which is soon to explode in my mouth. Candy Princess, as my gracious host, seats me at one end of a very long table covered with appetizers and walks far away to seat herself at the other end. Why do people always want to sit so far away from me? The midget candy people attend to my needs. They fill my goblet with something that foams over the top and smells of peach sorbet and a hint of dopamine. I

70

take a sip and my body drops twenty feet below me.

"That's an excellent choice of clothing," Candy Princess yells across the long table to me approvingly and breaking me from my high.

I stare blankly at my drink and then back to her. "Thank you," is all I can say about the neon green suit. "What is this stuff?"

"Oh you'd have to ask one of the candy smelters. I don't know what they put in it. Don't you like it? It's got a bit of a kick to it!" She giggles happily. It's infectious. A wide grin spreads across my face.

"What's that you're drinking?" I ask her innocently. "Is that cherry?"

"No, I don't eat sweets. This is tomato juice."

I guess candy treats can only be eaten in moderation before they grow tiresome and old. (damn, she told us she doesn't eat candy, don't you listen?) No.

"What was that?" she asks from too far away.

"Nothing," I say. "So what do you do out here? Are you alone in this magnificent palace?"

"Goodness, no," she responds. "I have all my candy people to keep me company. And occasionally I have new friends stop in too. Like you!"

CRASHHHH! Through the ceiling explodes a metallic figure glowing molten orange. The figure streaks downward in an instant, practically annihilating the serving table to the side of the hall. The smell of burning candy issues from the crater of where the figure landed. I'm on my feet and moving cautiously to the side when I hear a familiar robotic voice.

"Oh my! That did not go according to plan. Not one bit."

I jump up to the crater's edge, "The Robot With No Name?!" His frame is somewhat slagging and warped from the overheated reentry into the atmosphere, and metallic fingers have melted from his

71

metal head into what resembles a fucked up mohawk. He's riding on some sweet treads, but his hat and serape are missing. Jimmy better not have forgotten the retractable claws.

"Yes, it is I, the fabulous Robot With No Name!"

"You are *not* fabulous. Never say that again."

"Right you are master-friend."

"And I'm not your master-friend…you know what, never mind. What are you doing here and where is everyone else?"

"I'm afraid it's just me for the time being, sir. The storm is still posing significant problems."

"So they sent you here to piss me off?"

"Not at all. They sent me here to see if you are perhaps dead so if you wouldn't mind I'll have to check your pulse, sir." The Robot extends his arm to grab me, but I pull away.

"I'm not dead."

"Very well then. I'll just h-have t-to ki-kill KILL!"

"Um."

"Oh dear. My apologies sir, my circuits must have gotten s-ss-sparkled…I mean s-scrambled on the journey down. It was very rough but also remarkably fun. And since we've come to the conclusion that you aren't dead…that is the conclusion we came to, yes?"

I sigh with an exuberance of exacerbation, "yes."

"Of course, well then I have a message for you," and before I can even question him, the Robot's chest plate slides open revealing a video monitor. It flickers on, showing the Command Center of the Colossal Unity. There's movement in the background too insignificant to make out until something amazing fills the monitor. Emma.

"Victor. Vic, I don't know if this is even working. I think it is, but Jimmy just finished his work on RW2N," damn it! He's got her calling it that too! "I've been trying not to worry, but it's been three days," Three days? "I tried to get Ickby to take this whole damn thing down to the surface, which even I admit is pretty crazy, but he just refused saying that you were most likely dead or never existed. I don't know. Valiant seems certain that you are fine and—"

"Did I just hear someone say *valiant*?" asks an unseen, instantly recognizable voice.

"Yeah, I was just recording a message for Victor."

"Ah," suddenly Captain Valiant's face overtakes Emma's, "Victor, it is I, Captain Valiant! No doubt the mere sight of my magnificence will inspire you to persevere through any hardship. For this is the very smile that transformed the wicked Madame Malice into Mrs. Captain Valiant. The love we made was so vociferous, so plentiful that, frankly, people were disgusted. Manbot, from my notes, composed entire libraries of erotica about those days. A truly remarkable lady, whatever happened to her?"

"Uh," Emma interrupts from off-screen, "I'd really like to get on with this if you don't mind."

"Of course, but Victor, you must remain vigilant and remember to keep brushing your teeth!" With that, Valiant disappears and Emma is again the subject of my focus.

"Okay, I want to make this fast. The storm doesn't seem to be letting up so we're trying to come up with any other options. Jimmy mentioned something about working on jet packs and flying around the storm, but who knows how long that'll take. So in the meantime we're sending you RW2N. Jimmy said he did all the modifications you asked for plus a few of his own, though I'm not sure what those are, and he and Sera are working on amplifying the Com system so we can maybe get some communications through. Unfortunately Ickby is doing more harm that good an—"

Ickby comes on screen, practically shoving Emma out of view.

"Now *that* is at least the second time I've heard my name! Tell me what this is about camera! No! Fine. Whoever is listening to this, I have a very important mission for you. What I need is market research for my latest invention. Tiny wings for flies."

"Flies already have wings!" yells a far off voice. Sera, I think.

"What?! Is this true? What do you mean yes! You let me work on this for four yea—It was your idea! What am I supposed t— The crippled flies? Crippled flies can't afford to pay! I don't do charity cases..." Ickby's voice trails off as he walks out of view. Emma returns, her eyes following Ickby for a moment before looking back at me.

"I...I guess we should be sending this guy off. But Vic, I know...I know that you can," she stop, sighs before finishing. "Just be safe."

The video ends abruptly and the Robot closes his chest plate.

"She's very pretty," I was so distracted by Emma that I hadn't noticed Candy Princess sneak up next to me, still sipping on her tomato juice. "Are you two in love?" There's a dreamy tint to her voice. Suddenly I feel a bit sick from the smell of burning sugar and a strong metallic undercurrent. I keep my mouth shut in order to choke back my nausea. Thankfully the Robot With No Name buys me some time.

"And who is this lovely lady?" He asks.

"I'm Candy Princess!" She smiles, never falters.

"What a wonderful thing to be! I'm a kill-bot."

"Ooo! That sounds scary!"

"It might be, but I wouldn't know a-about th-the power source! Find the power source! Should I kill her sir?"

"What?!" It comes out in a croak. "Absolutely not!" I turn to address Candy Princess, "I'm sorry. For...for everything. I just—I need some air. I don't want to be a rude guest, but...how the hell do I

74

get out of here?"

She doesn't miss a beat; smiles politely and gestures for me to follow her. The robot and I follow her down a few corridors and come upon a stained rock-candy glass wall and similar doorway. She opens it, revealing a skittle's garden of delight. A concordance of rainbows glitters from wall to wall in epileptic synergy. Completely enclosed, save for a sunroof in the center that, in this storm, is transformed into a pentagonal Technicolor waterfall. "This is my most favorite place to come when I'm not feeling good. I hope you like it."

I look at her, our eyes meet. "It's beautiful."

She might be blushing as she gestures for me to enter. I let the Robot With No Name pass through the doorway first and seem to catch a glare in the eyes of Candy Princess as he goes through.

"Are you still hungry at all?" She asks.

I'd completely forgotten that we were in the middle of dinner when No Name busted everything up. "I—yeah I think so."

"You just wait here and I'll be right back, okay!" Candy Princess turns with a cheery smile and skips off.

When I see that Candy Princess is out of hearing distance, I start in on the robot, "What the hell is your problem?! Are you not programmed for etiquette?!" I can't believe the nerve of Jimmy not programming this hunk of metal with some simple goddamn commands to just shut-the-fuck-up! But what the hell is going on here?! "You said that I've been missing down here for three days? And what the hell was that blabbering about 'a power source'?"

"The pow- power s-sparkle is not a sparkle! It's out there!"

"No! No," I pause to recompose my question. "First, I said power source, not sparkle and I understand that a power source is 'out there', but *what* is it? And why the hell is it so important that you even brought it up?!"

75

"What's the power source, sir?"

"That's what I just asked! What is the goddamn power source!"

"Sir, I think you must be confused. Perhaps you were injured on your journey down here. I could take your temperature with my trusty probe."

"Keep your probes away from me, Robot!" I turn and move away from the Robot With No Name.

"They all believed you to be dead, sir. Emma was especially concerned. You didn't write, you didn't call, you abandoned—"

"Abandoned?! I've been on this island for ONE DAY!"

"Well sir, I imagine if you cons-consider 67 hours 'one day', then per-perhaps you are correct."

"67 hours?! How the fuck—"

"Ah ah ah! There's that naughty language again," Candy Princess makes her return, basket in hand. "If you keep that up I might have to spank you."

"Um," she really needs to stop saying things like that.

"I thought we could have a picnic," she gestures to the basket, "I don't think I've ever had one before and it sounds so wonderful."

"Yeah, I'd like that. Robot, get lost!"

"Right, sir. But how does one lose themselves?"

"Just go inside."

"Of course, sir. And should I send back the signal to the ship?"

"What, you didn't already do that?"

"I was supposed to wait for your orders."

"Well, do it."

"And should I contact you if word comes in from the ship?"

"Do whatever, just go."

I turn my attention to Candy Princess, not bothering to watch

76

No Name exit. She's still in her evening gown. Not like she's had time to change. I feel as if it should look out of place here, but somehow she's even more dazzling. The manic lights dance around, cling to every inch of her. Her dress, her skin, they pulse in unison. The same colors. It's impossible to tell them apart. I feel a strange perversion looking at her this way. I don't look away.

She lays out a blanket and the food. She never looks at me.

"Candy?"

"Candy Princess," she says earnestly, still not looking at me.

"Right, um, why didn't you tell me I'd been here three days?"

Now she does look up, a slight quiver grabs her lips. "Oh, oh gosh I'm sooo sorry. I was just so happy to see you awake and healthy and your stories were so amazing, I just..." She cuts herself off, bows her head and goes back to work. We sit in silence before I can't take it anymore.

"It's okay," I tell her.

And this time when she looks up she's smiling. Not at me, but for me. She smiles for me and it's all I can see.

It's a good night.

# Act II, Scene 3

Candy Princess explains that she has the entire day scheduled from behind my bedroom door, and that I need to wake up soon if we are to fit it all in. My problem, however, is that I have not slept this well since before the apocalypse. The pillows are laced with the scent of sweet honeysuckle melons and the mattress is a colorful liquid filled delight, most definitely cherry vanilla cream soda.

She knocks a little bit harder than before.

"Victor!" She sings my name, gently coaxing me from my stupor. "I want to play with you!"

I force myself out from under the sheets of the bed. How can I resist.

"Alright! Alright," I throw back through the door, "I'll be out in a second."

Wearing a clean orange sorbet suit, I step out into the hallway and meet Candy Princess. She smiles at me approvingly after looking over my dress. (of course she likes it, she *did* arrange for those clothes to be there!) Shut up!

Candy Princess chirps with laughter, and I blush a little realizing that I've done *it* again.

She dismisses me from my humiliation, while beckoning to follow her, "Come." And it's all I can do as she leads the way to a wing of the castle that I've yet to see. We pass what I count to be about thirty doorways before coming to a spiral stairwell and begin to climb. Tight vertical windows adorn one side of the tower which overlooks a large drawbridge that can barely be spotted in the hazy gray tones of the storm. It's immediately apparent that this castle was built for much more than your average medieval candy bombardment. This place could take years of pounding.

We reach the top room through a hatchway in the floor and Candy Princess closes it behind us. It's filled with paper. Maps, books, scrolls and hundreds of other loose leaflets are stacked or leaned up to the ceiling. Peering through the cracks in the book stacks, the wall look to be garnished in paintings and sketches I can't quite make out. A round table sits in the center of the stuffed room, uncluttered. Candy Princess briefly looks over one row of books before pulling an ancient looking volume from the rest. She places it delicately on the table and thumbs it open for me to see.

"This is my island," she gestures at an ornate map printed across both facing pages of the book. Candy Princess puts her finger down on a tiny arm of the blotch of land. "This is us, here. And over here," she points to another spot much further inland, "is the only source of fresh water on the island. There's a spring underground which swells up over a cliff face and drops sixty feet into a sapphire blue pool! When the weather breaks, I'll take you there!"

I point at a large dark portion of the map with trees and other vegetation drawn in. "What's in there?"

"Oh my!" Her face constricts as if I've uttered blasphemous words and she covers her mouth.

"What did I say?" I lean in, concerned but curious.

"Don't go *there*! That's where the monster lives! Oh, what a horrible creature!" Candy Princess looks extremely distressed and ready to break down. "We were just so lucky to have found you before he… before he…"

I wrap my arms around the shaking princess and try to help her fend off her nightmare. She relaxes considerably and I hold her more tightly in my arms, attempting reassurance. Moments which feel like an eternity pass before she leans her head back and looks up at me, doe-eyed.

BRATATATATA!

Machine pistol shots break out from somewhere far below in the castle. I react immediately, darting for the stairwell. Candy Princess follows close behind but I gain a lead taking two stairs at a time.

It's easy enough to find the scene of the crime as it's right in the middle of the hall. What greets me is fantastically horrific.

Robot With No Name has one tread resting on a lifeless candy person and an arm-attached machine pistol smoking from recent firing.

And that's not the only corpse.

# Act II, Scene 4

"**W**hat the fu—dge?" I catch myself mid-word as I notice Candy Princess giving me a stern look. It seems she's more concerned with my choice of language than the dead bodies on the floor of her castle. "What did you do, Robot?!" I'm not sure if I should pissed off or happy.

"I performed my duties as a kill-bot, sir. And might I say it was quite exhilarating!"

Ugh. I'm pissed. Why can't I even accidentally mind-wipe a robot and reprogram it as a kill-bot *and* have it work out the way I wanted? "You can't just go around killing people whenever you want! You're," I pause and lean towards the robot to whisper because I don't want Candy Princess to hear this kind of talk, "you're suppose to only kill people when I want you to."

"Of course, but I heard these particular people discussing the killing of other people. I deemed them a threat. It was a judgment call."

"You don't have judgment! You have programming," I correct.

"If I may, sir. Perhaps my programming should not lead me to believe I have judgment."

"Or perhaps you should shut up!" I turn to Candy Princess. "Look, I'm sorry about all this. He's pretty new at his job and, well, I'm not terribly attached to him so if you want me to dismantle him and stomp all over his circuitry, I'll do it."

She puts a hand to her mouth as her eyes grow wide. "Heavens no! It seems he was only trying to help and he said the guards mentioned killing others. They've never been the violent sort," what a weird sort for guards not to be, "so I'd like to ask what he overheard."

"Yeah," I sigh. No circuitry stomping today. "Go ahead."

"Hello there, Mr. Robot With No Name."

"Hello to you Candy Princess. Excuse me, but have we met before?"

"I, um," her face goes soft, but only for a moment, before bouncing back to life, "well yes! Last night at dinner."

"Ah, yes. Dinner. It sounds splendid."

"Oh it is! Truly it is. But, sadly, it's not dinner that I'd like to talk about. Can you tell me exactly what my staff was talking about?"

"Of course, miss. They were saying there will be more sacrifices soon. And I'm not sure that you are as familiar, but being a kill-bot I've taken it upon myself to learn all the language of death and to sacrifice means 1. to offer something, such as a life, to a deity to win favor or 2. the victim of a sacrifice."

"Oh," I start, "come on! That's your reasoning?! Two things. 1. Sacrifice can also mean just to give something up. Like say a kill-bot that you thought would be totally awesome and badass, but then turned out to be a typical robot douchebag. And 2. To use the word you are trying to define in its definition is just stupid. In conclusion, you suck! Now apologize to Candy Princess."

The robot starts to talk, but Candy Princess doesn't seem to be listening. She's got her hand to her mouth and is shaking her head. It's an expression that I, in my vast knowledge of body language, can easily decipher as worried . . . or trying not to vomit. Both not great things.

"What's wrong?" I ask.

"It's that awful monster!" she yelps.

"You think the monster is sacrificing people?"

"No, I know it is. Ever since whisperings of the monster began, people have started disappearing and stories have been passed around that some of them have been jumping into Candy Island's volcano, Mount Piñata."

"That's pretty crazy…but uh…Mount *Piñata* you said?"

"I did!"

"And it's a volcano?"

"Yep!"

"So when it erupts it spews out candy?"

"*Molten* candy."

"Uh-huh.  Well that just sounds so…" AWESOME! "terrible.
So terrible."

"Oh yay!  You agree!  Maybe we can go to town and stop this
silliness from happening?"

"Yeah sure.  Why not.  Robot, you're coming with us.  Keep
your mouth shut unless I ask you to speak, and if you dare kill anything
without my say so then it's *your* ass that'll be tossed into Mount
Piñata."

"Victor!" Candy Princess gasps and I snap my head around to
see what's the matter.  She offers an exaggerated frown. "Language."

"Sorry," I say as I follow her wherever she's going.

# Act II, Scene 5

The candy village is…not all that remarkable. Sure it's an entire town made out of candy and it looks delicious and under different circumstances, like if Candy Princess had been Candy King, the evil candy tyrant, then I would eat this whole place up and become Victor, devourer of worlds. That would be sweet. But that's not how things are and after hanging out in a candy castle, a candy town just can't compete. I'm so distracted by my dissatisfaction that I'm just now noticing how incredibly not wet I am.

"It's stopped raining."

"Yep," says Candy Princess. "Isn't it wonderful?"

"Well, sure. Do you think my friends can come down now?"

"Maybe! But Candy Island is prone to very severe electrical storms so maybe not too. Lightning is my favorite thing from the sky. So pretty!"

"Yeah, it's cool and I guess they'll get here eventually."

"Yay optimism. Oop! This is where we stop," Candy Princess comes to an abrupt halt in what appears to be the middle of the town on what I could only describe as Main Street. She clears her throat and I expect her to speak rather loudly, but she doesn't raise her voice one bit. "Hey everyone. It's me, Candy Princess. How are you today?"

"Um, I think you're going to have to speak up if you want them to hear you."

"Oh you, stop being so cute. I can't hardly stand it! Of course they can hear me. They're always listening for me." Then turning back to the empty street, "If you could all just come out here I've got a couple of quick questions for you guys. It won't take too long, okay?!"

I don't really have time to doubt her as almost immediately figures start pouring out of every door. A lot of them look mostly like

84

normal people. Or rather they look like people wearing a jumpsuit of extra skin. Some of them ripple beneath their skin in odd ways. Then there are the ones who are just straight up not trying. Like this one guy or girl or...well it's a giant candy cane with legs and a face that's walking right towards us. It flashes me a smile of razor teeth and winks at me. Either it's coming on to me or wants to eat me. It's definitely one of the five freakiest pieces of candy I've ever seen. We're surrounded, but they don't seem to be coming any closer.

"Good day, Candy Princess," says one of the sort of normal looking ones.

"Good day to you. To all of you!" The Candy People cheer. What an easy crowd. Maybe I should tell one of my hilarious jokes? Before I can decide on the proper one, Candy Princess quiets the crowd and continues on, "It's so lovely to see you today, but I have some unfortunate business to discuss. I'm so sorry. It's just that we've had some rumblings of sacrifices. Is this true?"

Nothing but silence.

"Come now, it's me, Candy Princess! You can tell me anything."

Silence still. Until a shrill sobbing voice bursts somewhere out of the crowd. "Oh Candy Princess please forgive us! It's that monster told them to do it and we were afraid it would come for all of us if we stopped them. Or even worse that what he said would come true."

"Now, now, no tears. Just tell me where they are so I can keep them safe."

"Um," says a candy voice.

"What? What is it?"

"Well, they sort of already left. Said they had to do it at sunset."

"Oh dear," says Candy Princess.

85

I sigh. I'm probably going to have to deal with this, aren't I? (seems like the right thing to do.)

Candy Princess is staring at me with a huge, giddy grin on her face. What's this about?

"Oh Victor, would you really do it?!" Aw fuck, I did it again. "Would you really go help those poor lost souls?"

I look around at everyone who just all happen to be looking right back at me. I shrug, "Whatever."

Candy Princess does a little skip and clap, "Everyone listen! This is my new friend, Victor, and he's going to go rescue our friends from the volcano, isn't that right, Victor?"

"Uh, yeah?" The crowd explodes into cheer. "I mean yeah! YEAH!!" The crowd gets louder, and I actually see a face I recognize. The white heart from my arrival. This time its face reads WE ♥ U. I'm supercharged now. "And then, and then after that! I'm going to go into that jungle and I am going to kill that monster!!!" (dude, what?) I'm gonna kill him so hard!

I look at the white heart again.

*KILL THE MONSTER*, it reads.

I blink.

*BURN HIM*, it reads.

"I AM VICTOR, MONSTER SLAYER!"

WHOOOOO!! (ugh.)

# Act II, Scene 6

It takes a while for the crowd to clam down, but eventually Candy Princess quiets them. "Now you can all go back to your fun, but first what do you have to say to our new friend?"

They all recite it in unison, "Thank you, Victor!"

I bask in the glory of me until Candy Princess turns to me, "And what do you have to say to them?"

"I-uh…well, um, your welcome?" She gives me a nod and the crowd begins to disperse nearly as quickly as it gathered. A few stragglers remain, mostly likely to get a better glimpse, and possibly a handshake, from the greatest hero this tasty island has ever seen. I am just so freakin' awesome.

Candy Princess leaves my side momentarily in order to say something I can't hear to this little taffy looking girl. The taffy girl must like what she hears because she smiles and practically nods her whole body before running off in the direction of the castle.

"What was that about?" I ask as Candy Princess returns.

"I just asked that adorable little thing if she could please run over to my castle and retrieve that map of the island that I was showing you. It made her oh-so-happy to be able to do it! I love making people happy, don't you?"

"Um."

"Of course you do! You're making all of us so happy right now!" She doesn't pause for me to respond or even to give me a little time to think of more candy metaphors that I've been slacking on. "We can go in here," she gestures to a nearby building and starts towards it, "and wait for the map. It's the best place on the whole island. Outside of my castle, of course." She laughs her candy coated laugh and I try and bite into it and taste the chocolaty goodness. I sure hope no one saw that. Embarrassing. Candy Princess ducks her head down to enter through the short front door of the building she designated as the second best place on the island, and I follow.

"This is where many of my people spend their free time!" She points to a large spa in which a few candy people lay and look blissfully oblivious to everything. "This is our sugar-re-coating bath," she points over to capsules suspended by thin legs, "and these are forming tables!"

"And what are those?!" I motion to some sexy looking tables.

"Well, where you come from it might be referred to as massage, but we candy people are not as soft as your kind."

Candy Princess continues to explain the day to day workings of the spa while I meander over to the liquid bath and poke my fingers inside. It drips viscously from my fingers back into the bath and after a few seconds, hardens into a shell. I put my hardened fingers to my nose but can only catch a faint smell of sugar. Candy Princess gestures out toward a patio area where many other candy people lounge about, and finishes her speech.

"...we're done will be completely new! Isn't it exciting?!"

"Uh... yes. Yes, very exciting," I say without having any idea of what she's talking about. She returns to the touring and, as she's not looking, I put my fingers in my mouth. A poetic mélange of sugary satisfaction erupts in my mouth. This is even better than her chocolate knobs!!

Then, right in my moment of oral ecstasy, Candy Princess turns back and catches me at it.

"Hi hua huss huvig hu hasse huv hu huger huell!"

She laughs, "So you think I taste good?"

I'm swimming for some response when the taffy girl returns from her errand and saves me from more embarrassment. She hands

Candy Princess one long scroll tied neatly in the middle with a colorful ribbon. Then, in an attempt to run back out the door she came in, she crashes face first into Robot With No Name. They both tumble out the door.

As No Name rights himself in the doorway, the taffy girl rises with him. She's impacted the robot with such force that her entire body is stuck to it. I rush to their aide and peel the taffy girl off. Where her face should be, there is only a negative impression of No Name's robotic features. Taffy girl begins to weep softly but Candy Princess overpowers her moans with a gentle melody of her own to reassure the girl, hands me the rolled map, and walks taffy girl back into the day-spa to be cared for.

Meanwhile, I'm left alone to reprimand this robot tag-along yet again! But really, I should be getting pissed off at Jimmy. If he'd actually listened to what I wanted this kill-bot to be like I wouldn't be having these problems.

If robots had tear ducts, No Name would be bawling. Perhaps I've been harsh on him in the past, but this latest reprimand takes the cake.

I unroll the map and order the robot to make a photo reference of it in his memory. Who knows what we'll run into out there, and it would surely be a good idea to have a back-up reference.

Candy Princess returns alone and hands me a bag.

"There's enough food and water for your short journey in there. I've also placed a small communications device for you to reach me if there should be an emergency. Now, if you'll please excuse me again, I need to make sure that poor girl is tended to."

With that, I'm on my own again.

The Robot With No Name and I wander down the adobe road through the main street of the town on our way to the bridge into this walled village. Little shops with bustling candy people go about their day-to-day business. I can't help but feel a little longing for freshly grilled steaks upon seeing so many butcher shops, and my stomach growls.

Upon reaching the main gate, armed guards open it and then lock it again behind us. Before us, golden brown and red grasses spotted with strange miscolored trees pepper the landscape. In the distance they grow thickly. We head for them.

# Act 2, Scene 7

We're barely within sight of the castle when we enter the woods. I haven't said a word to the robot since we left. It's been a hard walk due to sun direct exposure, and now a chill runs down my back from the temperature drop in the shade of these tall trees. Strangers to a strange land, we move onward. Cautiously.

(I don't think it's a good idea to be in the trees like this.) Oh great, you again. (I'm just saying that this place could be filled with crazy candy people and that monster.) The monster is in the candy jungle, this is clearly a candy forest. (how would you know?) Jungles are tropical, none of this candy looks tropical. This looks more maple syrupy. (sound logic.) As always. Besides, the jungles are on the opposite side of the castle. (the map made it look like they wrap around a bit.) Shut up. (it's just that—) Ugh, enough. I'll settle this.

The Robot just looks at me silently.

"Hey I'm talking to you Robot!"

"Does that mean I should also be talking to you?"

"Um, yeah. That is how these things work."

"Very well, and what should I be talking about?"

"The map and the jungles, dumbass. Are we going to run into the jungles? I mean, not that I'm worried or anything, I'm awesome. But clearly I don't trust myself despite said awesome. So what's the answer?"

"Well, at our current trajectory, yes we will."

"Will what?"

"Enter the jungle."

"Oh right. Damn it! So how do we not do that?"

"If we head slightly to the west then we should find a trail that will keep us outside the jungle and lead us to our destination."

"Of course, west…west? And west would be which direction? Not that I don't know, because I know! But I figure we should, um, test out your internal compass for its, uh, compassing abilities?"

"Oh I do love tests, sir. The west is to your right. Did I pass?"

"Uh…yeah? YEAH! The right is right." (so, what if his internal compass is messed up?) Then we'd go to the left, clearly. (but it's just that the jungles—) Are to the left, I know! Which is why we're going right. Keep up!

"Excuse me, sir."

"What do you want, Robot?"

"Well, if we are quite clear on which direction we are going would you perhaps care to contact the ship now?"

"Contact the ship? Okay, you've lost me there," I roll this last statement over in my head, "we can't contact the ship because of all the interference or whatever."

"That hasn't been an issue since the rain let up, sir."

"And why the hell are you only telling me this now?!"

"To show of my incredible ability to follow orders, of course! I kept my mouth shut until you asked me to speak just as you asked of me. You must be very proud of me, sir."

Oh my god…

"You know, when it first occurred to me that I could have my very own kill-bot I thought 'A robot that kills? And on my command! Well this might just be the best thing ever. It'll be like having my own Transformer. And not one of those pussy Transformers that can only turn into golf carts and never even run people over. No, one of those *hard* fuckers that turns into a jet and blows shit up.' So I ask you, is my very own Transformer too much to ask for?"

"Well, sir—"

"Nononono. NO! I'm still talking here. I mean, I almost saved the world. That's got to count for something. And I thought robots were supposed to be cool. But it turns out they're dicks. Obnoxious-vague-prophesying-and-whatever-the-hell-you-are-DICKS! Which is lame because you were supposed to be the Batman of robots, but without that rule against killing. Your one rule would be *killing*. And you could have said things like 'the only rule here is death!' and then killed a bunch of people. It would have been great. But you're no Batman, you're more like Jimmy Olsen. You're just another Jimmy. God I hate Jimmy."

"Uh, hey Vic."

"Great, now you even sound like Jimmy!"

"No, Vic just look down."

I do and I see that The Robot's chest is open again and Jimmy's dopy face is looking back at me. It's good to see that guy. "What do you want Jimmy?!!"

"We've been trying to get a hold of you since the com started working again," he says.

"Well you can blame your terrible personality for infecting every robot in the universe."

"Uh, okay."

"Just put Emma on already."

"Can't. She's in the shower, I think."

"You think? Well go check."

"O-okay."

"Wait! Scratch that. Her awesome body would just blow your mind and if you were to accidently see her naked I'd have to punch you in the testicles. Where's Sera or Valiant?"

"Sera's right here."

"Yeah, I want to talk to her instead of you."

Jimmy bows his head and mopes a bit before getting out of my sight and letting Sera take his place. Her hair is electric blue today.

"Hey," she says. It's like we've known each other forever.

"Hey yourself, buddy. Love the hair. Hope you aren't feeling *blue*."

"Nope, just like blue."

"I totally know what you mean, and you know what it reminds me of? That time that you were in that blue goo bath. You remember that time?"

"Yeah, that—that was like last week."

"Right, I know! We've known each other for so long, right?"

"Um."

"So what have you been up to?"

"Building jet packs so we can get down there."

"I heard about that. Jet packs are cool. You definitely need to get down here because I don't know if you know this, but this is an island of *candy*!"

"Why are you talking to me?"

"Just trying to catch up with my best friend, that's all."

"We're friends?"

"Not friends, Sera, best friends."

"I had no idea."

"Really? That's unfortunate. You want to know why I think that is? We haven't high fived enough."

"Okay…look, Victor, your com signal is getting weaker and we're starting to lose your tracking signal again too. We know you're on the move. Are you going anywhere in particular? We're going to be leaving here soon and we need to be able to find you."

"Actually, I'm headed to Mount Pinata. It's a volcano or something. Filled with delicious melted candy."

"Uh, you aren't going to try and eat it are you? Because that'll probably kill you."

"Nah, I've got to save some candy people from jumping into it. Heroic stuff, you know? Price of being a hero."

"That's what Valiant tells me...and everyone he ever meets."

"He's an amazing man, Sera. An amazing man." I look up to the sky and am reminded of the lovely grey of his eye. A piercing steel that's protective, so unbreakable. Sera still hasn't responded, "hey Sera, I said he's an amazing man, right?"

I look down, she's gone. The screen is dead. "What did you do to her, Robot?!"

"Nothing, sir. Communications have gone down again."

Crap. (what?) I wanted to give her a message for Emma. (what were you going to say?) Eh, it's not important. (it was about her awesome body wasn't it.) Not *entirely*.

# Act 2, Scene 8

We start again through the woods. I try and keep a quick pace to ditch my halfwit robot tag-along. The hiking is considerably easier now that I can dwell on the fact that I will soon be reunited with my band of adventurers. They will soon recognize my heroic heroicness when I, after having saved the earth once, proceed to save it yet again! And those grateful, creepy little candy folk will weep when in the presence of my heroism, thus making it all the more dramatic and marvelous when my friends show up just in time to witness it all. They will bow to me. Except Emma and Valiant, of course. They can just clap. Sera's cool too. But Jimmy better bow.

My foot suddenly goes heavy causing me to wobble. I try to regain my balance by taking another step, but tug as I might, I can't move. I fall sideways and land unusually comfortably onto the…ground?

I've apparently stepped into a bubblegum trap. And much like the more naturally occurring sand trap, I feel myself slowly being pulled down.

"Okay, okay. I remember seeing that guy on this survival TV show talk about this…Beaver? Beaver was his name. But yeah, he definitely talked about getting out of sand traps. Don't move too much. Uh, take off clothes to spread your weight over the viscous surface. FUCK!"

I can't move my hands. Actually, I can't move anything. Bubblegum isn't quite the same as sand. I sink a little bit more.

"Terribly sorry to intrude upon your bathing, sir, but shouldn't you be more concerned with the quest you've undertaken rather than leisure sports?"

No Name strolls up nice and close to the edge of the

bubblegum. I wouldn't be the least bit surprised to see him drop into it and submerge with me just to watch my face turn blue-violet as my lungs suck on bubblegum. He must be less than an inch away.

"Forgive me sir, I dare not move any closer to this pool since its molecular makeup will most definitely prevent me from assisting you as I have been programmed. But please, you should get a move on if we still wish to prevent those poor candy souls from being lost."

"I'M STUCK YOU BRAINLESS ABOMINATION!"

"No sir, simply shed your skin and use it to walk on and don't touch the pool again."

"What do I look like, a fucking snake?!" I think Jimmy forgot to use the set-up wizard to adjust the robot's settings to '*human* master' as opposed to '*disgusting reptilian alien* master'. "I can't shed my skin, robot." I'm done with him. "Just record my dying moments and broadcast it back to the ship so they can see just how useless you really are."

"Useless is not the correct term you're looking for, sir. I believe you are looking for quite the opposite word since I would be very useful in reversing the effects of the pool by grinding up some—"

"Oh! OH REALLY! Who the fuck do you think you are? Mr. Wizard? I don't care about science! Science is for pussies! Just get me out of here!"

"Yes sir, right away! Oh boy, I get to use science now!"

"I said science is for pussies!" But the Robot is too busy doing stupid-ass science to hear me. (you could be a little more grateful, you know.) I just tell it like it is, science = for pussies. (you can be a real douche sometimes.) For true. I'm always having to clean up the mess of a bunch of pussies. (dude, gross.) Oh great, the Robot is coming back.

"Now as you can see I've brought back the following—"

"Why are you talking, Robot? When did I ever give the impression that I was interested? Just get me out of here!"

"Right away, sir. Oh, this is so much fun!"

"Whatever, just hurry up. I've got heroic adventures to get back to because eventually I'm bound to come across my very own spaceship. Like all great adventurers eventually do. Then I'll…well, I don't know what comes after that. Captain Valiant didn't get past the spaceship part. But one things for sure, it'll kick ass."

Robot With No Name picks up a variety of similarly colored rocks, grinds them to a fine powder, lights it on fire, pours a liquid from an opened gasket on his chest and, smoldering, throws it at the gum. I can smell the reaction and the gum turns brittle. No Name cracks most of the gum away, enough to free me, and drags me away. Crusty pink barnacles cling to me like a gay version of the creature from the black lagoon.

Maybe I can melt this shit off. (or you could just chew it off, it is bubblegum after all.) Aw damn! That's your best idea ever. Time to get to work!

After a bit, the Robot interrupts my expert bubble blowing, "Excuse me, sir, while the bubblegum trap was quite a lovely time perhaps we should get back on the move?"

My initial response is, "perhaps you should go die" but my mouth is so full of gum that nothing really comes out. I have to spit it out. Yet another example of this robot ruining my life. I finally get around to saying fine, "but from now on you go first, Robot." He doesn't protest, just takes the lead and starts on the way.

"Because I'm a good trap detector?"

"No, because you're expendable and I hate you."

"Oh, very good then!"

We walk for awhile and it's nice and quiet, but I hate walking so, "Hey No Name?  How much further do you think this volcano is?"

"Just about 3.2 kilometers, sir."

"Kilometers?  Seriously?  Those are for prime ministers and serfs and shit.  I'm American goddamn it!  I don't respect your kilometers."

"To be fair, sir, we aren't in America."

"And to be fair, I Jesus'ed your obnoxious ass just a few days ago and if there's one thing I know about Jesus it's that he demanded satisfaction from his disciples.  So give me miles already!"

"That would be 2 miles, sir."

"See, a nice round number even.  But 2 miles?!  That's like a 20 minutes walk."

"And that's just to the base, we'll probably have to climb some."

"Ahhhhhhhhhhhh, bullshit," I sigh. "Carry me."

# Act 2, Scene 9

"Hey No Name, how long have we been rolling now?"

"About 10 minutes, sir."

"Balls." (well, on the bright side we're halfway there.) Yeah, but on the suck side we've still got halfway to go. (at least the trees are starting to thin out so we should be able to see the volcano soon.) And that's good why? So I can see the mountain I have to climb and not want to do it anymore? I already don't want to do it. Hmmmm. (what?) I was just thinking that—(no, that's a bad idea.) You don't even know what I was going to say. (of course I do!) Oh, so you're a mind reader now? That's ridiculous! Anyway, I'm pretty sure you'll be surprised. (just say it.) Okay, so what we do is stop and relax for awhile. Maybe snack on the foliage. Then just leisurely walk back to town and tell everyone we were too late. Problem solved. (yep, that's terrible.) No, it's easy. (I thought you wanted to be a hero.) Even heroes fail, it's how they overcome that defeat that truly defines them. (you're being defeated by your own laziness.) And I've already come to terms with it. Is that not heroic? (no!) Well, it's the thought that counts. (no, it's the trying that counts.) But everyone will *think* I tried and they'll love me for it. (we'll know you didn't.) And I already love myself. (okay, but what would Emma say?) She'd probably say "Oh Victor, you're so manly. HOLD ME NOW!" (she doesn't talk like that!) I think I know her well enough. (fine! What about Valiant then?) Well he would . . . damn it. Then we'll do this for Valiant!

"Excuse me, sir?" No Name intrudes.

"WHAT, ROBOT?!"

"Sorry to disturb you, but I believe there's a jungle bush trying to get your attention."

"I thought you said we wouldn't end up in the jungle!"

100

"We haven't, we're next to the jungle."

"No Name, you are dangerously close to, um, to something."

"What thing, sir?"

"Shut up. And stop telling me bushes are trying to do things. Bushes can't do things."

(actually, I think he may be sort of right.) Did you not just hear what I said about bushes and doing things? (well it's not so much a bush as—) You shut up t—

"Viiictor."

HOLY CRAP! A talking bush! (it's not a talking—) No no, I'll handle this.

"Hey bush! First question: Are you God? Second, if you are God can I have superpowers? Third, why do I even have to ask for superpowers? It's bullshit, God."

"I am not a bush and I am not God," a blue candy person moves out from behind the talking bush.

"Oh!!! Hey there little guy! Did you see this talking bush here?"

"There was no talking bush, Victor," says the blue candy dude. Clearly he missed it.

"Sure there was, you were standing right behind it. Here I'll get it to say hello. Hey bush! Say hello to this blue guy."

Silence.

"Hmm. It must not like you."

"Victor, aren't you curious as to how I know your name?"

"Not really, I'm pretty famous. Although I am curious as to why you sound so similar to that bush."

"I AM THE BUSH!"

"Nah, you can't be a bush and a person. That's ridiculous."

"Okay look, I was never actually a bush. I was always me, just

101

behind a bush."

"You are the bush, you aren't the but...look man, this conversation sucks. Not that I mean any offense, but you should probably take some anyway because you're terrible to banter with. Now I've got other things to do so I'm going to take off and—"

"He says you will come to him, Victor!"

"He who? The bush?"

"Not the bush! The Great Hard One!"

"Um?"

"The shining light in the vast darkness of the candy jungles. Some would call him a monster—"

"Oh hey! I've heard of him."

"—but he is no monster, he is a saint that will lead us to a better day. And you, Victor, shall come to him."

"That's cool. I've got to kill him sometime," I start to walk towards the base of the mountain, yet again.

"You won't kill him."

"Sure I will. I'll be all 'hey monster, you're dead meat' and then I'll make it so. Maybe have my kill-bot do it."

"Who should I kill, sir?"

"Yourself if you don't shut up."

"It's not in his nature!" yells the blue candy freak because I'm pretty far away now. "He is eternallll!"

We leave the little antagonizer behind and begin the ever harder duty of climbing the growing slope. After a few minutes I stop. It occurs to me that I've been able to see the mountain for quite some time, yet I haven't seen any sign of Candy People climbing it. (maybe they're just sitting at the top?) Uh, I can see the top. They probably already jumped. (but it's not sunset yet.)

"Actually, sir, I believe I can offer a possible explanation for

102

this," I don't recall asking for his opinion. (oh just listen to him.) Fine!

"Explain, Robot. But do it fast."

"<sub>EEEEEEEEEEEEEEEEEEEEEEEEEEEEEEEEEEEE</sub>"

"Aw CHRIST! What the hell was that?!"

"It was me explaining as fast as I could, sir."

"Well slow it down!"

"Ah, my apologies. I assumed you could interpret ultra-sonic frequencies."

"I think my ears are bleeding."

"As I tried to explain, when I was making my way down to Candy Island—"

"No, seriously! Are they bleeding?"

"Only if you are bleeding invisible blood, sir."

"What the crap! I can bleed invisibly?"

"Shall I continue?"

"Sure, why not. I'll just stand here and slowly die from invisible blood loss."

"Very good. So on my way down to Candy Island I got an immaculate view of the entire island. And might I say it made me quite wish I could breathe so that I could have had my breath taken away."

"I don't care. Get to the point."

"Well I very clearly spied a lip at the mouth of the volcano, perfectly suitable for camping and certainly not visible from our current vantage point."

"No Name, I mean this with all due offense because I really hate you. You're a malfunctioning piece of scrap metal and you can't be trusted."

"Of course, sir, but I do have it all archived in my memory. I could make a scrapbook for you!"

"A scrapbook? Why would I ever want that?"

"Captain Valiant says that scrapbooking is one of the 15 great inventions of man."

"And naturally I'll expect that scrapbook in my hands by the end of the night."

"Of course, sir."

"Now where was I? Let's see…malfunctioning scrap metal, trust issues, hate you…did I mention hating you?"

"Yes sir, several times."

"Good, good. You can't hear that word enough."

"I do love words!"

"Just another reason to hate you, but that's beside my point, which is that I'm actually going to trust you on this one, because if you're wrong I can always push you into the volcano."

"That's sounds like fun, sir."

"It certainly does, No Name. It certainly does."

# Act II, Scene 10

"**O**kay, so we're just about to the top and I can only presume the sun will set eventually, so here's the basic plan as I see it. We'll charge over this supposed 'lip' and if you're right, Robot, and I really hope you're not—"

"I'm quite right, sir. I can hear voices very distinctly just over the ridge."

"Well, that sucks, but fine. So we'll ambush them and I'll yell 'GO GO KILL-BOT NET!' and you'll deploy your kill-bot net, capturing the sugar-filled sacraficees and we'll drag them back. Safety for them and glorious praise for me."

"An excellent plan, sir. Where do I get this net?"

"You don't have a net?" I sigh deeply once. And then even deeper a second time, "You are a constant disappointment, you know that. On to plan B then." I causally stroll over the ridge at the volcanoes top. I see three candy people sitting near the mouth of the crater. None of them look like normal people. They look delicious! Looking up at me, they don't say a thing so I hunker down next to the nearest one. A woman carved from caramel.

"Nice day," I'm breaking the ice. I'm an excellent ice breaker. "Perfect weather for a picnic or, I don't know, a *sacrifice*?"

Still nothing, although the caramel woman smiles at me. It's unsettling. No matter! I know exactly what to do.

"You know, I was just like all of you once. In love with sacrificing." (what?) Trust me; I heard this speech back in school during DARE. It'll work. (oh balls.) "Sure it wasn't always at the top of a volcano, truth be told it didn't really matter where I was. I could be in my house, at the back of a dark alley, or in some sleazy, run-down bathroom. Anywhere that I could score a sacrifice, well I'd be there and I'd do whatever it took.  Because sacrificing made me feel good, made me feel special.  Like for a few brief moments my shit life had meaning.  Sure, at first it started out fun.  Something to do when I was bored with friends.  But before I knew it I was sacrificing myself everyday.  Constantly driving around town looking for guys to give hand jobs to in the hope that they might hook me up with a sacrifice.  That was my life.

"Until one day I woke up after a particularly wicked sacrifice binge and I realized that all this sacrificing was killing me.  That if I didn't stop right away I'd end up dead.  Oh maybe not that day, or the next day, but one day I'd sacrifice myself and I wouldn't wake up the next morning.  So believe me, I know where you're coming from.  When a scary, charismatic monster says go jump in a volcano it all sounds like great fun, but eventually you'll just end up with a penis in your hand.  Or maybe your mouth.  Just say no, kids.  Just say no."

Silence.

This is good, they're letting it all sink in.  You can't rush these things.

A lot more silence.

I must have really made an impact.

Finally: "Uh," stammers a little blue guy who looks freakishly like that little blue guy hanging around the talking bush, "He's not really a monster at all."

"Look, I'm not here to apply labels to the monster or to pass judgment about his horrible deeds.  I'm just saying that Candy Princess says he's a monster and monsters suck.  Is Candy Princess ever wrong?"

"Well," says the little blue guy, "she's always been very good to all of us."

"You can't be seriously listening to this guy!" exclaims the

106

caramel woman next to me.

"He has a point though. Candy Princess has never asked us to jump into Mount Piñata before. And I didn't even want to do this in the first place. I'm just filling in for my brother since he's sick."

"Wait!" I feel the need to interject. "Does your brother look a lot like you? Because I talked to a guy who looked just like you at the base of the mountain."

"Did he look sick?"

"Well he was alarmingly blue, and that can't be healthy."

"Um, that . . . that's natural."

"Really? Hmm, then he looked fine, I guess."

"That is so typical! He's always shirking his responsibilities off on me. Well not this time, no sir! I'm going back to town."

"M-me too!" yelps a rock candy girl. Or I assume it's a girl, but maybe that's just how all rock candy sounds.

"Fine!" the caramel woman stands up, "But I won't betray the word of the Great Hard One!"

"Sure, if that's how you feel," I tell her, "I won't stand in your way. It's your decis—GO GO KILL-BOT NET!"

She looks at me. Nothing happens.

"Um, where's the net?"

"I still don't have one, sir," says my worthless kill-bot.

"Ah, that's right. Oh well, two out of three ain't bad." (oh come on! We can still do something, it's not like she's jumped ye-and there's she goes.)

Before I can respond to myself the air streaks oddly and goes BOOM! By the time I'm able to re-gather my bearings I see four people floating down to me.

Emma, Valiant, Jimmy, and Sera. And Emma is holding a squirming caramel woman. Eventually I notice Ickby way off in the

107

distance. Apparently he's in no hurry. Emma drops Caramel as she lands and immediately the candy lady dashes for the volcano again. But Valiant grabs her, valiantly, as Emma rushes hug me. She's soft and smells good.

"Awesome jet packs," I say.

"It's good to see you," she says.

"You too," I give her a look-over with a smile, "and with what you're wearing I can pretty much see everything," she blushes and tries awkwardly to cover up. It's cute.

"Hey Vic!" says Jimmy while Ickby finally makes his touchdown.

"Oh, christ Jimmy!" I cover my eyes. "Unfortunately I have to say the same thing about your outfit."

"Right, well that's because we needed to reduce the friction for our flight and our normal clothes would have ripped right off. Luckily the CU had this amazing material that—"

"I don't think I asked, Jimmy. Just stay out of my direct line of sight and everything will be fine."

"Um, sure thing, Vic."

"Victor, my friend," exalts Valiant, "excellent to see you still living. I never doubted it for a minute. You and I are cut from the same mold. Unkillable heroes is what we are. Now Lieutenant, if you'd kindly take this woman off my hands so that I might stretch and pose."

"Certainly Captain," responds Sera as she takes handle of Ms. Caramel. Once Valiant turns his back she deftly clocks the writhing Caramel in the back of the head, knocking her out.

"So this is Candy Island," states Valiant as he places one foot on the lip of the volcanoes mouth and looks out toward the setting sun. It's a picture for the generations. No Name better put it in my scrapbook.

"So is, like, everything here candy?" asks Jimmy.

"It is Candy Island. Just pick something up and try it," I say.

Jimmy grabs a handful of soil and shovels it into his mouth. "Pffft! It's dirt!"

"It's *candy* dirt!" I tell him.

"But it tastes like regular dirt."

"Dirt flavored candy dirt. It's to add to the realism, obviously."

"O-okay?"

"Hmm," mutters Ickby, "dirt flavored candy dirt? What about candy flavored dirt dirt? Tasty and nutrious. Must make a mental note...DRATSTICKS! Where's my mental note pad? Has anyone seen my mental note pad?!" We all just ignore him.

"Anyway," I say, "we should probably get back to town. It's only a couple miles from here so we can get there before it's too dark. They probably have celebrations planned for me."

"Ah, unadulterated praise," lavishes Valiant, "it's one of my favorite parts of *adventuring*! Lead on, Victor." Emma grabs my hand before I start and down the volcano slope we go.

This would be a lot easier if I also had a jet pack.

Damn you, Jimmy.

# Act II, Scene 11

In the diminishing daylight we can see the bonfires from over half a mile away. The rest of the crew doesn't seem too concerned, as they've never been to the candy castle, but fear mounts in my gut. The monster has come out of hiding to retaliate for our offenses back at the volcano. I just know it! One of his brainwashed candy minions must have been able to get word back to him, and then launch a siege on the castle grounds. Laying waste to the unprotected village beyond the outer walls of the castle, they've probably perform unmentionable grotesque acts upon the happily ignorant candy folk. Like popping out eyeballs and devastating their brains with assorted candy genitals…shit! That was supposed to be unmentionable.

We get closer and I can hear the screams from those poor tortured candy souls. Why is there music? Is this some new form of torture? I pick up our pace.

"Alright, everyone quiet down. Turn off your lights."

"Vic, what's wrong?" Emma asks.

"It's a raid!" I whisper.

We keep down and hide behind the last line of trees before the open village grounds. It is seconds too late before we notice Ickby running towards the nearest bonfire.

"PARTY!!!" he exclaims wildly.

I hold our friends back and prepare to see the moron scientist ripped to shreds by the candy mob that runs towards him and then throw him upon a bonfire. But it doesn't happen.

They lift him in the air, maybe three feet high, and pour bubbling multi-colored liquid into his eager gaping maw and over his pale complexion. Apparently he learned how to party on one of his CU excursions.

"Vic," Emma begins patiently, "this is *not* a raid."

"I give Ickiness maybe ten seconds more before they take him apart. Wait for it…"

"Sweetie, remember back at the volcano how you said there would probably be a celebration for you?"

"Yeah, and now it's being ruined by some orgiastic murder ritual! Any minute they're going to start eating each other."

"You poor, crazy man . . ."

"I know, Ickby is screwed!"

Emma kisses my forehead as my angry terror grows, "Look," she says, "I'm going to go infiltrate this orgy and do as the Romans do."

"An imperialistic takeover. Good idea, I'll stay here. They know me. But you might want to take someone with you to watch your back."

"Sure, Sera you want to go to the orgy with me?" Sera shrugs and Emma takes her by the hand. I can't help but reflect back to a time in my life when hearing a woman invite another woman to an orgy while I watched was all I really wanted. But those were simpler times. Times when I still thought robots were cool and that orgies were more about sex and less about cannibalistic candy people out to eviscerate me. And as the two of them walk towards the fire, I can't help but reflect on just how incredibly hot those jetpack outfits are.

Emma and Sera join the fray and are immediately accosted with those multi-colored drinks. They drink. That wasn't part of the plan! Perhaps they've gone so deeply undercover they've forgotten which side they are on. That's when I see Jimmy join them. He's drinking too. They all start dancing.

OH.

MY.

111

GOD.

I know what's happening. It's so obvious, why didn't I see it before. Those multi-colored drinks are clearly some sort of cultish super kool-aid brewed deep in the dark heart of the Candy Jungles. It's turning them all against me. Soon they'll be one; a hive mind of mega-death controlled by some unseen monster. Except to them I'm the monster. They'll hunt me. And one day, they'll catch me. Tales will be told of the day they killed the Legendary Victor. But not if I kill them all first. I turn to my only remaining allies, Captain Valiant and that crappy robot. But no! Captain Valiant has left my side. He's making his way towards certain doom! I must stop him.

"Captain Valiant!" I whisper. I've no doubt he'll hear me. The man has ears like a fox. I assume foxes hear things well. But Valiant doesn't stop. Damn it! I'll have to risk it. I grab some mud and make a circle around each eye as a makeshift disguise. No one will notice me now! Rushing to Valiant I reach him just in time.

"Ah, Victor! Excellent of you to join me. We shall join this party together," okay crap! He can see through my disguise. But then again, what can't he do? No matter, I'll just get to the point.

"Sir, I have reason to believe this is a *death* party."

Valiant pauses. And then he laughs. "Calm down my friend." Valiant boldly steps forward to greet the approaching horde with open arms. "We have returned from the mouth of hell itself, *victoriously!* Now if someone could snap a picture of me with my adoring new fan club, I'll be needing one for the scrapbook."

"But Captain, there's a monster on this island and monster's love death parties, probably."

He grins, "Victor your undying vigilance and commitment to *adventure* is nearly as *valiant* as my own. But you have much to learn. So worry not, I've been to enough parties to know a death party when I see one."

"Well, if you're sure."

"Victor, I'll make you a deal, if we die here tonight then the Adventure Galley is all yours."

"Well then let's party!"

The little colorful people swarm around us and usher us into the extravaganza. It doesn't take Emma long to find me and wrap herself around me.

"I see you'll come for the Captain, but you never come for me," she slurs slightly. I think she's drunk. She hands me a glass of that crazy liquid everyone is sipping on. Blue now and gently dissolving to grey. Never static; an ever changing rainbow in my hand. "Wait until it's purple," she says, "purple's the best."

So I wait.

Grey gives way to red becomes purple.

I drink.

The world expands and pops. A bubblegum burst of violent orchids. Ultra sexy, funky, tight. My pores expand; sweat euphoria. Makes me cool. In my chest my lungs laugh as my liver laments its loneliness; wishing for the companionship that my kidneys share.

My pores contract. I exhale imaginary fire. I get hot. The wind shows me a voice. I close my eyes and it touches me. A jolt of exuberance mixed with the caress of familiarity. "Victor," it exclaims, engulfing me. Lips press against mine, the taste of berries inside me.

Emma.

My mouth melts into hers. Fantastic and . . . and sugar coated? Uh-oh. Not Emma.

I open my eyes.

Candy Princess is in front of me, beaming. Emma is to my left, steaming. I find that in times like this a good rhyme lightens the mood.

113

I feel better already.

"Uh," says Emma. Candy Princess, oblivious to her presence until now, latches on to her.

"Hi! You're Emma, right? I saw you on Victor's adorable robot. You looked so worried and that made me so very upset! But I took very good care of Victor and now he's our hero! Even if he's being very rude right now by not formally introducing us."

They both glare at me. It might be awkward if I wasn't so damn purple.

"Right, well…Candy Princess this is Emma. Emma, Candy Princess. And before you ask, yes that's her actual name and she's also a princess."

"Oh," says Emma.

"Thank you for that wonderful introduction, Victor. Now, Emma, I hope you won't mind if I borrow him for a few minutes. We're all just dying to hear of his heroic exploits."

"She's making a pretty good point about how great I am. I shouldn't deny people that, Em."

"Um," Emma replies.

"And of course you can join us," Candy Princess grins. "I'm sure you have many tales to tell. We'd certainly love to hear more of Victor's great escapades from a different perspective!"

"N-no. That's okay; I'll catch up with you later. I think I need a few more drinks first."

"Good idea, Rainbow Rhapsberry Cream is so very tasty. But don't drink it when it's grey. You'll just end up with delusions of invisibility and that only leads to very inappropriate behavior. Come on, Victor, everyone is waiting," she begins leading me towards what looks like a circus tent before turning back to say, "it was so wonderful meeting you, Emma!"

114

We enter the tent and it's filled with nothing but mind melting color. Rainbow Rhapsberry Cream flows from every corner as candy people dance and sing. A small group is near the back of the tent banging on skullish bongos. Valiant, Jimmy and The Robot With No Name are already inside being merry and all that. We drink pitchers of Rainbow Rhapsberry Cream throughout the evening and congratulate each other on a mission accomplished. No Name recites the adventure in clips of sound bites stolen from the real world while I add color commentary to make me sound almost as cool as I actually am. The candy people cheer or shrink in excitement and fear at our recounting. Eventually Sera and Emma join the crowd too. At first her glances are a bit cold, but as the evening progresses they soften and by the time I'm finished she's laughing with everyone else.

She comes to me, "Hey you!" sticking her finger in my chest. "You're mister hero, Mr. Hero." She kisses me hard. Too hard, really. My lips mash against my teeth and I taste blood. It's okay though. As I wipe the blood from my mouth, I notice Candy Princess smirking at me, eyes glazed over. But Emma pulls back my full attention. My face in her hands; there's no other place my attention could be. "Dance with me," she whispers. And I do. With her head rested against my chest she looks up at me, a goofy grin plastered on her face. "You know what I've been doing?"

"Drinking," I say.

Her grin gets even goofier. "Soooo much!"

"I could hardly tell."

"Thass because Ima lady and ladies are always not showing things."

"At least you're feeling good, right."

"Oh I'm not juss feeling good I'm feeling *stuff*. Like after Candy Sweetass took you away I started drinking all green which made me go 'Whoa! What's all this about', right?  And then Sera she was saying 'drink it blue, Emma' cause she's talking to me and her hair would change to whatever color she was drinking so I did it!  And that made me all like 'yeah', you know?  Which is when I started drinking it was almost purple again, but still sort of red and that make me all ROWWR!  Thas my mating call so you know and you know what that means."

"You want some more Rhapsberry Cream?"

"That's not the kind of cream I'm looking for," she smiles sloppily.

"Emma!  That is by far the filthiest thing you've ever said to me.  Thank you."  I look around for Candy Princess in order to politely excuse myself, but she's nowhere to be found.  So I say fuck it and whisk Emma out of the tent.  Only one problem, I've no idea where to go.  Luckily it's dark so—

"Excuse me, Mr. Victor," says a tiny candy fellow.  This better be good because I've no time to waste.  "Are you retiring for the evening?"

"Sort of, although I don't see how it's your business."

"I didn't mean to intrude, it's just that we've set up a very special tent for you this evening and—"

"Take me there, good man!"  He guides us through town and leaves us outside a rather fancy looking tent.  Inside it's beautiful and splendid and all that stuff.  Who cares.  I grab Emma.  Nothing else matters.

I'm in the process of trying to figure out how to get her damn jetpack suit off when she says something unpleasant, "Dr. Icky!  What are you doing?"  And in return I hear something even worse.

"Nothing nothing, not a thing.  You can't even see me so I'm not here to be doing anything.  And it's Ick*by*."

I turn around only to wish I never did. There's Dr. Ickby sitting in the conner. Completely naked. "Get. OUT!" I yell.

"Get out? Why I'm not even here! If I were here you could see me, but clearly you can't as I'm quite invisible so you must be mistaken about my presence. No please, continue with your clumsy intercourse."

"You aren't invisible, we can both see you!"

"Hmm, curious. Could I really be visible? No, I'm quite certain that's an untruth. Ah-ha! You must also be invisible. Note to self, once you find your mental note pad take note that invisible people are visible to other invisible people."

"Just go away! Spy on Jimmy or something."

"As if that one is in any danger of intercourse," he says as he exits the tent, still naked. "Your mating habits disgust me."

Finally alone I turn back to Emma. Thankfully she knows exactly how to work that flight suit.

"Hey," she says. I think she tries to wink.

She lies down.

I follow her.

The sound of drums carries through the night. The world beats softly; gently. Constantly transforming, never static. The night builds to a frenzied rhapsody. The air made sweet with imperfections. A breath out of rhythm. Then two. Things get erratic. Unraveling towards a crescendo. Everything falls. Softly again. The drums diminish; stop. The night exhales.

The party's over.

# Act II, Scene 12

The Candy Jungle.

I wait.

I hide.

The scent of licorice and sweet death surrounds me. Engulfs me. It's the smell of false candy. The kind old people try to give you not realizing it tastes like necrotized flesh. Probably because they're too busy decomposing to notice. Every second I stay hiding I get stickier, and every second that monster gets more, uh, monstrous. Doing weird monster things to my friends. My Emma. And to think, the morning started out so well…

*Gentle warmth and amber glow intertwine to wake me from an entirely rejuvinating sleep. If not for the rising temperature inside our tent I'm certain that the soft pillows and silk sheets would keep me completely under awhile longer.*

*I stare at the gorgeous creature stirring beside me, watching the delicate rise and fall of her chest as she breathes ever so slightly. Before her dreams are also broken by the new day I suck up and savor each quiet moment, closing my eyes as I do.*

*Candy Island.*

*Awesome. I'm still on Candy Island.*

*I keep expecting to wake up from this fairy tale back at the office with my swimming-fish-screensaver before me. I'd have passed out, sleep deprived and overworked at my desk, before the apocalypse. Was this my subconscious trying to tell me something? Did I secretly long for some semblance of normality?*

*No. I've been here a week now. Completing life-saving work, getting stronger. I am a hero and every minute I stay I rise to the ranks of 'legend'. Otherwise, I'd be what? Promoted to head of inventory?*

*Everyone gets everything they want. I want it all, and for my heroism they've given me a monster to slay.*

*I sense a black velvet ready to snuff out my consciousness once more. I feel Emma stir.*

*"mmmmictor?" It's a sweet sound, a sleepy sound. I know that the battle is almost lost, but I reach out, caressing her cheek.*

*And then nothing.*

*For how long? Only a second or two?*

*"You ever gonna wake up?" Emma's voice, wide awake, tugs at my consciousness. I grumble, shake my head. "Everyone is waiting for us at breakfast." I must have been out longer than I thought.*

*"Mmph," I say, eyes still closed.*

*She kisses me and I inhale sharply. That's when I catch it, something lingering in the air. My eyes burst open.*

*"You smell that?" I wonder. "Do you smell that?" Emma glares at me, bemused, but I don't care. "Waffles! I love the smell of waffles in the morning. This one time I ate something like twelve waffles. There was syrup everywhere. The smell though, that cakey smell. Smells like—"*

*"Victor," she interrupts, "we have to go."*

*I stretch and search for my clothes, noticing with a tinge of disappointment that Emma is already fully dressed.*

*She lies back on the bed and watches me hunt for each article of clothing. Smiling faintly, giving no indication that she intends to help despite her earlier impatience. "Are we going into the jungle today?"*

*I nod as I locate a stray sock. "We might as well get this over with," I lower my voice, make it all ominous. "We are going to the worst place in the world," Emma rolls her eyes, "you might not believe*

119

*it, but I can tell from seeing the maps in the candy castle's tower. Possibly days away and miles down a river that snakes through so many unknown traps and trials, like a main circuit cable which plugs right into that terrible monster. We simply need a boat and we will be delivered to the lair of the creature. I'm sure Candy Princess will help us with that, though."*

*Emma gives something that's a mix between a sigh and grunt as she throws my shirt in my face. "Hurry up, I'm hungry." I struggle a bit with my shirt, still not wholly awake, and just as I pull my head through, Emma's face pops into view. She kisses me swiftly. And we're off. Waffles here I come!*

But that was long ago. Hours even. It was a different life, where candy was sweet and sugary. Not like in the jungles. If only we could have eaten breakfast forever. I was willing to at least try. But everyone else had other plans. Because I'm a hero. Because there's a monster at the heart of this jungle.

*"Any idea how to kill it?" Sera asks no one in particular.*

*Valiant laughs heartily in return, "Lieutenant, I've yet to encounter a monster I couldn't kill!"*

*"I bet Victor hasn't either," Candy Princess beams at me from across the table. Next to me, Emma rolls her eyes and grumbles something I can't quite make out over all the praise I'm receiving.*

*I can't help but grin at the compliments and state how truly magnificent my magnificence is, "You are absolutely correct, Candy Princess! I have an uncanny ability to find the weakest link in my enemy's armor and exploit it." Suave satisfaction drips from my self congratulations. "One does not survive so many days on the run without being a master in his field, and I am a master of death!"*

*Sera chokes on a square of waffle.*

*"We are so lucky that the gods have brought you to us,*

120

*Victor," Candy Princess continues. "Before, it seemed there was a black empty hole in our hearts and lives. With you here, my hero, our village has become a home."*

*Emma turns her head away, visibly agitated, and then looks around the table.*

*"Are you looking for the syrup?" Candy Princess asks without any recognition of Emma's agitation. "Victor, you need to fill Emma's nooks!" She exclaims cheerfully.*

*Everyone at the table looks wide-eyed at Candy Princess in silence. An awkward moment passes before Candy Princess starts in again, "So about getting you a boat…"*

I wipe the sweat from my brow and taste it. Don't ask. I just thought I'd give it a try, and *damn it!* Licorice. This place has gotten into my skin.

I gotta have a plan. I need to quit simpering about and do something heroic. Like swinging in on a rope out of the trees yelling really loud, or kamikazing a jet into their camp only to eject at the last second, landing to save my friends, strapped to the back and chest with assorted projectile and laser weaponry. *That* would be heroic. However, neither of these seems possible without that damnable Robot With No Name. But, any way about this, I can feel that there will be casualties.

How many people have I killed already? There were all kinds of monsters, but I don't count those. Killed so many that I've lost track of the count. But, this time, I feel that it will be a human. One of my own.

As a hero that shouldn't matter. I should know that my friends will always be made to suffer. But it does matter. And now that I think about that's even more heroic. Still, I should have made them stay behind. I should have made them stay with Candy Princess.

121

*"I think we're gonna need a bigger boat," Jimmy says gleefully upon first glance of our odd means of sea travel. A rainbow steamboat of confectionary delights. Sugar, glucose syrup—or perhaps hydrogenated palm kern oil—certainly some gelatin to hold its shape. All the colors are there: Red 40, Yellow 5 and 6, Blue 1 and 2. It's glorious. When no one's looking I take a bite out of it. Fruit flavored. Natural and artificial.*

*I love candy.*

*"Well, we do have plenty of other boats if you would like more space," Candy Princess smiles at Jimmy.*

*"Oh, um, I didn't really mean that. It's just something I've kinda—"*

*"Shut up, Jimmy," I sigh.*

*"It was just a joke, Vic."*

*"A stupid one," Jimmy's smile fades as he turns his head to the ground. Sera pats his shoulder and whispers something. I don't really pay attention to his reaction. "Let's just get this done."*

A flash snaps me out of my reverie. Before I can question its origins, the sound of thunder answers me. Another storm? Or just a continuation of the one that's threatened to drown me since my arrival?

I hear the rain sheet the mint canopy above. It's a while before any makes its way down to me. And even then it's only a few drops at a time.

Drop

Drip

Spearmint water mixes with licorice filth. It's sickening and strangely refreshing.

Drop

Drip

I inhale violently.

Drop

Drip

The day is growing dark.

Drop

Drip

Drop

Drip

*Bloop*

*Blip*

*Bloop*

*Blip*

*The sound of the steamboat that's not a steamboat soothes me in maddening duality. Violet bubbles escape the steam stack, float a few feet, and burst into clouds of pixie dust. I breathe phantom sweetness to an unending candy coated melody of Purple Haze.*

*Bloop*

*Blip*

*With Emma next to me it's easy to forget everything else. The distance between us is negligible, almost unnoticeable. A slight shift and we'd be touching. She's laughing with Sera about something. I miss her.*

*Sera's a blazing orange today, or at least her hair is, allowing her to melt effortlessly into the ship. The ship itself would be easy to see from miles away anywhere else but here. In the Candy Jungles it looks just like the rest of the surrounding.*

*Jimmy is near the back of the boat tinkering with the world's worst kill-bot while Captain Valiant dictates tales of adventure for me to listen to later.*

*Ickby is nowhere near any of us, pacing around mumbling nonsense, no doubt. I don't even know why he's here at all.*

*An overcast sky and our spirits are high, despite sailing towards some unseen monstrosity. Or maybe because of it. I'm pretty sure we all like killing things. Either way, at this moment the day is perfect.*

*And then:*

*"Stop the boat!" Ickby yells with unnecessary volume. "Stop it now! Hurry hurry, not much time."*

*Sera jumps up and powers down the boat. It drifts to a stop with everyone on guard. Except for Captain Valiant who looks calm as ever.*

*"What's the emergency, Doctor?" Valiant asks ever so valiantly.*

*"It's dire, Captain. Exceptionally so. So dire that it's looped back into normality. Frightening."*

*Valiant never loses patience, "Would you care to fill us in?"*

*"I'm hungry."*

*Seriously, that's what he just said.*

*Sera barks a short laugh before laying back down.*

*Emma reclaims her spot next to Sera, "You know Dr. Ickby, we have plenty of food on the boat."*

*"Blech! Don't want it!" He shakes his head erratically before shooting a finger out towards the jungle, "Want* that*!"*

*"I'm not sure it's safe to just eat random things in the jungle," Emma responds, but she's no longer paying any attention to Ickby.*

*"Of course* you *wouldn't be sure! But I am. I'm much smarter."*

*"Just let him eat whatever he wants," I finally sigh. "I really wish you'd stayed with Candy Princess."*

*Ickby, about to jump off the boat, freezes. "Staying at the castle was an option? Why wasn't I informed? Once we've eaten we'll turn this boat around. Boats are the worst form of transportation. I've done research." He doesn't wait for a reply; he just jumps off the side of the boat and swims to the jungle.*

*"It's settled then," Valiant declares, "we picnic." Without another word he rips off his shirt and dives in after Ickby.*

*None of the rest of us seem too keen on swimming so Jimmy maneuvers the boat closer to the river bank and we all make our way to shore just as Ickby is retuning with an armful of bright pink berries, already snaking on them.*

*"So, how are those?" Emma asks.*

*"Incredibly terrible, actually," Ickby answers while continuing to pop berry after berry into his eager mouth. "They taste like dry fire. Sensational. Try some."*

*Everyone declines.*

*We eat in silence, mostly just enjoying the day. Until Ickby ruins it again.*

*"Uh-oh! Are the rest of you seeing what I'm seeing? No, no. You wouldn't be. That's insanity."*

*"What are you seeing?" Sera asks, though she doesn't seem to care and never takes her eyes away from the overcast sky.*

*"Hmm, you know voices and feelings. The usual. Although," his eyes fix on Sera, "you're getting brighter. That can't be good."*

*After a moments pause. "Ah! I see. Poison! Dratsticks."*

*"Wait, what?" Jimmy looks confused.*

*"Ugh. Try and keep up. These berries are poison. Obviously. My chest is now a cold inferno and my heart should be exploding in about 6 minutes. Very unfortunate."*

*He looks directly at me. "This is all your fault."*

*"Me?" My jaw would have dropped if Ickby ever made any*

*sense or I cared.*

*"Yes, you never should have let me eat these berries. Poor leadership. I'll hate you forever," as he speaks, he shambles down to the river and lays down in the water.*

*Emma jogs over to the river bed. "Maybe we can help you? We'll at least get you back to town and find a doctor."*

*"There is no hope. And I don't want your help. You're all very bad helpers. The evidence is in my dying. Now if you would all please help push me down the river."*

*"Why?" I wonder.*

*"Because water burials are very prestigious. Great honor. You're very uneducated."*

*"It's only proper to give a man his dying wish," states Valiant. "Remember that, Victor; it's one of my* valiant *tenets for being a better you."*

*More than one of us sighs. I do it because of my distaste for pushing things.*

*"Oh, one more thing," Ickby stops us, "Captain, would you like the Colossal Unity?"*

*"It would be an honor," Valiant replies.*

*"Of course it's an honor, but it's mine. You can't have it."*

*And with that, we shove.*

*He floats downstream still talking, "Thank you all. I'll try not to hate you as much in death," he cranes his neck towards us, "except for you, Victor!"*

*Watching Ickby float away is unusually soothing. At least for me.*

*Everything is quiet.*

There's nothing but the rain and thunder now. The calm pitter-patter is gone, replaced by a panicked torrent beating away my sanity drop by drop.

The thunder roars, challenging me.

I start to rise.

I prepare to kill.

*The walk is killing me. I miss the boat. But we all decided a surprise attack was best. No good sailing straight to the monster. Still, I hope it's not much further. I'm always walking way too much.*

*Spirits have been muted since Ickby's bon voyage. Even mine, and I'm not sure I even liked him. But I hate seeing Emma frown. Only Valiant speaks now. Endlessly narrating our entire ordeal so that he can relive it over and over again.*

*I could listen to him talk forever.*

*And then a rustle.*

*And a whisper.*

*Something scurries in the depths of the jungle.*

*I see eyes all around us. And something says my name.*

*A voice yells "RUN!" and nothing makes sense anymore.*

*I search for Emma but she's not there. I'm moving. Did she run first, or did I? I trip and tumble down a shallow slope. I hit the bottom hard.*

*This all seems very familiar.*

*My mind wants to quit on me. My body refuses. But slowly. I take too long. When I finally get back to where it all started there's no sign of anybody.*

*Scratch that, there's one thing. My kill-bot may be worthless, but he's heavy and his treads leave a very clear path to follow. That's what I do.*

*Eventually I find myself just outside the monster's camp. It's too bright. I search around for cover and it's not long before I find a nice gooey black pit. I don't hesitate to jump in. All too late I notice*

127

*the pile of corpses in various stages of decomposition. The sweet candy flesh of the most recently deceased is darkening, melting into the pit. My love for candy gets the better of me. I take a bite out of the nearest one. EWWWW! Licorice. No matter, I'll endure. I'll wait until dark to strike. The liquefied candy flesh will give me the perfect cover. No one will see me coming. No one. So that's the plan. The Candy Jungle.*

*I wait.*

*I hide.*

*The scent of licorice and sweet death surrounds me—*

(um, are we done yet?) Huh? (well, we've been over this already.) Well, yeah but I'm trying to get in the mood. You know, for killing. (okay, but it feel like we were going to be caught in some infinite loop.) Hmm, I guess you're right. Just give me a second. Killkillikilldeathkillkill! OKAY LET'S DO THIS!

This is the end.

I emerge from my candy death pit, dead candy people dripping from every inch of me. I make my way back to No Name's tracks. I ready the weapon I built from a nearby candy tree. (it's a stick.) Yeah, a really sharp one.

"Hello, Victor."

Um.

"You've finally come to see the Great Hard One."

I turn to see the little blue guy from when that bush was talking to me. He's totally ruining the killing mood. Guess I'll have to kill him first.

"Would you like me to take you to him?"

Well, I'll definitely kill him later.

He leads me to the largest grass hut in the clearing.

"He's right inside," he says before leaving me. I open the

doorway and enter. This is going to be so easy. And then I see it and stop.

No.

NO!

It can't be!

"*You* are the monster?"

The horror.

"I AM THE ROBORACLE."

The *horror*.

# Act II, Scene 13

"**I** AM THE ROBORACLE."

"I know who you are, so stop saying that," Maybe it should be a relief that the monster I came to slay is just my extremely obnoxious, vaguely prophetic, former robot companion, but the problem is he's *extremely obnoxious*. He's always saying things like "I AM THE ROBORACLE" and "THE FATES SAY YOU ARE BONED". The best part of being a space slave was not having to hear him every day.

"THE ROBORACLE WONDERS WHERE YOU'VE COME FROM. VICTOR."

"I don't have time for this. Where's Emma?"

"THE FATES DEMAND AN ANSWER. WHERE HAVE YOU COME FROM?"

Arrrhg.

"From outside!"

"HOW FAR FROM THE RIVER?"

"What? I'm not an odometer! Go measure for yourself."

"THE ROBORACLE'S MOTHER WAS AN ODOMETER. SHE WOULD TELL THE ROBORACLE STORIES OF HER TRAVELS EVERY NIGHT. 10 MILES. 15 MILES. 68.3 MILES. THE NUMBERS RARELY REPEATED. THE ROBORACLE WAS ENTHRALLED. THEN THE FATES PLAYED STYX FOR THE ROBORACLE. AND THE ROBORACLE NEVER SPOKE TO THE ROBORACLE'S MOTHER AGAIN. IS THAT WHY YOU'VE COME. VICTOR? TO LISTEN TO STYX?"

"I *came* here to kill a monster."

"IS THE ROBORACLE A MONSTER?"

"Well there are stories about you pimping cannibalism, and

judging from all those corpses I got acquainted with I'm inclined to believe them."

"THE FATES BELIEVE. AND THE ROBORACLE CONCURS. THAT CANDY WAS MADE TO BE EATEN."

"I—hmm?" Damn his superior robot logic! "Look, I'm a hero so I have to do hero things, okay."

"NO. YOU ARE LAME. YOU WORK IN A CANDY SHOP EATING CANDY. THERE WILL BE VOMITING. A DIABETIC COMA IS INEVITABLE. IT WILL LEAD YOU TO HELL. TIME FOR STYX."

"No it is not time for Styx! It's time for—"

"Victor!" Emma! "You finally made it," I turn to the hut's entrance, "we wanted to go look for you, but the Roboracle said you'd be here soon and—Oh sweetie, why are you naked?"

"Huh, I forgot I was," Emma holds a very twisted frown as she struggles hard not to smile. It's a look I know quite well. Emma isn't alone, the whole gang is here. "I needed camouflage to sneak in."

"Uh huh," she humors me. Sera, however, is keeled over in hysterics.

"Well, it seemed like a good idea at the time," I trail off at the end, shoulders slouched, almost dejected.

Captain Valiant claps me on the shoulder. "Do not fret, my friend. It was a *valiant* effort. It's not the clothes that make the man, but rather his ingenuity and genital prowess. You'll learn this many times over." He lets out a hearty guffaw and poses by my side. It's so freakin' great.

"I really wish you wouldn't encourage him so much," Emma shakes her head, but we don't pay her any attention. We just pose.

"How cool is this, though, Vic?" Jimmy interrupts our epic Grecian pose, "The monster was just The Roboracle all along."

131

"Cool, Jimmy? You think it's *cool*? There's nothing cool about robots!"

"Jeez, man, you don't have to be so pissed off."

"Oh don't I, Jimmy? (1) I hate robots. (2) I didn't get to kill a monster. (3)," I point at the Roboracle, "Fuck this guy! (4) I'm cold. Would you like me to continue because I'm pretty sure I can get all the way to seven and—holy shit! Ickby?"

"It's Dr. Ickby and that you're noticing me just now speaks volumes about your perceptive capabilities. I'm stunned, actually. I figured you wouldn't notice me at all. You're very dense. Almost blind. You probably have very poor intercourse skills. You should have let me watch. You need evaluation."

"Um, how is he not dead?" I ask.

Before anyone else can speak, "He as in me? Already forgot I was in the room. Imbecile. The poison was a misdiagnosis. Heartburn. You should have recognized it. More terrible leadership. Candy people fished me out of the river. It's nice to see you again."

He smiles at me and I go back to ignoring him. That's the best way.

"THE FATES SAY YOU MUST ALL LEAVE HERE."

Finally something I can get behind.

"AND YOU WILL TAKE THE ROBORACLE WITH YOU."

"Hmm, let's see...PASS!"

"THE FATES DEMAND IT. THINK IT OVER WITH SOME STYX."

"Fine! Jimmy, grab the monster and let's get the hell out of here. I need to get my clothes anyway."

Sera, who has managed to recover at least a modicum of composure through all of this, rips down what appears to be a curtain

132

and tosses it to me.

"I'm getting really sick of looking at that," she says.

Emma helps wrap it around my waist, making something close to a grass skirt, before we head out of the hut.

"So what is that black stuff all over you?" Sera asks as we step outside.

"Decomposed Candy flesh," I answer. I'm so nonchalant.

"What?!" more than one voice echoes back.

"Apparently Candy flesh gets all black and gooey after they die. Tastes like licorice too."

Emma's jaw drops almost comically, "You tasted it?"

"Only one bite."

She does a little half dance half squirm that's unbearably cute, "Ew ew ew ew. I don't think I can ever kiss you again. Eeeeeew!"

"Psh! Like you haven't had disgusting things in your mouth."

Before Emma can respond—and she clearly plans to—that little blue guy pops up again.

"Where are you going with the Great Hard One?" he asks.

"Away," I say.

"No, that won't do," he says.

"And yet here we go," we continue to causally leave the freakish little camp.

"No, you don't understand. We won't allow it," suddenly Mr. Blue is joined by a pack of candy people. They bare their teeth and snarl rather impressively.

I groan. This could be unfortunate.

"We might want to walk faster," Sera whispers.

I nod and we all increase the tempo of our strides. Except

for Ickby.

"Hey, Ickby!" I hiss. "Pick it up!"

"And listen to you," he starts, "no thank you, but thank you. I rate you as a leader a 4. That's out of 10. So I do the opposite of what you tell me now. I'm quite confident it'll all work out."

The Candy Pack has increased, and several of them are licking their lips. I propose to everyone that we run. They approve this measure with their feet.

That's when the Candy Pack strikes. Two of them launch themselves at Ickby. The rest come for us. I can barely hear Ickby over the horrible ripping sounds. He's not screaming, though. He's scolding.

"Ow! You're biting me. That is very backwards. Very. Hasn't anyone told you that you're candy. Maybe I'll try eating you."

And then:

"Damn you, Victor. This is the second time you've gotten me killed. I still hate you forev-*"

I think that's the point his throat got ripped out. Oh well.

"No Name," I pant, lungs burning. I really need to work out more, "kill everything that's not us!"

"It would be my pleasure, sir."

The dark jungle ignites in a steady *ratatatat* as the scent of gunpowder and burnt sugar blanket every breath.

It's a great life.

# Act II, Scene FINAL

The trip back to the castle is a blur. I'm still high from all the gunpowder. I vaguely remember re-boarding the boat, but it isn't until we dock that my senses fully recover.

I start preparing for another celebration. If last night was any indication, tonight will rock my socks off. I can already taste the Rhapsberry Cream on Emma's lips.

Sure I didn't actually slay the monster, but I made sure there would be no more candy cannibalism in the jungle and I'm pretty sure that's good enough. Besides, I'm already being punished by having to travel with The Roboracle again.

The Candy Castle is quieter than I expected. Of course it is late so maybe we'll just party in the morning. I could sure go for some waffles. And maybe a Coke.

Strange. I had expected to at least be escorted in by some of the villagers.

Wait!

Oh hell yeah!

I know what this is! A surprise party. I don't bother telling everyone else, though. This way they'll be surprised, but I've got to get to work on my surprised-face. The perfect expression pops into my head just as we make our entrance.

I jerk to a stop. This is not what I had hoped for.

The Candy Castle is in shambles. Dead guards litter the floor. A sudden urge to call for Candy Princess grabs me, but I quell it. What if the people who did this are still here? We can't alert them to our presence.

We follow the trail of destruction to the dining hall. And there, huddled in the far corner, is a tear-stained Candy Princess.

She struggles to find her footing as I approach. I help her as much as I can only to have her fall into my arms. She mutters something about robots and an amulet. There's no time to make sense of any of it as we're both startled by the sound of The Roboracle.

"THE FATES FORESEE A BURSTING PIÑATA."

"Is that a bad thing?" Jimmy asks.

A low, hard grumbling answers him. The grumble grows louder, more insistent, and the earth quakes beneath us.

This can't be good.

I look down at the princess in my arms. She smiles. It's weak, but genuine. I don't know how long I stand there. Long enough for the shaking to stop—except for the girl in my arms—and long enough for Sera to have started strapping something on my bare back. It's a jetpack.

"Don't worry about anything," she says.

"RW2N will control everything remotely," she says.

"Hopefully," she says.

It's a whisper over the never-ending growl of an angry mountain.

Candy Princess strokes my face, gently ushering my eyes back to hers. A plea that's barely a sigh escapes her lips.

"Don't let me go."

And then a piñata bursts.

Surprise?

# Interlude

The Thing's stomach grumbles.

Alas, now is not the time to dine.

So the Thing waits.

Sometimes sacrifices must be made.

Roborotia Publishing

## Characters you should know:

**Victor** – likes Coca-Cola

**Emma** - likes cinnamon jelly beans

**Jimmy** - likes cutting his skin off

**Captain Valiant** - likes adventure

**Sera** - likes secrets

**The Roboracle** - likes Styx

**Candy Princess** - likes everything

**The Thing** - likes sunsets…

**…AND THE WORDS JUST KEEP ON COMING!**

# ACT III, Scene 1

"You can let go now," I tell her.

She only shakes her head.

Her face is hot and wet against my chest.

She won't stop shaking.

Or maybe that's just the jetpack.

I've no idea how to shut this thing off.

# Act III, Scene 2

I let the heat wash over me; scald me. My skin is red from the exposure. But it feels good, like I haven't showered in days instead of hours. I scrub until I bleed in some places. Still the faint aroma of licorice batters me with each breath. I must have gotten some up my nose. I start breathing through my mouth. I should probably get out soon, find out what happened to Candy Princess before Candy Island exploded. For that matter, what happened to the Colossal Unity? It was just gone, only the Adventure Galley left in its place. No big loss. Kind of annoying though.

I turn off the water and cough. My lungs still haven't expelled all the candy ash. Stings but tastes good. I dress quickly and head off towards the Captain's chambers.

Everyone is waiting for me.

Jimmy, Sera, and Emma are all seated comfortably on a leather looking couch. It's probably made from the skin of a Fliperisakiss. Those freaky space whales can be made into anything once they're dead. Valiant is posing with the robots—it still pains me to have to pluralize robot now—in a corner nearest to Jimmy. Valiant is no doubt dictating some masterful diatribe that I'll listen to later. Candy Princess, who's wanted nothing to do with robots since we got back from the jungle, is prettily perched in the opposite corner, her frilly dress, barely hanging on to her candy body, scorched from our escape and grey with ash. No one else bothered to shower or change, they didn't really need to as much as I did, so they're still smattered with dirt and ash. Sera makes it work for her, however, by changing her hair to dull silver. Jimmy, on the other hand, is blue now. This wasn't the case when I last saw him. He was a mess back then. Or a different kind of mess, at least. All singed and burnt with his scalp looking as if the hairstylist decided to use a blowtorch instead of scissors. He must have been the last to blast off from the Island. I laughed when I saw him then and he surprised me by laughing back. I laugh at him now and he just bows his head, dejected. But I think I see a bit of a smile as Sera dabs more blue—presumably that same phoenix stuff she bathed in earlier—on his head. I'm sure he likes the attention.

I sit down in a love seat next to the couch, nearest Emma, and Candy Princess slides over, taking a place at my feet. Emma glowers when she notices Candy Princess' migration. All I can do is shrug.

"Ah, Victor," Captain Valiant takes a few steps my way, "you've rejoined us. Excellent! I was just finishing up a lecture on proper *adventuring* décor that I hope you'll take to heart. But that's something for later. We've filled Candy Princess in on our time in the jungle, but were waiting for you to hear her tale."

"She knows about The Roboracle?" I ask and Valiant nods.

Candy Princess looks up at me sheepishly, "I don't like that he's here. The things he did, that he can do…I don't trust him."

"I don't like that he's here either, but don't worry about it," I reassure, "he's mostly harmless. All he does is occasionally spout off weird cryptic nonsense that only makes sense after it happens. Otherwise he just listens to Styx and pisses me off."

Candy Princess taps me on the foot as if to scold me. Language, of course.

"The Roboracle has helped us out plenty, Vic," Jimmy interjects.

"Jimmy, I know he's your friend, but eventually you'll have to admit that your friends are retarded."

"We never would have found you or the Adventure Galley without him," Emma says without looking at me.

"Fine, so he's useful once in awhile, but we're supposed to be letting Candy Princess tell us what happened to her."

She sits in silence for a while, but eventually she finds her voice.

"I…well it's hard…I remember that I was in the dining hall preparing for your return," she follows the thought and her whole body smiles, "I had this big party planned with balloons and specially trained singing woodland creatures," ZWHA?! Why didn't I ever see those? And as if she is reading my mind, "I wanted to introduce them to you earlier, but the storm had them taking shelter on the other side of the island. I guess they're all gone now."

Tears well in her eyes, but only one spills over, carving a line through the ash still caked on her face. She doesn't wipe it away, "I'm sorry I—anywho!" She forces cheer, "I was getting ready for the party when I heard some commotion with the guards. I worried that something had gone wrong in the jungle; that the monster was coming for me. And then, when I saw the first one, I was certain I was right. No, worse, I was sure that the monster had infected your minds and convinced *you* to get me. Because that first robot looked just like that one over there," she points to No Name, "except that wasn't true. Not when I really looked. It was…less deformed than yours. They all were. And there were lots of them."

"Ah, the Dread Space Pirate Robots," says Valiant.

"You know them?!" She exclaims.

Valiant nods, "All too well, my dear."

"Hey," I feel like adding my two cents or whatever, "were they going on and on about some power source nonsense? Because that's probably our bad."

"Why? What is it?" The tears have nearly evaporated as her eyes blaze with curiousity.

"Who knows? They're just crazy robots."

144

"Oh, well I don't recall them saying anything about a power source but I was so very scared. They killed all the guards so easily. And the woodland creatures. Oh my! The unspeakable things they did to those poor things, but even then they never stopped singing. The robots only seemed insistent about one thing. A very old amulet of mine. It's the most beautiful necklace, I'm sure I showed it to you once, Victor."

I don't remember any necklace, but I nod anyway.

"It's so wonderful and hardly ever the same color twice. The jewel is said to have been retrieved from the heart of a star. Of course I never believe in silly stories like that, but golly it's pretty! And it's been in my family for generations. Father told me it was called the Amulet of Anexia. Kind of a funny name."

Anexia? Where have I heard that before? (Entheus. The Immoral Many. The Donnanatrix.) Oh right! Hey—

"The Roboracle! Where the hell is Donna?" I ask.

"Um, Vic," Jimmy jumps in, "that's kind of a touchy subject. There was a pretty nasty break-up after you got abducted."

"So you're telling me that the only decent part about having The Roboracle around isn't even around? Weak."

"THE ROBORACLE MISSES DONNA NATROIS."

"Yeah, well way to go with sucking so hard and making her gone. She might have actually been useful with all this. She probably knows some way to track this Anexia amulet."

Sera rolls her eyes sarcastically, "Sure, that's likely."

"She and this Entheus guy knew all sorts of convenient stories."

"Who the hell is Entheus?" Sera asks.

"Uh, the Inspiration of Anexia! Everyone knows that."

"Yes, Lieutenant," Captain Valiant chimes in, "you really

145

should have known that."

HA!

"And perhaps this Donna Natrois women would be useful, however, if it's a pirate we seek then there is a much simpler first course of action." Ever the master a dramatic effect, he pauses *valiantly*. "The Brothel of Infinite Sadness is our destination."

Sera surprises me by actually giggling. She leans toward Emma, "You're gonna get a kick out of this place. It's wild!"

"But first things first, rest. To enter the Brother weary is to kiss a beautiful lady at dawn before brushing your teeth; ill-advised. So, Lieutenant, if you'd show the Princess to her quarters—"

"It's Candy Princess, actually," I interject unconsciously.

"Oh, if you prefer Princess or," she tilts her head back to smile at me, "or Candy, well that's quite alright. And Captain? May I have a room next to Victor?"

"As you wish, Princess," he nods to Sera.

She nods back in reply to his silent order. And so we head back to our rooms with Sera leading the way.

# Act III, Scene 3

"**I** don't like the way she looks at you," Emma says.

"Who looks what now?"

We're alone in our room, about to climb into bed. Emma stares at me, "Huh?"

"What?"

"Candy Princess!"

"What about her?" I ask.

"The way she looks at you. It's…it's unnatural. Like you're her favorite dessert but for some reason she wants to have sex with you."

"Awesome."

She hits me.

"Ow."

"Look, I don't want you leading her on, okay."

"Come on, Em, I'm not leading her on. She just lost her home and needs a little comfort is all."

"Which is all the more reason to set boundaries. She's a sweet girl, but she's vulnerable right now and *you* are what she's latching on to."

"Yeah, you're totally jealous."

"Fuck you," she throws herself into bed and gobbles up all the covers in one angry gesture, leaving her back to me.

"I can't help it that I'm so dreamy."

"Only when you look in the mirror, sweetheart," her voice has a bite to it, but it's not all that hard. I'm sure she's got that little half-smile creeping around the left corner of her mouth that would make any sane person delirious with the kissing fever.

I lie down and try for sleep. I don't get very far though,

because suddenly I hear a tapping. You know, like something gently rapping, rapping at our space port window. (that was terrible.) Well, I'm tired.

"Could you please stop talking to yourself in poorly plagiarized Romantic prose," Emma scolds, "I'm trying to sleep."

"Sorry, but didn't you hear that?"

"No, I was sleeping," she growls and presses a pillow over her head.

*Tap tap tap*

"Okay, you had to have heard *that*!"

"Yeah yeah," we sit up and look to the window. Instead of seeing space and stars and junk, there's just white. And a little pink. The pink reads HELP ME. Then I see the hand going tap tap tap again.

"Hey! I know this guy. It's a giant candy heart I met on Candy Island."

"Huh, weird," Emma studies the thing outside our bedroom window. The pink now reads LET ME IN. "Kind of cute though."

"We should probably go tell Sera or the Captain so that we can help it," I say.

Neither of us move.

"When you say 'we' you mean *me*, don't you," says Emma.

"Thanks for offering! I'll stay here so it does freak out and float off into space."

Emma sighs and grumbles. Well, sort of. She actually says "grumble, grumble, grumble" as she sulks off to retrieve help.

Unfortunately that doesn't have the desired effect and I get suckered into the retrieval operation anyway. I was too tired to say no. I also can't resist jettisoning a robot out into space. If only briefly. We tie a braided steel cable to No Name and the other end to the ship wall then seal him into the airlock. It takes the robot mere minutes to find

148

the candy heart and bring him back into the airlock. The robot seals the chamber and opens the inner airlock. I shiver as a cold blast of air rushes past Emma and me. The big little candy heart flashes a smiley face across his front-side and then jumps a 180 to read THANX across his back-side, if it could be considered either a front or back.

The chalky little heart starts trying to spell something out, "G, E, O, R, G," when I notice that my sight is becoming a little fuzzy. I shake my head. No change. I close my eyes and pinch the bridge of my nose, holding my eyes shut.

"Victor..." Emma starts worriedly.

I snap my eyes open to see her faint, and just barely catch her blurry form before she hits the cold metal floor. Through the haze, it looks like she's breaking out with green spots. My head swims as I catch a few words being shouted down the corridor by whom I can only imagine to be Valiant.

"...masks out... space contaminants..."

I let the waves pound in my brain and can no longer resist its strength. I go dark.


*Candy Princess shatters my solitude by sticking her tongue in my ear.*

*I tell her I'm trying to read, but she continues undeterred. I try to do the same. She's winning this battle so I change tactics. I attempt to bore her with fascinating details. I explain to her in very simple terms that what I'm reading is of the utmost importance. I tell her that Steel Canyon issue number 26 is a very special issue. I say that Entheus has just ripped the arms off one of the Immoral Many— Plantera, I think—and is demanding that he sign a release for the damages he's caused.*

*She starts to nibble.*

149

*Clearly she doesn't understand the magnitude of contract negotiations to a world class adventurer. Captain Valiant does, but she doesn't seem to care.*

*Something wet drips onto my shoulder.*

*I wipe if off, expecting saliva, but it's red. Blood. Sometimes women get overzealous when placed in sexual situations. I just want to read this fucking comic book. Candy Princess distracts me further with a soft caress to the back of my neck while wandering the other hand to my inner thigh. Multitasking really pisses me off.*

*I throw the comic book across the store and rip my shirt off. If she wants it now, by Valiant, I'll give it to her! It's at that moment I notice a yellow glow enveloping Candy Princess. It's nothing, she tells me, noticing my curiously worried gaze. It's just my C.U.N.T.S she says. I stare down at her nether region. She slaps me playfully and tells me that it stands for Compact Utility Nano Tech Shield, silly. The inevitable question then dawns on me; what does she need a shield for? And then blaster fire scorches comic books off the racks. That's the last fucking straw.*

*Jimmy shouts to protect the VIP from behind the counter and tosses me a laser rifle. It's like I've been created to do this, to be a supernatural killer. I jump out into the mall corridor and without use of the scope—who needs one?—I go all Duck Hunt on their asses, firing off four shots and watching four armored enemies drop to the floor, head-shots for all. But it's not enough.*

*An alien garbles something and drops an electrical ball which stops me cold. My arms and legs are twitching as the creature approaches, pointing a plasma rifle in my face. This must be the end.*

*Before it can even register in my mind, dwarf pink elephants and candy canes maul and eat the alien, then pick up instruments and begin a candy parade. They march off down the corridor singing*

150

*something that dimly registers from my youth.*

*A man without a face pulls me to my feet and asks me to kill him and a giant hummingbird comes forth and speaks of nectar for life. I turn to the man with no face and find Sera instead. She pats the bird on the head and says no one needs life when they have power, before it plunges its beak deep inside her. She laughs and explodes into 22 rays of impossible light, all made to illuminate one thing.*

*Emma.*

*I smile at her and wave. She's shakes her head unhappily and ignores me, shopping intently for shoes at the store a few windows down with a massive sign which says that they'll pay you to wear their shoes. As if she'd wear shoes for money. Her feet aren't whores.*

*Candy Princess tells me to forget about Emma and blows softly. . .*

. . . softly into my ear and I open my eyes. Everything is blue, blurry. Or I'm blue? No, still not right. I blink hard. And then it makes sense, surrounding me is blue, and like a Phoenix I am reborn. Or at least restored in some fashion. Quite comfortable, I start to close my eyes but am yet again interrupted by that strangely erotic breeze in my ear. With a scent of honey on top!

"Are you awake?" Candy Princess' voice envelopes my consciousness and dips it in melted sugar. I turn towards it.

"Relax and let the healing happen," she brushes a bit of hair from my face, "close your eyes. You won't be able to see too well with them anyway."

Questions run through my head, "What?"

She anticipates my confusion, "Relax!" She pushes me down into the bath. "Those goshdarn robots! Pardon my language, but I just knew that they were no good. How it managed to save my little heart I'll never know. It couldn't even follow the simple steps of re-entry from deep space. And now you've been exposed to a space virus and it's done something awful to the both of you."

"Both," I try to get up again thinking of Emma, needing to see her, but again Candy Princess pushes me down.

"She's fine. Can you see over there?"

I strain to look across the room and can only see a bluish blur before what I make out to be a wall.

"She's in another bath healing along with you. But Victor, you're so strong it seems you heal much faster!"

She coaxes me to settle back into the healing solution and giggles a little as I do.

"Huh?"

"It's been a long time since I've been alone with a naked man."

I can feel the heat flaring in my cheeks and neck as the realization of my nudity comes to focus.

"You look so good I could eat you!"

"I am very sexy," I mumble.

"Yes," she says, barely more than a sigh. She's so close that I can feel the heat burn from her cheeks. Or maybe that's still me.

"Well," I sink a little deeper into the bath, "don't let her hear you say that." I intend it more as a joke, but that tone must still be hanging out on the other side of consciousness.

"Oh goodness! Have I offended her? I would never—"

"S'okay, no worries."

"It's just that, Victor, you're the greatest man I've ever met, but I'm sure you hear that all the time. Especially from her," she smiles brightly.

"All the time," I lie.

"But I should make it clear that I would never try and take you from her."

"Sure, sure," I struggle to keep my eyes open and it doesn't go unnoticed.

"Oh you poor thing, still so exhausted! I should have realized."

"Mmmfine."

"Hush and sleep. You'll want to be fully rested before we get to that brothel. If there's one thing I know about men it's that they love their brothels!"

"Um," is all I manage before I fall back into sleep.

# Act III, Scene 4

"**D**id she ever tell you about the bubblegum dragon she used to have?" Emma asks while I'm still trying to get the last bits of blue goo off me.

"Huh?"

"Candy, she must have told you. It's a great story."

"Um, no."

"You didn't like it? Oh wait, you mean she didn't tell you. You'll have to ask her about it."

"O-okay?"

"She a pretty amazing woman."

"I thought you didn't like her."

"I never said that," Emma hands me some clothes, "I said that I didn't like the way she looked at you."

"And?" I inspect myself in the mirror one last time.

"I still don't, but we had a nice talk while you were passed out and she's just really genuine and sweet."

"You said that about her before."

"Well this time I mean it," she scowls. "And so we're clear, I still don't want you leading her on. She's really nice, so you be nice back. Just not *too* nice, you know?"

I don't know, but I nod anyway so as not to propagate this conversation any further. I like to talk, sure, but only about things I like to talk about.

"Come on already and let's go. Sometimes you're such a girl when you're getting dressed."

I deliberately slow down the buttoning of my shirt, leading her to smack my hands away and finish the job herself.

"And you call me impatient," I say.

154

"I'm just anxious to get caught up to speed on everything. Get the scoop on all the happenings and what's up with the brothel and all that."

"Oh, so that it! You're just a filthy little sex crazed school boy."

"Girl, sweetie. I'm a girl. And besides, it's supposed to be so far beyond just sex stuff. It sounds fascinating."

"Uh-huh," I offer up an exaggerated wink.

She rolls her eyes, but otherwise ignores me, "So Sera said everyone would be waiting for us on the bridge," she opens the door and walks out. I hurry to catch up with her, but unnecessarily as I find her waiting just outside the room, a goofy grin on her face with her tongue barely sticking out between her teeth. She takes my hand and drapes my arm around her shoulder just before standing on her toes to kiss my cheek.

This is how we walk to the bridge, like a 50's greaser and his gal off to our favorite malt shop. Except we're in space and our clothes are hardly retro so in hindsight that simile was piss-poor. I do wish I had a cool leather jacket though. I wonder if Valiant would approve. I'll have to ask.

The Bridge is as dull as always. A bunch of buttons and switches I'm not allowed to touch. I'm not sure why. My track record with switches might be a bit iffy, but I'm pretty intuitive when it comes to buttons.

Everyone is spread throughout the room. Valiant sits in his captain's chair looking like some sort of Renaissance statue with Jimmy nearby tinkering with the robots. Candy Princess, for some crazy reason, is brushing Sera's hair. But it's someone else who notices our arrival first. The white heart is standing at my feet.

Its pink letters read HI.

"Hello there," Emma says back and the heart extends its cartoon hand to her and then to me.

"Oh, right," I wipe my hand on my pants, just to make sure all the blue goo is gone, and shake its hand.

Emma kneels down, "Do you have a name?"

Suddenly the pink reads GEORGE MCMANORBURY

I blink and it reads VI

"That's a very distinguished name," says Emma.

"Yeah, totally," I say. "I'm going to call you Chalk."

The pink swirls and solidifies again, NEATO it reads.

"Right, right," I say as I pass the little dude up. Got important things on my mind. I pass up Sera and Candy Princess, noticing Sera's discomfort with whatever Candy is doing to her, but who cares. "Captain Valiant?"

"Ah, Victor," he says, swirling his chair my way, "good to see you on your feet and fully clothed. How are you feeling?"

"Just fine, Captain, but speaking of clothes, what is your take on leather jackets?"

"Leather you say? Is that procured in some way from the fliperisakiss?"

"Cows actually."

"Space cows?"

"Um, Earth cows."

"And what do these cows do? Wait, scratch that. Have your kill-bot prepare a presentation. If I'm impressed then we shall turn the ship around and all get leather jackets!"

"Yessir!" No Name better not fuck this up for me.

I turn around to go back to Emma, but find her and Sera joining me instead. Candy Princess sits where Sera was, cradling that little Chalk fellow in her arms.

156

"—slave quarters, the com-room, even the engines," Sera is clearly in the middle of explaining something. "She just had to see everything and know exactly how it all worked. So I agreed to a makeover just to get her off my back."

Or I guess it was the end. Didn't sound very interesting anyway. I decide to interrupt them with my newly provided quest, "We need to go back to Earth and kill some cows right away."

"Uh listen, Victor," Sera begins, "other than you just butting in and interrupting me, we're about a million miles away from Earth at this point, or have you forgotten about those dread space pirates we're chasing?"

"I thought they were chasing us?"

"Do you ever pay attention to anything?!"

"Nothing I'm not directly involved in, so about those cows?"

"Gah! Am I the only one around here who hasn't lost their mind?!"

"Um, yeah," I'll ask Emma nicely, "maybe you and me can go to Earth and drag some co—"

"No cows, Victor," she commands sternly, taking the initiative, "Sera, can you maybe fill us in on this 'brothel of sadness', or whatever?"

"No need!" Valiant interrupts. "Ask your questions and I will answer!"

"Okay, where is it? Do we get to visit some exotic alien planet?" Emma's eyes twinkle with excitement.

"Not exactly, my dear, but an excellent question. Tell her why lieutenant."

"Yessir," Sera rolls her eyes, but Valiant doesn't notice, "see the brothel is located on a giant asteroid, but in order to evade certain intergalactic authorities the asteroid jumps from port to port, never in

157

the same place for more than a few days."

"Then how does anyone find it?"

"They send out an encrypted signal."

"Shouldn't these space authorities be able to track that, though?"

"Of course, but who do you think the majority of the patrons are? The authorities always officially show up just after the brothel has jumped away."

"Uh-huh, uh-huh," I interrupt, "that's all very boring, but now for a *good* question."

"Fantastic suggestion, Victor. Next question!" Valiant is excited as ever.

"I've hea—"

"Ah, show of hands please?"

I shoot my hand into the air.

"Victor," Valiant calls on me.

"So I've heard some rumors about the females they keep there. Some of your slave crew was saying that they had multiple—"

"Victor! Excellent question!! Let me answer that…in my quarters!" And then under his breath, "I have some scrapbooks dedicated to the matter."

"Oookay, so that's not happening right now," says Emma.

"But Em, you know how much I love scrapbooks!" I say.

"You probably don't even know what a scrapbook is, but if it's that big a deal you can make your own once we get there," YES! "…wow, I already regret saying that."

"Pardon me," Candy Princess says from somewhere behind me, I'd almost forgotten she was here, "but how long until we arrive?"

"According to the latest transmission," answers Valiant, "the brothel is currently in the Celestial System which is no more than 12 hours away."

"Actually, sir," Sera interjects, "it's probably going to be a few days before we get there. The brothel is due for a jump soon and—"

"Then we should hurry. There are so many things to see in the Celestial System that we wouldn't want our passengers to miss. The Old Star alone is—"

"Not exactly safe, sir," Sera gives Valiant a look I don't care to understand. Not when I have presentations and scrapbooks to prepare for. No Name is going to be one busy worthless pile of junk.

"Ah of course, Lieutenant," Valiant concedes.

"But I've heard the Celestial System is absolutely beautiful," beams Candy Princess.

"It's overrated," says Sera, "and not somewhere we should be right now."

"I thought we were all about danger," Jimmy says, poking fun. I'd almost forgotten he was here. Those were good times.

"We're about *adventure*, Jimmy," I say and smile towards Valiant. He nods in return. Sweet! Now back to my plans for procuring a leather jacket...

"Besides, Jimmy," Sera says, ignoring me almost as hard as I'm ignoring her, "Emma and Victor need to rest up. They've been through way too much these last couple of days."

"Hey," Emma says, "we'll find cows, right Victor?"

What? I mean, "HELL YEAH WE'LL FIND COWS!"

Emma sighs. "That's not what I said at all."

"I'm pretty sure that's what I heard."

"I'm sure, but what I said was 'we're fine now, right'."

"Oh...well maybe you are, but I'm pretty cold."

"Oh dear! Do you still have a fever?" Candy Princess rushes to me, placing her hand on my head. "You don't feel hot."

"Right, because I'm cold. Like from my shoulders downward, to about my waist. It's weird."

"That sounds troubling!" Candy exclaims.

"I concur. But what, *what?!* Could fix this ailment?"

Candy shakes her head worriedly while Emma mutters something under her breath that sounds very unladylike.

"Wait! I know! A jacket might warm me up. Perhaps one made of cow?!"

"Quickly! We must slaughter a cow and drape it's skin over Victor immediately," shrieks Candy Princess, and then she turns to me delicately, "Don't worry, I'll find you the most beautiful cow to wear and then we'll have a great feast!"

"Uh, thanks?"

"And with that I think," Sera says, "I'm going to go…elsewhere."

Jimmy jumps up. "I'll come with you! If—if that's okay?"

"It's fine, come on." And Jimmy, with The Roboracle in his arms and No Name tagging behind, follows Sera off the Bridge.

"Those two are just the cutest, don't you think?" Candy Princess titters with a crinkled nose.

"Um," I say.

"Oh that reminds me! George over there was telling me the most precious story. You must let him tell you!"

"George?" I say.

"Chalk," Emma whispers to me.

"Oh, right."

"But actually," Emma starts up again, "I was probably going to take off too. Still a bit worn out, I guess."

"Okay," I say, "I'll tell you all about the story if you're still awake later."

"Um, I was—I was kind of hoping you'd want to come with me," she pauses and bites her lower lip before adding, "maybe" with a smile.

"I'm not really tired."

"Okay," Emma turns, dejected, and walks out the door.

"Oh Victor, I think you do," Candy Princess says, "look a tad sleepy. Don't you think, Captain?"

"Hmm," begins Valiant, "Ah yes, certainly. Sleep is very important to the intrepid *adventurer*. Go on, there will be plenty of excitement in the days ahead. Besides, Emma would surely be of great assistance in scrapbooking."

I shrug and head off after Emma.

"Sleep tight!" Candy Princess exclaims as the Bridge doors swoosh shut behind me.

I catch up with Emma about halfway to our room, "Valiant says you might have some good scrapbooking tips." She doesn't respond. We walk the rest of the way in silence.

When our cabin doors shut I ask, "What do you want to do?" My voice brimming with cheer.

But apparently not enough, "Sleep."

"So you didn't need me here," I say.

"No, Victor, I didn't *need* you at all."

"You made it sound like you did."

"Sorry. You're free to leave."

"Nah, I'll stay. Captain Valiant says sleep is very important for us heroic types."

"And you certainly wouldn't want to disappoint the great Captain Valiant, would you."

"No, Emma, I *wouldn't*."

"Great. Good night."

161

"Yeah," I say.

The lights go out, but, unfortunately, I don't. I feel like I've been asleep for a week. Maybe I have. So I just lie there and wait. It's all I can think to do.

It takes a long time.

# Act III, Scene 5

The days pass.

## Monday

Or at least I'm calling it Monday. Calendar dating and Pacific Standard Time don't have much meaning in space. Maybe I should come up with my own, more awesome, calendar and time system. Or at least get No Name to do it for me. That robot has to have some use. Anyway, Sera is telling us that the Brothel has just moved and its new location is about 3 days away.

"Is that going to be enough time for us to get there?" Emma asks.

"Yeah, it'll be plenty," Sera answers. "The jumps usually happen every 5 to 7 days."

"That's good to…"

Christ, this is boring.

## Tuesday

"Come on, let's go," Emma says. She's really antsy today. Sera told her about this planet that will soon be visible that's supposedly really something else, but she wouldn't be specific about it for some reason. I'm really hoping it's Cybertron so I can show our crappy robots what robots should be. So it's off to the Observatory. I didn't even know the ship had one, but usually there's nothing to observe in space other than more space so why would I ever think a space ship would have a room devoted to looking outside.

We run into Jimmy, Sera, and the robots on the way. Good, this should be a humbling experience for those two. (we don't even know what we're going to see.) Maybe not, but I'm sure it will be *more than meets the eye.*

"What?" Sera says.

"Yes?" I ask in return.

"Just ignore him," Emma says.

Jimmy laughs.

"THE ROBORACLE FORESEES MUCH PAIN."

"What's new," I say as I notice Candy Princess and Chalk down the hall. Seems they're joining us too.

They both wave, but before I wave back, a hand grabs my arms from behind. What did we end up doing with those dead slaves again?

"Victor!" Ah, not a space zombie after all, only Captain Valiant, "Just the man I was looking for. I'm ready for your presentation."

"Now?" I say.

"Can't it wait, Captain?" asks Emma.

"I'm afraid not," Valiant chides, "procrastination is not one of the *Valiant Virtues.*"

"Okay!" I say. "Come on No Name, let's do this thing!"

"With pleasure, sir," No Name follows me as I follow the Captain to his chambers.

Valiant takes a seat in what I can only assume to be his favorite chair, "Wow me, Victor."

"No problem!" I say. "What I am proposing, sir, is a *Moo*dest proposal," pause for laughter and/or applause…nothing? Tough crowd, "Right, well you see cows say moo and, um, No Name take it away!"

"As you wish, sir," begins the Robot, "The earth species B. Taurus of the genus Bos, subfamily Bovinae from the family Bovidae of the Order Artiodactyla of the Mammalia Class in the Phlyum Chordata in the Kingdom Animalia, coloquilly known as 'cow' have a plethora of functions. These include: menial labor, providing dairy

164

products—such as milk an—"

"Stop right there," Valiant interrupts, "would this be the same milk that makes vanilla ice cream?"

"The very same, sir," answers the Robot.

"And can a cow both produce milk and leather all at once?"

"Not exactly, sir," says No Name.

"Then I'm sorry, Victor, but I can't risk the loss of ice cream. You may go join the others now."

I sulk out of the captain's chambers with No Name at my side, "Milk?! We're trying to sell him on leather and you bring up milk?! What kind of info-bot are you!"

"The kind that is a kill-bot, sir."

"Yeah, well you suck at all of that too and I wi—"

"Victor, wait," Valiant calls from behind. Perhaps he's changed his mind! "I almost forgot to show you my scrapbooks."

Well, at least that's something.


## Wednesday

"Hey Emma, come here," I say as she passes by Candy's room.

"There you are," she says, "I've been looking all over for you. Guess I should have looked here first," there's a tone in her voice that I can't quite place. "Hey Candy."

"Hellooo!" Candy whistles back.

"So what have you been doing here?" Emma asks.

"Teaching this guy," I motion to Chalk, "some tricks. Check this out!" I make my thumb and pointer finger into a gun and aim it at Chalk, "BANG!" Chalk clutches himself and falls to the floor. "Now read the words!"

"'I AM DEAD'," she reads, "cute, but he's not a dog."

"I know, but this is its favorite trick so far."

165

"*It* is a he and he has a name," she says.

"Right, Chalk, but—"

"No, *George*. You can't keep doing that, Victor."

"Doing what? Besides, he likes it. Right little buddy?"

Chalks chest reads U R RIGHT!

Then we high five.

"Fine," Emma says, "anyway I was hoping you'd come have some lunch with me."

"In a little bit, I've still got a couple more tricks to teach this guy."

"So dinner then," her voice is flat.

"Sure," I say, "sure."

## Thursday

"There is it," Sera says, "The Brothel of Infinite Sadness."

Finally.

# Act III, Scene 6

It takes us a good fifteen minutes to transmit identifications and be provided with docking platform coordinates. There's a slew of traffic near this hub of debauchery. Imagine the best science fiction movie produced on Earth then throw that image out the window. Nothing can prepare an untravelled human for the sight of a main intergalactic hot-spot.

A ship about the size of a football whizzes by our window. Mammoth ships even larger than the CU float around in an orbital pattern. Too large to dock on the astroidial rock. The creatures within them? Unfathomable.

I can't wait to land.

With all the docking mumbo jumbo finished we finally get to deboard or unboard or disboard…we get off the damn ship. And this is what I see:

A rock.

Now don't get me wrong, this is probably one of the two nicest rocks I've ever seen, but I was expecting some Cirque du Solie stuff.

(it's just a docking platform, man.) Yeah, but there should still be, I don't know, dancing tigers or something.

"What was that?" Valiant asks.

Damn it.

"Nothing, just thinking out loud," I say.

I follow the captain through the docking platform doors and that's when it hits me, a wave of incense, latex, and broken English. A pointy headed alien with red skin immediately assaults us with gibberish.

"ηελλο τηερε, τακε τηισ φλψερ."

"What now?" I say.

The alien taps it's ear twice, "Ah, English. Very good, yes? You'll take my flyer, no. Every of you," it hands me, hands all of us, a flyer, "for making with the fun, see?" It skips away after that, as I examine the flyer.

There's a picture of several dancing aliens. I think they're women and I think they're supposed to be sexy. It's hard to tell. I guess if you hold it slantways and squint with your right eye it's kind of hot. There's some writing too. It says in big letters "Chronotastic Dance Party!" and below that in smaller font "From the birth of a universe to the death of time. Why just live it when you can dance it!" I flip it over to see if there's anymore information, but all I see is a complex diagram. What do I look like, an architect?

Suddenly Sera jumps on a shiny trick-of-the-light and starts pummeling it.

"You thieving malformed glimmer!" She pulls my wallet from a shimmering, barely visible appendage of some creature she is still wailing on, and chucks it back to me. Valiant pulls her off the thing and kicks what seems to be air, and the shimmering reflection of light floats quickly away.

"You will have to be more careful with your possessions, Victor. You could lose everything in a place like this," Valiant gestures to my wallet.

"You're right, I'd hate to lose another one of these. There's not much leather left in the universe!"

"And I will need to be careful with the ship." Valiant eyes around, then focus' on Sera. "I'm sorry my dear, but I'll need you to stay with the ship until I get a few matters sorted out."

"Emma's the best fighter we got," I pitch-in for safety's sake.

The captain pauses, "Emma? Do you want to stay?"

"Oh yes, Captain! I'd *love* to stay aboard the ship. There's just *so much* to see!" She exclaims sarcastically and turns to walk silently back to the ship's door while Sera follows after. Without turning back, she extends her middle finger to the air. Oh boy.

"Jimmy, please go with the ladies," the Captian requests.

"But I wanted to see more..."

"Jimmy! *Please.*"

No Name picks up Chalk and The Roboracle and rolls to follow the Captain as he's already started his way into the passageways of aliens. I follow and it occurs to me that Emma would have enjoyed seeing some of these bizarre aliens.

Candy Princess turns from a street vendor with something glowing softly in her hand. She skips over and hands me the glowing orb then smiles. It feels much like a warm marshmallow, but without the heat.

"Eat it," she encourages me.

I do and my mouth tingles with excitement.

Further through the mercantile corridoors she buys a set of what look like wristbands, but instead she clamps them around each of my ankles. She holds my hand in support as I slowly drift eight inches above the floor.

"Now control your movement leaning only very slightly where you want to go."

I push myself forward and whizz quickly away from the group. I slam into a stack of crates, and can hear the Roboracle laughing.

We follow the Captain through an eight foot hatch with a symbol emblazoned upon it. Inside smells like vinegar, and the air assaults my eyes like pepper. Valiant doesn't flinch, showing a complete indifference to the change. A slug-like organism, hooked into several hoses suspended in the ceiling, points a dozen tendril sensors at me, apparently fascinated by my wheezing and crying.

The sensors all shift to Valiant except one which stays trained on me.

"Ωηατσ γοινγ ον ωιτη ψουρ φριενδ"

"ηε δοεσν϶τ λικε τηε αιρ," Valiant seems to be explaining. "λοοκ, ι νεεδ το ρεφυελ μψ σηιπ. στανδαρδ φαρε?"

"ψου στιλλ οωε με φορ τηε σλαϖεσ βυτ I κνοω ψουρ γοοδ φορ ιτ. I εξπεχτ παψ βεφορε ψου λεαϖε."

Valiant nods to the slug creature and motions for us to leave. I'm the first one out the door.

"What was that about?"

Valiant breathes deeply of the outside air, "Supplies, my friend. We need to go back to the ship and await its arrival."

"Captain," Candy Princess say sheepishly, "there are a few other things I'd love to look at while we're here, if you don't mind."

"Of course, Princess," he turns to me, "Victor, don't be too long, I'm sure everyone is anxious to get inside."

"No problem," I say, "but would you mind taking the robots with you?"

"Not at all. See you back at the ship."

Valiant turns back the way we came, the robots at his heels, as Candy Princess is already browsing various items that I can't even begin to describe. Out of laziness, not because I don't know how to describe things.

I lose track of Candy for a moment before she pops up behind me, reaching around to place something over my nose.

"Breath deeply," she says.

I do and I jump, "Holy crap that's coke! A cola, I mean. Except for the air. I always knew my lungs were missing something. I must have this always!"

Candy Princess giggles as I continue to inhale the sweet, caffeinated sexigen. Because it's like sex and oxygen combined. (I got it.) Just making sure.

And Candy is still laughing when:

"I see you're still talking to yourself, you unbelievable bastard!"

"Huh?" I have no idea who just said that.

And then my face is stinging like I just got a paper cut. That's when I see the tiny paper girl floating in front of me.

"Donna?" aka Donna Natrois, aka The Donnanatrix, aka the sometimes leader of The Immoral Many—a group of super-villains from a really crappy comic book. She's pretty cool.

"Don't 'Donna' me, prick!" she screams at me. "How long was Emma gone before you picked up this trollop?!"

"I'm a trollop?" says Candy, "that sounds adorable. Like a lollipop. Thank you angry paper lady, you're very sweet."

"I," starts Donna, "um, what?"

"I am also saying what," I say.

"You don't get to say what to me, standing here like Emma never even existed!"

"I don't know what you've been inhaling, clearly it wasn't this fantastic space coke, but Emma is back at our ship. Which is where we're headed now."

Donna's voice drops to a whisper, "Emma's at…she's here?"

"Yeah, and you might as well come with us. Everyone else always does."

"Oh, okay," she says.

Donna seems dejected as we all head back to the ship. I guess she really wanted to kick my ass.

# Act III, Scene 7

"**I** said I was sorry," which is true, I've already said it.

"And I said I don't want to talk about it, Victor," that's also true, Emma did say that.

"But—"

"'But is talking. Just drop it," she says without looking at me. She's done her best to avoid looking at me since I got back, which to be fair was about a minute ago, but I don't like it.

"Fine, but if I was allowed to talk I'd tell you about how I ran into Donna."

"Donna the Donnanatrix Donna?" Her interest is piqued, but she's still looking everywhere except where I'm standing.

"I don't actually know another," I say, "she's catching up with The Roboracle right now, or something, and she was pretty pissed when she saw me with Candy Princess."

"Really," she tries to keep her voice flat, but a smile twitches— albeit briefly—across her lips. And for the first time she looks at me. "Oh yeah, she got you pretty good. Let me see if I can find you a band-aid." Emma gets up and heads for the bathroom.

"That's okay, I don't need a band-aid."

"You have no idea what you need," The sound of water starts and stops before Emma comes back out. "I have no idea what any of the crap in there is," she wipes my cheek with a damp cloth. It stings.

I smile.

She drops her eyes and turns away.

"I'm going to see Donna," she says.

I follow her.

Donna and The Roboracle are engaged in some argument, I think.

"YOU MUST DO AS THE FATES COMMAND." Or, who knows, it could be foreplay. Stupid robot has no inflection.

"I will do it," Donna says. Yeah, I'm starting to think foreplay, "I told you I would when last I saw you, but never presume what I *must* do."

"THE ROBORACLE MISSES DONNA NATRIOS."

"And I you, my love, but I cannot be a slave to fate. To conform goes against the very fabric of my immoral code. How I wish you had stayed away. I don't want to be a part of this."

Emma clears her throat loudly, "Hey, Donna!"

Donna places a paper hand on what I guess you'd call The Roboracle's cheek before zipping over to us, "Hello, Emma."

"Thought I would save you from the awkward reunion over there," Emma points to The Roboracle and Donna sways in acknowledgement, "it's good to see you."

"Yes, well unfortunately I can't stay long. Work and all. Immorality waits for no one. You know how it is."

"Work?" Emma wonders.

"At the Brothel."

"Oh wow, yeah that make sense. We're headed there now."

"I kind of figured."

"Ha, yeah. We are *here*, after all. Hey, maybe you could give us a tour?"

"I really don't have much time."

"Awwwww, come on. Please?"

"Ugh. Don't insult me with politeness! I'll show you a few points of interest I guess. But that's all I have time for. Really."

"Thanks, Donna! I'll go get everyone else," Emma scurries off leaving me alone with Donna and The Roboracle.

"Yes, I'll take you to the Brothel, but none of you have any idea what you have coming," and then with a sigh instead of a laugh, "mwahaha."

"So you're still doing that, huh?" I say.

"Shut up," she says.

Yep, the gang's all back together. Well, except for Entheus. He's confetti now.

Donna ignores me and flutters back over to The Roboracle. I don't want to see whatever they might do so I decide to leave the ship and wait for everyone on the docks. Captain Valiant is already there, but he's dealing with those aliens he was talking with earlier. I can't understand a thing they're saying. Minutes pass and I'm bored. There's a space brothel mere meters away and I'm stuck waiting in silence. This is almost as bad as the time when I used to have to work for a living. Just thinking about it makes me want to vomit. I'm feeling a heave coming on when Sera interrupts.

"Sir, everyone is ready when you are."

"Ah, serendipitous timing, Lieutenant, I've just finished up here myself."

"Captain," Emma says, "did you have a chance to meet Donna yet?"

"Yes, albeit briefly," he turns to Donna, "a pleasure once again, madam." Donna nods back.

"She works in the Brothel and is going to show us around," Emma says.

"Most excellent, I do love tours! Lead the way."

We follow Donna as she weaves through the docks and past the markets, bringing us to a rather ordinary looking door. It opens.

"This is the Brothel of Infinite Sadness," she says. I don't know what I expected. Probably just a motel where there were aliens and sex. This isn't that. "This is The Garden."

174

A sprawling moonlit walkway in full bloom, much longer than it is wide, lies before us. Marble archways, covered in vines and flowers I've never seen, line both sides. A glowing fountain seems to mark the halfway point from the entrance to…I don't know where. The ground is soft and moist and perfectly trimmed beneath me. The air is vibrant with the scent of spring time, vanilla, and something almost familiar. Something that gets my blood racing. Lights twinkle on and off in mid-air, fireflies without substance sing a near silent song that I feel with every breath. Looking around, it's obvious I'm not the only one affected. Everyone's breathing seems heavier and Chalk reads WOW. Even Donna's voice softens. "The Garden is technically little more than a hub, linking each facet of the Brothel together, but it's not unusual to find people gather here for a moment of quiet after an exhausting day. This is our heart and it refreshes all who pass through.

"The archways you see," she continues, "are the gateways to, well, everything. This one here, for example," she points to the second arch on the left, "will take you to the Effluvium Elysium, where each breath is a gift greater than the last."

Jimmy chuckles, "It sounds like you've given this tour before."

Donna shrugs. "I do a lot of different jobs here. Occasional greeter is one of them."

"Oooh," Emma squeals, "what's 'N'Tissa's Concealed Kiss-es?"

"That's where the most beautiful women in the universe tattoo poems of epic struggle, sorrow and love beneath your skin with their very kisses. And in moments of perfect bliss or despair they illuminate to reveal your soul to the world. They offer an assortment of ethereal liquid piercings as well. You can pierce your muscles with the blood of an enemy to counter his strengths in battle, thread your heart with the joyful tears of a loved one to keep them with you always, or take the sweat of a lover's passion to penetrate your . . . um," Donna clears her throat, "that over there leads to the Maze of Muses. You can achieve greatness if you can find your way to the end of the maze. Very few have ever made it. I don't recommend going there. This one is where I've been working lately," she points to an arch just past the fountain that reads "The Sound of the Sirens"

"I didn't know you sang," says Emma.

"I'd love to hear you sing!" exclaims Candy Princess, while Chalk has a big ME 2 written across his chest.

"No no, I don't sing. I'm sort of a bouncer. If not for me a lot of people would just go in there and die, which isn't a problem really. It just costs more. Anyway, I really wouldn't recommend going there either. Not that I want to tell you what to do here, although...what are you doing here?"

"Looking for my amulet that was stolen," Candy Princess says with cheer.

"Wow," laughs Emma, "I almost completely forgot about that. But hey! It's great that we ran into you, Donna, her amulet was called the Amulet of Anexia. Can you tell us anything about it?"

"Sorry," Donna says, "but I've never heard of it. Once stole the Armoire of Anexia though."

"I never would have thought you'd not know about something from Anexia," I say.

"It's a big universe, jackass, and that's not even including trans-dimensional travel. Working here I've met at least ten entities named Anexia. Look, I wish I could help. But this time—this time I just can't."

"Don't worry about it," Emma reassures, "we already know who has it. I just thought you might have a fun story to tell."

"Not this time, but look I'm running late. Some foolish thing

176

could be starving to death as we speak, without paying for it. I'm sure the captain can take you the rest of the way."

"Indeed I can," replies Valiant.

"Thanks for showing us around a bit, Donna," says Emma, "we'll see you around?"

"Uh, yeah. Sure," Donna says as she flits off and disappears into the "Sound of the Sirens" archway.

"She was acting kind of weird, don't you think?" Emma asks me.

"She's always weird," I say back.

"You can never just back me up, can you," Emma says.

"I thought I was."

"Whatever," she scoots past me, "Excuse me, Captain, I don't me to be a buzz kill, but Donna brought up the whole money issue and I know it's stupid, but I never actually thought about that before, and, well, Victor, Jimmy and I don't really have any money."

"Ha! My dear I have saved this rock from every kind of danger imaginable. Captain Valiant and his friends never have to pay! Now let me show you to the *Valiant* Suite. They named it after me, you know."

# Act III, Scene 8

As it turns out, the Valiant Suite *is* pretty sweet. Soft beds, luxurious bathrooms, a roof with adjustable scenic settings, plenty of space booze, there's really nothing not to like. But after a few days even a suite this great can start to feel confining. It's not that I haven't been out, I have. However, the brothel trips have pretty much just been about gathering intel on the Dread Space Pirate Robots. As expected, the word is that they're never away from here too long and we've even learned a few of their most frequented establishments while here. All that means, though, is that I spend my time scouting the places out, just waiting for some robot to show up. As a matter of fact, Valiant and I are planning to meet up and do just that in a few minutes. So far, company aside, it's been horrendously dull. Couple that with Emma still doing a damn good job of avoiding me and this whole trip has been a bust. I've hardly seen, let alone talked, with her since we got here and I get the impression that going out and brotheling it up probably won't help matters. Which sucks since is seems she's been keeping herself plenty busy. She was already gone when I woke up this morning and I didn't expect to see her again until late, so it surprises me when she sneaks up behind me and kisses my neck.

"So I have an idea," she says.

"Oh yeah," I say.

"Let's get tattoos!"

"Seriously?"

"Yeah, come on! It'll be fun."

"I guess, but—"

"But what? I'm giving you permission to get all kissed on by beautiful women while you watch me get kissed by women too. That sounds nice, right?"

"Yes, mostly nice."

"Just mostly, huh?" she rolls her eyes with a half smirk, "Okay then how about we get one of those piercing deals? I'm ready to work up a sweat if you are."

"Now," I say.

"Now? Yes now! But I suppose you have something better to do."

"Yes—I mean no! Not better, just something. I've got to meet Valiant."

"Of course you do."

"The pirates could show up at any time."

"So I keep hearing."

"This is important."

"And I'm not."

"I didn't say that."

"You don't have to *say* anything! You'd rather find a stolen necklace than fuck me."

"Well that was crass."

"Ha! So now we have to take verbal cues from Princess Perfect even when she's not around? Fuck that! And fuck you."

"Fuck me?! You're the one who's been ignoring me since we got here!"

"And you've been ignoring me since I showed up to save your ass from a lifetime of slavery!"

"First, I lead a fairly successful slave rebellion without you. And second, maybe try cutting me some slack while I try and save the universe here!"

"Please spare me the hero bullshit. You're a fuck up, Victor. That's all."

"I think I should probably go."

"Fantastic! We wouldn't want you to miss your chance to save Princess Peach's necklace!" Emma storms into the bathroom and slams the door, "I bet she'll let you clean her pipes when you're done."

"What?"

"It was a Super Mario reference, dumbass!"

"Oh."

It takes me a bit to gather myself, and by the time I do I realize I'm already out of the suite enroute to meeting the Captain.

What the fuck was that all about? (you being an oblivious asshole?) Unlikely! She's probably just menstruating. That would make me cranky too. Hey is it weird that I kind of want to play some Super Mario now? (weird, inappropriate, insensitive.) But such a great game.

I'm hardly paying attention when I turn the corner. What I see freezes me in my tracks. Candy Princess is down the hall giggling with a robot. But not just any robot, a traitorous motherfucker of a douchebag robot. Manbot!

I jump back around the corner instantly feeling like kind of a dick for not rushing out to save Candy Princess. It could compromise the mission, but then again she's sort of the reason for the mission and I'd hate for her to get robot raped. What would Valiant do? Undoubtedly something awesome and—

"Hello, Victor!"

"Eeeek!"

Candy Princess titters, "I scared you!"

"Um, no I—what? Nevermind," I say, "are you being followed?!"

"By whom?"

"That evil robot you were talking to. Did he threaten you?"

"Oh my no! He was ever so polite."

180

"He's one of them, Candy."

"Silly Victor, he looks nothing like them," Candy smiles.

"That was the Captain's old servant droid, Manbot"

Candy Princess gasps, "What should we do?!"

"You just go back to the suite and don't leave. Tell the others to stay put too. I'll contact Valiant."

"Be careful," Candy says as she skips off towards the suite. Content with her safety, I touch the transmitter in my ear.

"Captain, we have trouble," I say.

Valiant's voice cracks loud and eager through the device, "I know, Victor. I was moments away from contacting you."

"You saw Manbot too then."

"Manbot? That treacherous whelp! No Victor, and unfortunately he'll have to wait. I'm trailing a squad of them right now. Come quickly."

All thoughts of feuding with Emma are completely wiped in the face of finding the robots' master and deactivating its circuits. I run down a large bronzed staircase, through street peddlers and their wares, going the opposite direction of the ship, to catch up with Valiant.

The transmitter guides me directly to him. He waves me to silence as I approach and then speaks in softer tones.

"Down there," he points past the narrow passage directly ahead of us. "They just went inside."

"How many?"

"Four."

I draw my revolver and Valiant motions to continue following the Robot Pirates. We cautiously hunt them for several blocks, each second expecting their superior robot senses to detect our following presence. Every footfall draws us further from the mass center of the asteroid's populace and into its dirty underbelly. I know this hair standing on my neck can't be a good sign.

In surprisingly short distance, the robots, with us following, are the only signs of activity. Red and pink coral-like funguses choke shattered and broken shadows of former structures. The tangled, erratic patterns they form are the only things that draw my attention behind us, alerting me to the swift, soundless motion of two robots preparing an ambush. It's a trap.

I let fly a 45 round which connects with the head of the first and sends gears zinging. I hear alien metals clash behind me which I can only assume means Valiant is slicing his way through the other two machines with a saber.

A laser-ray burns a hole in the meat of my thigh and the final robot behind us draws a blunt mace from its back. I dodge its blow, but only because I'm collapsing to the ground from the new hole in my leg. The laser-ray glows brightly again as it slowly recharges. It fires and burns the ground I roll away from. One bullet takes the laser—and its entire arm—away from the robots use. It stands over me, nonetheless, and, with its remaining arm, raises the mace for a killing blow.

Valiant cleaves the machine's hand, but the bot opens a small compartment, pulling another sidearm and aims at Valiant. Before it can fire, however, I put a bullet in its head.

Cruelly, the robot without arms plays a recording which begins with a chuckle, "Well, I can tell you that I am genuinely surprised that you made it to hear this. Ah, but it will bring the news I'm going to give so much more of that *human* element." The robot's feet start to glow. "This was a diversion."

He need not say anything more for me to understand, to strain against the pain and pull myself off the ground. I have to get back to the suite. Back to Emma.

The ever-glowing robot continues the pre-recorded message

but I don't listen. I let rage overpower the pain and Valiant helps me to run as fast as possible back to Emma. I pray that she has fought them off long enough.

We don't quite outpace the force of the explosion from the armless robot's self-destruction and it knocks us flat to the ground. It's a good thing we didn't stick around to hear the rest of that recording, and it's an absolute miracle that neither Valaint or myself were hit with robot shrapnel. I roll onto my back and a fresh pain bursts up my leg. Valaint drags me to my feet without a moment to lose and suddenly all hope drops, as before us stands a cadre of the Space Pirate Robots.

I have to try to find the silver lining…more distractions must mean that Emma's still fighting!

I'm able to shoot two of them before we are forced to take cover. I pop the revolver's cylinder open and stuff a new half dozen shells into it. Valiant reaches over the top of our cover and blindly fires with a boot gun. I hear the electrical burning sounds of a mid-section impact on another robot.

"We gotta get outta here!" I yell.

A laser-ray cuts through our cover.

"Quite so," smirks Valiant.

I don't think I've ever seen him so thoroughly enjoying himself. (except maybe when he's scrapbooking.) Good call.

He fires off more blind rounds, "What was that about scrapbooking?"

"Nothing?" I peek to see how many pirates we're facing and count six or seven before ducking back to avoid a flash of laser. "Nevermind. Look over there!" I point to what resembles a huge drain pipe but tilted out of the asteroid's surface at about thirty degrees.

"That's not the safest bet," Valiant tries to dissuade the presented escape route, but another laser cutting through our cover and burning an outer layer of skin off my shoulder convinces him there aren't any other options.  I swing my 45 around the side and plug a pirate square in the torso, knocking it backward with the force of a sledgehammer.

Return fire concentrates where I just shot from, so Valiant and I pick ourselves up and make a dash for the pipe.  We dive the last few feet and find the inside to be a smooth glass slide that carries us rapidly down.  We stop as it levels out onto a five tunnel split.

"As I was saying," reminds Valiant, "it's probably not the best idea to try and beat the Maze of Muses.  Any wrong turn in here could mean our sudden end."

"Let's get it over with then," I start towards the tunnel second from the fifth.  "I won't give up until I know Emma's safe."

# Act III, Scene 9

I haven't stopped running since entering the maze. I don't know how long ago that was. Not long, but still possibly too long. I haven't taken anytime to take much note of the surroundings. As far as I can tell the maze is a vaguely beautiful elephant graveyard. Except the elephants are people and aliens and stuff like that. Though there could be elephants here or some weird alien race that looks like elephants. There are worse places to die, I suppose, but dying isn't on my agenda today. Or ever really, but certainly not today.

"Victor," Valiant says from slightly behind me, no sign of strain in his voice whatsoever, "perhaps we should slow down and think about where we're going?"

"Captain," I pant, "normally I'm all for your advice but here's something I've learned: The faster you move, the faster you get where you're going. Thinking just wastes time that we don't have to spare."

"A very *valiant* statement, my friend. Would you mind if I use that in my next book?"

"Seriously? That would be great, I—" Before I can finish, I trip and crash down in a pool of something. How I hope it's not some sort of alien bodily fluid. I look around as I stand. "Wait, this is The Garden."

"Yes, very impressive! I think you may have beaten my record."

"That was it?"

"I should have had more faith in you, my friend. The maze has never been much of a match for true greatness."

"Ah forget it, let's go!" I break into a run again.

The suite looks fine from the outside, except that the door is wide open. At first glance I don't see anyone. I'm not sure if that's good or bad, but—OH NO!  Why God? WHYYYYYYY?!

"Chalk?!" the giant heart is flat on his back and white as a sheet, which is actually sort of normal except there isn't a single pink letter on his chest.  "Aw little buddy, did those pirates kill you?"

I blink and his chest reads NO.

"Oh, well then get up," I say.  Chalk is struggling to his feet when suddenly Valiant pulls his weapon, pointing it at the bathroom door.

"Identify yourself immediately or I will kill you," he says.

I don't hear or see anything.  Do robots have cloaking devices? (what, and sound dampening devices?)

"No, Victor.  There's someone or some*thing* in the bathroom. Speak up or die, scoundrel!"

"I-it's me, Candy Princess."

"Oh," I say, "okay come on o—"

"No!" barks Valiant.  And then in a whisper, "Some robots can modify their voices to sound like anyone.  Ask her a question."

"When's my birthday," I yell.

"I don't know, you never told me," she answers.

"I'm pretty sure that's true," I murmur to Valiant.

He sighs.  "Okay, just come out very slowly Princess."

The bathroom door slides open and Candy Princess delicately peeks out.  Valiant, satisfied, lowers his weapon and Candy rushes towards me with a fierce hug.

"Victor it was so horrible!  I went to freshen up and all of a sudden there was this huge commotion outside so I hid and kept absolutely still until just now."

"Where's everyone else?" I ask as calmly as possible.

"Jimmy, Sera and the robots weren't here at all.  It was just me, George and Emma.  Is she not here now?"

186

"Where'd they take her?!" This time I'm not so calm.

"I-I didn't—" Candy stutters, but it gets interrupted by Chalk tugging on my leg. His chest reads DOCKS.

I start running again.

I'm almost to the entrance/exit of the Brothel when I run into Jimmy and Sera coming out of one of the arches.

"What's going on?" Sera asks, already running after me.

"Emma has been kidnapped or robot-napped!" I yell back, never slowing down.

"What?" Jimmy says.

"Look Jimmy, I don't know the proper term, okay. All I know is some robots have been doing some sort of napping with my Emma!"

I duck and weave pretty awesomely through the crowds, assuming everyone is still following me, but I can't be bothered to check. When I finally get to the docking bay, however, I'm forced to stop.

"How do we know which ship is theirs?"

Valiant pulls up along side me and surveys the ships, but before he can speak a lanky, well-groomed gentleman approaches us.

"I believe I may be of some assistance," he says. "You're looking for the pirate ship, are you not?"

"Um, yeah," I say hesitantly.

"I take it you're Victor," he says. "A man out to rescue his lady will always be leading the pack. Even when in the company of a legend," he nods at Valiant.

"Who the hell are you?" I ask.

"I thought that would have been obvious," he smiles, "why I'm the Dread Space Pirate Robots."

"Holy crap! You're a terminator?!"

The Dread Space Pirate Robots laughs, "I hardly know what

you're talking about, but I'm just a man. A man who loves thieving."

Those of us with weapons immediately draw them, pointing them at the pirate.

"Come now, can't we be civil about all this?"

I cock my revolver.

"If you kill me now, my robots will kill the girl."

"How do we know you even have her?" Valiant interjects.

The pirate taps his ear and says, "Show them."

A ship not too far from the where the Adventure Galley is docked opens, and a gaggle of robots inch ever so slightly out to reveal a bound, gagged and unconscious Emma. At the head of the pack is Manbot. Valiant turns his gun in that direction and Manbot actually chuckles, "Now Captain, we wouldn't want this pretty girl to go the way of your lovely Lollipop, would we?"

Valiant's face goes crimson, but he lowers his gun. At the same time I hear him say under his breath, "Lieutenant, ready the Galley."

In the hopes of distracting the Dread Space Pirate from Sera's departure and to buy us time, I start to talk: "So let me get this straight, you're a pirate whose name is Robots and you also use robots to do all your pirating?"

"I know it seems a bit on the nose, but I've never shied away from the obvious. I prefer to embrace it. It makes life much easier."

"Seems kind of cheap to me. I mean what kind of pirate has a bunch of stupid robots do all the fun stuff?"

"The successful kind, my friend," The Dread Space Pirate puts a hand to his ear, "I'm sorry to cut this short, but it looks like our ship is ready for departure. And don't worry too much about your girl. I only need a date for the dance. It shouldn't take too long, unless I have to wait for all the best times, but even then I get bored quickly. I'll

188

give her a shuttle afterwards and send her on her way. If you're lucky you might find each other before she runs out of oxygen."

With that he disappears behind the closing doors of his ship while the rest of us make a mad dash to the Adventure Galley. I get to the bridge just in time to see the Pirate ship launch from the docks. The Galley is prepared to launch as well, docking orders be damned, when everything implodes and the world goes black.

A millisecond later I breathe again, but the stars have changed and the pirate ship is gone.

The Brothel of Infinite Sadness moved.

# Act III, Scene 10

"**W**hat are we going to do now?!" I think I might be panicking.

"What we are going to do, Victor," says Captain Valiant, "is relax. Worry is the testicular cancer of heroes."

"The hell?! That's stupid!"

"Victor, I don't think you understand. That was one of my Valiant rules of heroism."

"Oh…well in that case it's alright, but I still don't see how I'm supposed to relax when Emma is being held captive by dozens of robot pirates and one devilishly suave pirate guy. I've seen those romance novel covers. Women can't resist pirates! They might be probing her orifices as we speak. HER ORIFICES!"

"Ah, but Victor," Valiant grins, "we know exactly where they are going."

"We do?" I'm puzzled. "Because all I heard him say was something about a dance."

"Exactly," says Valiant.

"Exactly what? Are we going to fly to Shermer, Illinois and go to prom? That seems like a bad idea to me because 1. I think it's fictional. 2. I don't have a tux, and 3. While I kick far more ass, I'm not Jake Ryan!"

"What the hell are you talking about?" Sera asks. "Look, it's really simple, there's only one dance where there are 'best times' to miss. The Chronotastic Dance Party!"

"Um."

"There were flyers for it plastered all over the markets and docking bay."

I shrug.

"You were handed one, we all were."

"You mean the architect party? I threw that thing away."

"I saved my copy!" Jimmy exclaims.

"Jimmy, don't interrupt when we're talking," he's a rude bastard sometimes. "Why would anyone want to go to that anyway?"

"Ugh," Sera sighs, "first of all architects build buildings, not machines. If anything it would be an engineer party. Second, those are instructions on how to build a time machine so you can get to the party."

"Whoa whoa whoa! Next time let's just start the conversation with time machine. Now we've got all the time in the world! Sera, you just cured my testicles of metaphorical cancer. High five!"

"No."

"Later then. There's no hurry for anything now that we'll eventually have a time machine in the future."

"I'm afraid it's not that simple, my friend," says Valiant. "The Chronotastic Dance Party exists outside of the time-stream. It's always moving forward."

"You know, I've seen, heard, and done a lot of crazy, non-sensical things these last few months, but that makes no sense."

"Be that as it may, if we don't hurry Robots and Emma could be there and gone before we even get there."

And the ball cancer comes back with a vengeance.

"Jimmy," I bellow, "why haven't you built the damn thing yet?!"

"Vic, I don't know the first thing about building a time machine."

"That's what the instructions are for! You look at the picture and make a thing that looks like the picture. Besides, I'm pretty sure you told me you built a time machine once before."

"Actually, that was you from the future who told you that."

191

"Well then you know you can do it!  Christ, how little self-confidence do you have?  Do you need your parents here shouting words of encouragement?  Because they're dead Jimmy and it's about time you move past that."

Jimmy looks down, dejected.

"Don't worry, Jim," Sera reassures him.  He's such a pussy sometimes, "I'll help you."

"Good," I say, "and Roboracle—"

"I AM THE ROBORACLE."

"Yes, I know.  Go play them some Styx song.  Musical montages always make things go faster."

"I once mounted a turret on a Lamborghini," I hear Jimmy telling Sera as I leave them to build my time machine.  Valiant paces along with me.

"We'll have to have a plan when we get there," I tell him.  "I don't want to go in there half-assed.  This is *Emma* we're talking about."

"Yes, of course.  You do need to calm down and help me figure out our best course," Valiant ponders.  "I believe I have some spectacular ballroom wear in your size for the event!  You must come with me right away!"

He wasn't lying.  Spectacular hardly cuts it.  If James Bond and Tony Stark had a kid and he was raised by what's-his-name from The Great Gatsby, that kid would be me right now.  If I was to look up classy in the dictionary, it would probably read "elegant" or "stylish".  And then I'd say, "Thanks dictionary, I already knew that.  Why did I just waste 30 seconds looking that up when I could have been looking at myself."

That's how good I look.

Still, it seems to be kind of overkill.

"You're sure this is what we should wear to the dance party? It sounds like it might be more of a casual thing. Kind of like matching clothes might mean you're overdressed."

"Victor, success is a lady who must be carefully seduced, and Valiant's rules of Seduction begin with foreplay. Under the heading of foreplay you will find several subheadings, of which dressing to impress is second—preceded only be proper hygiene—and eventually these steps will lead any woman, physical or metaphorical, into your bed. Follow my rules, Victor, and success will come whenever you desire."

There's a knock at Valiant's door.

"Enter," he says.

The door hisses open and Candy Princess and Chalk skip inside. "My, my, my! So very handsome!"

"Thank you, Princess," says Valiant. Chalk climbs on to Valiant's bed and gives us a look…I think?

"What do you think, little buddy?" I ask.

His white chest flashes a bright pink I'D DO U.

"That's very disturbing," I say, "but awesome!"

"To what do we owe the pleasure, Princess?" Valiant inquires.

"I was looking for Victor actually," she says and turns to me," I was wondering if you'd be my escort to the dance?"

"Oh," I say," I don't think that's really necessary. It's just a lame party."

"Actually," Valiant interjects, still admiring himself in the mirror, "The Chronotastic Dance party is far from lame and happens to be mildly dangerous for singles. There are certain species there that will take a person arriving alone as an open invitation for mating."

"That doesn't sound that bad," I say.

"And it's not, until they proceed to lay eggs in your intestine,

193

chest cavity or eye sockets. Trust me when I tell you that you don't want aliens hatching out of your eyes."

"Hmm, in that case I will definitely escort you."

Candy Princess bounces up and down, beaming. "Oh boy! I'm going to make the most loveliest dress ever. I'll be such a great date! I better get started. Come George, you can help me."

Chalk hops off the bed and waves goodbye as he follows Candy.

"I guess you'll be going with Sera to the dance then," I say as I change back into my regular clothes.

"Yes, the Lieutenant will be my date."

"Cool. So have you two ever, you know…"

"Had hours of exuberant sexual intercourse? No. First and foremost that would be highly unprofessional. And second, the Lieutenant is a fine young woman; I would never give her my *valiant* and *adventurous* love only to rip it away. I have seen it destroy women before."

"Goddamn you are awe-inspiring," I say.

"I know."

"Okay, what about Jimmy?"

"Jimmy? No I've never been intimate with him either."

"That's good to know, I guess, but I was wondering about the dance party?"

"Ah, I suppose if we can't find him a date he'll have to stay behind."

"Aww, that's too bad. I think I'm going to go break the good news to him!"

"Enjoy," Valiant says, hardly paying attention as I take my leave.

I find Jimmy in Engineering with Sera and the robots, fiddling

194

with some such nonsense—that hardly looks big or awesome enough to be a time machine—and speaking it too. "Come on, man! Why won't you tell me where you disappeared to back on the brothel?"

"THE ROBORACLE DOESN'T KNOW WHAT JIMMY IS TALKING ABOUT."

"If it was Donna, you can just say it was Donna."

"THE ROBORACLE WILL NOT COMPUTE YOUR WORDS. PLEASE LISTEN TO STYX."

Listening to these two talk is like listening to a deaf guy try to rap. It makes saying this all the easier. (like you didn't want to tell him anyway.)

"Tell who what, Vic?" Jimmy asks.

"Jesus, Jimmy! Can't a guy talk to himself loudly without you eavesdropping? By the way you can't go the party. So how's the time machine?"

"What? Why?!" Jimmy looks pretty confused.

"Because I'm trying to save Emma here! I thought you were her friend."

"I was talking about the party."

"That is old news, now we're talking about time machines. Is this it?" I start examining an odd shaped contraption. "Where's the flux capacitor?"

"But Vic, I was kind of looking forward to the party and I'm actually a really good dancer and—"

"And I'm sorry God hates you, but I don't make the rules."

"You usually do," Jimmy mumbles, at which point Sera finally joins the fun.

"Actually, Jimmy, as much as I hate to say it...Victor is sort of right. I should have told you sooner, but it just didn't cross my mind."

Jimmy frowns.

195

"I'll explain later, okay," Sera say apologetically.

"Good," I say, "now that that's cleared up, what's up with the time machine?"

"It's almost done," Sera says, "we just need some spare parts, but we'll pick those up on Earth."

"Earth, again?"

"It's the closest resourceful planet."

"But we travelled for days to the brothel, we don't have days to save Emma and get Candy Princess' amulet back. Probably."

"Yeah but the brothel jumped to a location a little closer than we were before. Plus we picked up some fuel there so we're traveling at super-luminal speeds right now. We'll be there in a couple of hours."

"Did you say super-luminal?" I ask.

"Yes," Sera says back.

"Important question! If the Adventure Galley was to race The Flash, which one would win?"

"What about Superman?" Jimmy asks.

"Superman? Is your last name Olsen? Honestly, I have no idea what it is."

"Well it's—" Jimmy starts, but I won't have it.

"That wasn't an invitation for your life story, Jimmy. This isn't some slow and steady wins the race bullshit, this is *real*!"

"Superman's not slow," says Jimmy, he just won't let this die.

"Can Superman travel at super-luminal speeds, Jimmy? Can he?!"

"Electric Superman could."

"Electr—You would dare bring Electric Superman into a serious conversation? I'm sure you heard this a lot from your parents, but it bears repeating, you are a constant disappointment. Now if you'll excuse me, Sera and I were trying to have a conversation."

"No we weren't," Sera says.

"See what you did, Jimmy? One mention of Electric Superman and everyone is pissed off."

"Look, Victor," Sera starts, "we're really busy here so if you don't mind—"

"Helping? Sure thing! What can I do to help?"

"You can leave," she says.

"Cool! I'm good at that. How far away should I go?"

"Preferably out of earshot."

"No problem," I say, "Now watch this, Jimmy. I'm going to show you how to complete a task. I'll yell from time to time and you tell me when you can't hear me anymore."

"Um," Sera and Jimmy say together as I scurry off.

I wish I had somewhere to go, but everyone is busy preparing for something. Maybe I'll go work on my dance moves. (aren't you going to yell back at Sera and Jimmy?) Eh, too much work.

# Act III, Scene 11

We've been back on Earth about an hour now. Jimmy finished the final tweaks on the time machine—which to my disappointment looks neither like an Irish sports car or a phone booth, but more like a watch instead—pretty quickly. He's good with these things. (yet instead of ever complimenting him, you belittle the poor guy.) Yeah, he's a good kid.

"Thanks, Vic!" Jimmy yells from somewhere nearby.

"I thought I told you to stop eavesdropping," I yell back.

"Sorry."

Anyway, now we're here to test the time machine, at the site of my greatest victory. (victory, giant fuck up, it's all the same, right?) Right.

"You're positive this is the place?" Valiant asks.

"Yeah," I say and point to a patch of scorched earth, "that's where the house used to be."

"Then let us do this," he says and we walk over to Jimmy, Sera and the time machine.

"Okay Vic, this here," Jimmy points to the face of my pseudo-watch, which has a bunch of numbers and whatnot on it, "is where you put in the date and time you want to go to. Then all you have to do is hit this button over here," he points out a button near the bottom of the contraption. "And when you want to come back just hit it again. Got it?"

"Yeah yeah, dates and buttons. Just let me do my thing!"

"So you know the date and time you're trying to get back to, right?"

"Of course I do. Probably." I punch in something that looks pretty much correct.

"What's this thing you're going back to retrieve, anyway?" Sera asks.

"Something totally amazing," I say. I push the button.

"It's his—" I hear Jimmy start to say and then

*ZAAAAP!*

Holy crap! That was tingly! Hey! There I am with Emma. Now I'm pointing a gun at me. This is awesome! What was I here for? Oh yeah! "Don't burn down the house yet!" I yell at myself, "You've forgotten," I feel heat and look around, "oh, right then. I guess I'm too late. That's embarrassing. You can stop pointing that gun at me."

"Give me one good reason not to shoot you dead," I said way back in the past to my future-self who is now my present-self in the past.

"I'm you from the future," I say because I'm pretty sure I said it then.

"As if I'm averse to killing myself? I would know better!"

I've got a point. If I were me, I'd probably kill me if I showed up from the future all mysteriously yelling at myself, but I think I know how to convince me against futurecide, "But I'm *you* from the future." Ha! How do you like that logic?!

"Your added emphasis on *you* is a compelling argument," I knew it would work! "But does it outweigh my desire to kill a time traveler?"

Ooo, good question.

"Knowing me, no," I say back from the future. How could I forget #27 on my list of life goals?

"Exactly! So you've come to terms with death then?"

Well, I had a good run.

"Oh, Jesus," Emma takes the gun from my past-hand so I no longer have to worry about it presently. She's a life saver, "he's clearly

199

you from the future."

"On second thought, Emma makes a valid point about you being me from the future. Consider yourself lucky."

"So let me get this straight," Emma starts, turning her attention from me to me. "You have a time machine—"

"Yeah, Jimmy made it," I interrupt.

"Whoa!" exclaims someone who is face down in the dirt with a sword sticking out of his back. I think it's Jimmy, "I make a time machine?"

"Shut up, Jimmy!" I yelled at some point in the past.

Emma just brushes the little exchange aside, "You have a *time machine* and you were still late?"

"Yep."

"Then just go back a little further and fix this."

"Can't. No time."

"You have a *time machine*!"

"Right and I came back to see if I could retrieve my wallet before going off to save you from the Chronotastic Dance Party."

"Hold up," me from the past interjects, "I dropped my wallet in the house?"

"Yeah," I say presently, in the past.

"Aw, fuck!"

"What?" asks Emma.

"It was great wallet," both me's say at once. Emma opens her mouth to speak, but instead just shakes her head and turns her back on us.

"Anyway," I say to my past self, "I have to get going. I'll see you all…" damn it, I have to make this a memorable exit. Ah here we go, "IN THE FUTURE!" It's awesome because it's true.

I push the button again.

*ZAAAAP!*

"—wallet," Jimmy finishes. Everyone looks at me.

"You really went back in time to try and get your wallet?" Asks Sera.

"And he failed," Jimmy laughs.

"I didn't fail," I say.

"I *know* you did," Jimmy says.

"Okay, fine! Maybe I did, but do you want to know why, Jimmy? It's because of your defeatist attitude. Now excuse me while I go change for the party."


What else is there to do but brush my teeth during the flight? Yep. First rule of party-going is to freshen up before the kissing. And I plan on a lot of it when I save Emma.

Jimmy can laugh all he wants but if it weren't for me telling myself in the past I'd still be with Emma, I think my life may have been for the worse.

I spit the plasma gel space-toothpaste into the sink and straighten my hair in the mirror.

Come to think of it, we hadn't been apart since the apocalypse. Every day spent as if we were the last two people in the entire world. (except for all that time you were a slave and then again on Candy Island.) *Every day* as if we were the last two people in the entire world. (*sigh* whatever.)

Startled, I spin at the pull on my pant leg. Chalk stands back a little at my reaction and has SHE'L BE OK written on his chest.

"Was I talking to myself again, little buddy? You gotta stop just sneaking up on people like that," I tell him while turning my attention back to dressing for the party.

We must be nearing the Chronotastic Dance Party by now.

201

"Alright," I motion for Chalk's attention and strap a small 9mm pistol to my ankle, "that's gonna be for you when shit hits the fan. I want you at my side drawing that pistol at moment's notice!" He looks like he understands, "You got it?"

Chalk springs forward and swipes the gun quickly from its holster and aims it around the room. He drops the clip, confirms the hollow points, jambs the clip in and slides a load into the chamber.

"Alright! I like what I'm seeing here."

Chalk flicks the gun's safety and slides it back into my ankle holster.

"Now everyone keeps saying that people need dates unless they want alien eye babies, but since you aren't technically people and have no eyes I'd say we've got nothing to worry about with you."

I ♥ DANCE appears on his chest.

"We all do, little buddy, but most importantly, we have to rescue Emma. I don't want to live without her. She stirs something inside of me that I thought couldn't exist. A sort of parasite that, when she's gone or smiles or laughs or scowls or talks or looks at me or away, stabs at my bowels and keeps me awake at night, wanting only to be near her. And that parasite's nam—its name is Love. It's a wonderful thing, Chalk. Like something from a fairy tale... So you're gonna stick by me and if I, for some reason, can't get to my gun you pull it and go to work."

CAN DO he reads.

"Our primary objective is Emma, our secondary objective is the amulet and our third...endary...um our other objective is to enter and win a pairs dance competition in which the onlookers will say 'that man, that *Victor* has stolen my heart as clearly demonstrated very literally with his tiny heart that dances beside him. It's as if my heart has leapt out of my chest to join him in a dance so soulful, so glorious that I would weep were I to allow my vision to blur for even a single moment. But I cannot!' at which point we'll probably get a trophy or something."

Chalk's chest is blank.

"Exactly, they'll all be speechless."

CANDY Chalk prints on his face.

"Candy..." I trail off.

PRNCS his face reads

"Candy Princess?" I stupidly repeat.

READY he reads

"Oh!  Yes, ready for the event!  Why didn't you say so?"

.  I take one last glimpse in the mirror and rustle my hair again before hustling to the bridge and finding my date so we can get on to this party and on our way to saving Emma...

...and possibly, the world. (or universe.) Whichever is bigger.

"Were you talking to me, or yourself," I turn around to see a very glammed-out Sera.  Multi-colored hair all frazzled about with knee-high boots, spandex and a short skirt and glitter and glowing things all over.  Even her skin seems illuminated.  If I wasn't infected with Emma's love bug I'd be pretty turned on right now.  Actually, I still am.  But it's completely plutonic.  Mostly.

She takes a quick glance at me, "Please tell me you all aren't dressing like that."

"Um," I say.

"It's a dance party, damn it!"

"I, uh, we dress for success, you see, um, because it's like foreplay with sexy ladies and all those sexy ladies like foreplay and fancy clothes.  So by wearing fancy clothes we turn them on which allows us to succeed at success and, um, give them orgasms?  I think that's how it goes."

Sera stares at me for a long time, "…you guys suck."

She sulks past me, down the corridor, and I follow. We find everyone else at the helm watching empty space all around us as we near the dance party address coordinates.

"Great!" I say, "It doesn't take a genius to see that it was a FALSE INVITE! Damn it all! Emma's orifices have been probed by now!"

Everything crashes down upon me; the gravity of my failure. The dance party was an illusion all along. A ploy to lure us into their emotionally baited death trap. Only a matter of time now before they fusion blast a doorway into the Adventure Galley and storm-troop in with blasters firing.

I jump into a tuck-roll which lands me behind sturdy looking cover and draw a break-top 45 revolver.

Bring it on you cowards! I will have my VENGEANCE!

"Victor, don't fret," Valiant attempts to aid, "We're in the right place, so as much as I appreciate the importance of combat drills, this is hardly the time for it."

"Don't deny what is plainly in front of our eyes, Captain. It's nothing, by the way. Nothing!"

Candy Princess somehow emerges from the impossibly small group as if staged for the theater, "Please, this won't save Emma." Her candy hair is done in intricate curls and she wears the best looking dress I'd ever want to eat. "The Chronotastic Dance Party is an eternal moment of space. Bodies in the universe grow and disintigrate in time, but time endures. This is where the party is."

"She's right, Vic," says Jimmy, "just chillax!"

"Chillax? Jimmy that term should have died with your family."

"What the hell, man! That's like the third crack you've made about my family dying!"

"Whoa, Jimbo! Chillax, dude. Take comfort in the fact that, even in death, they bring joy to so many. And what are you doing here, anyway? You can't g—" and that's when I notice it. "Jimmy! Oh Jimmyjimmyjimmy."

"What? You said I needed a date, so I figured," he motions to his left, where The Robot With No Name is standing, dressed as a woman.

"I had no idea you were so hard up, man."

"I just needed a date," Jimmy tries to laugh, it sounds forced to me, "it's not like we're going to do anythi—"

"Ut-ut. It's none of my business, Jimmy."

"Victor is right, it's none of anyone's business," says Valiant as he nods to Sera, almost bowing, and takes her arm in his, "now everyone link up, and don't forget your dates!"

Candy Princess looks at me encouragingly, "Is it a date?"

She is very pretty and I do need to get a move-on to save Emma. Candy Princess puts out her hand like Sera, expecting chivalry, bravado and all that. I do like Valiant and nod before taking her arm in mine while she touches the captain's other arm, Jimmy and his 'date' grab Sera, and Chalk holds on to my leg. I hit the bu—*ZAAAAP*!

# Act III, Scene FINAL

——tton.  My thoughts are suddenly drown out by a heavy thrumming bass while insistent strobe lights threaten to induce seizures.  The scent of sex, drugs and rock & roll engulf me.  Daring me to dance.  As if I would ever back down from a dare.  My hips begin to gyrate as my feet tap to the beat.  But no!  I must resist.  Emma first, then the amulet, and only then comes the sweet release of dance.

"Alright everyone," Captain Valiant takes charge, "the party is massive, we'll do best to split up into pairs in order to cover the most ground.  And do stick with your dates very closely until you've established yourself as unavailable."

I give him a thumbs up, "Chalk, you're with me and Candy."

"Oh, and Victor," Sera says, "try not to lose the time machine."

"Bah!" I scoff, for if ever there was a time to scoff it is now, "I don't lose things, Sera."  I'm not sure if she hears me though, as she and Valiant are already weaving through the mass of people.  Or whatever you'd call these things.  Candy Princess, Chalk and I head off to the right, mostly because we were the right most of the couples so it just made sense.  The music dies out and an excited voice comes over the speakers.

"And that little ditty was brought to you all the way from the Burbidge Chain, where they make music just like their ladies: Hot, fast, and completely tone deaf!  Coming up this infinite-hour in time's most happening party that always is, we're gonna dive right into the Milky Way for Earth's Cretaceous Period!  Do the canary with a pteranodon or try to out jive a Tyrannosaurus-Rex!  Why did the dinosaurs go extinct?  Because they're about to get out danced so hard the only solution for their disgrace is mass suicide!  It'll be hari kari reptile style!  And then get yourself ready for the greatest dance competition until the next one..." the voice keeps on going but I can't hear it anymore. Not when I see her on the dance floor. Elegant like a swan, sexy like a swan at the end of Swan Lake when the swan is a hot, sexy princess again, she dances. She's encircled by dozens, but I can pick Emma out of any crowd. I rush to her, Candy Princess still in hand, knocking people out of my way as I go.

I grab her shoulder, "Are you okay?"

"Hey buddy, I don't," she turns to me, "Victor!! Hey baby," she sloppily hugs me and she smells like sweat and alcohol as she simultaneously sips from a drink she's holding. I feel drunk just standing near her. It's wonderful. "Dance with me!"

"Sure thing!" I say before Candy Princess tugs on my sleeve.

"Now that we've found Emma can we try and get my amulet back?" she whispers politely, her breath almost as intoxicating as Emma's. I don't have a chance to answer.

"Candy Princess," yells Emma, "Caaaandy. Princesssss. Hey Vic, do you think she tastes like her names says? Because I loooove candy. I'm fucking hungry. And thirsty!" She pounds her drink. "Let's dance!"

"Um, okay. But first we need to get Candy's necklace back."

"No, no! First you need to not be a jerk and dance with me."

"It's just that I had this very specific plan laid out and—"

"And plans are meant to be forgotten when you drink a lot of this," she hands me her glass, "hey what?! It's empty? Who drank my thing, huh?!"

"We can get you another one after we deal with the pirate," I say.

"Ugh! You're such a buzz kill. Fine!" She takes my hand and yanks me off the dance floor towards a private table and the Dread Space Pirate Robots.

"Here!" she says. "Give us that amulet I said stuff about now so we can do something I want to do, please."

"At least she's polite when drunk," says Robots. "Hello, Victor. Glad you could make it. Quite the party, no?"

"Just hand over the amulet, okay," I say.

"Business it is then. Would this be the amulet you're referring to?" He pulls a necklace from under his shirt.

"Ha! Like I would know," I scoff.

"Yes that's it!" Candy Princess yips. I hadn't noticed until now that she's cowering behind me, hiding.

"And who might that be?" asks Robots, subtly trying to peek around me. "Your voice is familiar, Miss. Have we met?"

"You should remember?" I answer for her. "Your robots attacked her and stole from her."

"They are prone to doing that from time to time. But the problem is, this little piece of jewelry happens to be, let's say, special to me. And if she's saying I stole it from her then…well I guess it could be true," he laughs, "I never did keep track of whom I steal from, and she does sound familiar even if she won't let me get a good look. Either way, I won't part with it easily."

"Fair enough, I propose a contest."

"Hmm, intriguing. I suppose you wish to have some sort of dance contest?"

"Um, actually that never occurred to me. I was kind of thinking of a staring contest."

The Dread Space Pirate Robots laughs, "Oh you're serious aren't you? Very well, a staring contest it is. Have a seat and a drink and we will begin."

As I take my seat across from him Candy scurries from behind me to behind Emma.

"This is stupid," blurts Emma, "you suck at staring contests. I want to see someone get their ass kicked. Where's Sera? She'll dance with me with drinking. Ima go find her." She starts to walk away.

"This is too scary for me," Candy whispers my direction, "I'll go with Emma."

"Looks like it's just the two of us," says the pirate, "shall we begin?"

"Indeed we shall. Let's stare!"

And so we do, for a really long time. (it's been maybe 6 seconds.) In staring contest terms that's probably equivalent to 12 hours.

"Excuse me," my opponent interrupts, "are you talking to yourself?"

"Maybe. Does it make you nervous? Like enough to blink?"

"No. In fact, I don't need to blink. My left eye is glass and the right is electronic. But I'm sure you knew that."

"The things I don't know would astound you. But I don't need you to blink because I just had my candy heart friend take the 9mm from my ankle holster, which means he's most likely under the table. Pointing it at, how can I put this in robot type terms? Let's say your nuts and bolt."

A quizzical look flashes on his face, "A bluff, as if I'd look down so easily."

"Chalk, give him a little tap," I notice the pirate jump a little, but he doesn't flinch. "But whether you blink or look down or don't doesn't change the fact that there's a gun held by a trigger happy little heart ready to castrate you violently. Victor's guide to winning contests, rule number one: If at all possible, go immediately for the balls."

He stares at me a moment longer before looking down, "Well

played."

"Thanks, now the amulet please."

"Of course," he takes the necklace off and hands it to me, "I may be an untrustworthy, lying, cheating, murderous thief, but if there's one thing I've learned over the years it's how utterly dangerous candy can be. Best of luck, Victor, perhaps we'll meet again someday. Now if you'll excuse me, I must go dance off this shame." The Dread Space Pirate Robots disappears into the crowd as Chalk hops onto the table and offers up a high five. I don't leave him hanging.

We look around and notice that Emma and Candy Princess didn't go too far, so we head off to join them at the bar they currently occupy.

"Hey Em, you just missed my ultimate moment of triumph!"

"Psh! Whatever."

"We can dance now!"

"We can what, no! You had your chance to do what I said we should do but you decided everyone else's thing is more important than my thing so now you can't touch me."

"You're very drunk," I say.

"And it was great 'till you showed up and made it, like, whatever."

Candy Princess comes over from the other side of the bar and hands Emma another glass, "You forgot your drink over there, Emma!"

"Did I? I don't remember that, but it sounds good to me. See Victor, she cares about what I want and need and drinks, Victor."

"I'm not sure you need another one," I say.

"Well I'm not sure I care about what you're not sure of," she says as she downs the drink in one swallow. "Mmmm, tastes like fun! Let's go dance, Candy!"

"I'd love to, thanks!"

210

I follow the two of them onto the dance floor, trying to get Emma to talk to me. It takes almost an entire song, but finally I get her attention.

"Oh, it's still you. I said I don't want to dance with you so go now."

"Maybe we can go back to the ship and talk about stuff?"

"No, Victor. I want to have fun and feel good, but you...*you're* making me feel bad. I feel bad now so leave me alone."

"Come on, Em," I touch her shoulder, she brushes it off.

"Fine, then I'll leave."

"Can't we have a good time together? I just beat a legendary pirate in a duel of wits. I want to celebrate."

"Oh how could I forget what *you* want. 'Later Emma, I need to be a hero now. Not now Emma I want to listen to Captain Valiant lecture me on the history of boring. Leave me alone Emma, I'm fucking busy with my shit Emma.' You don't get it!"

"Emma I—"

"Exactly that's it, right there! You you you I I I me me me."

"What?"

"Emma emma emmaemmaemmaEMMA! That's not even my name you fucking lunatic!"

She starts weaving her way through the crowd and I do my best to follow.

"Victor!" Candy Princess intercepts me, "I really need to excuse myself to the ladies room, so don't worry okay," she smiles, but for the first time it looks forced.

"Um, okay," I shrug her off and continue chasing after Emma, but I've lost her in the overwhelming sea of people. I'm completely turned around with no idea where to start looking.

Another song ends and a voice pops back over the speakers.

"Alright ladies, gentlemen and all those other genders I don't even want to think about, it's time for the 8 trillionth and 53$^{rd}$ in our infinite series of ultimate dance competitions. Introducing our first couple, they're known as 'A Hero and his Heart of Gold'. Everybody let's hear it for Victor and Chaaaaalk!!!!"

"Say huh?" Are they talking about me? I feel a tug on my pant leg. Chalk is standing there with SIGNED US UP! on his chest.

"Um," I feel like I should keep looking for Emma, but on the other hand maybe space is the best thing? I don't know.

I hear the crowd cheer as I look back down at Chalk, his chest says LET'S KICK ASS

He's got a point. To walk away now would be forfeiting.

The music starts.

I can't *not* dance.

Emma will be fine.

I have to dance.

She'll be fine.

Besides, it's like I said earlier…I don't lose things.

# Interlude

The Thing follows the girl off the dance floor, happy to be distanced from the blaring music, if only briefly.

The Thing has work to do.

The Thing can't help but admire the girl's beauty from behind and suddenly feels a pang of regret in the pit of its stomach. Or perhaps that's only hunger. It's hard to tell in this situation.

The girl enters the bathroom.

The Thing is pleased to find it large and empty.

The girl sprints the last few feet. Forcing a stall open, she begins to vomit.

The Thing approaches and reaches out to her.

"Let me," it says, grabbing the girl's hair and forming it into a pony tail, "we wouldn't want any of that getting in your hair."

The girl turns to see the Thing and weakly smiles a smile of thanks. And of familiarity. A very pretty smile, interrupted by another wave of vomit. This one worse than the first.

"Oh," the Thing says, "I'm so sorry you have to go through this. I really did want it to be quick." The girl tilts her head toward the Thing again. Her face flashes with confusion. Or perhaps it's just nausea. She heaves again.

"I really had no idea what to expect," says The Thing, "it's a very special poison that's supposed to react differently for everyone." The girl whips her head around. She's full of fear and tries to say something.

The Thing thinks it might be "you" but she can't be sure. The Thing puts on her best pouty face, "You seem to be taking it especially poorly."

The girl can't seem to stop vomiting.

"I do hope you won't hate me too much for this," says the Thing. "I'll always consider you a dear and true friend, Emma. This is all for the best. You'll see," the Thing giggles, "well I guess maybe you won't, but you have my word! Just like when I told you I'd never try and take him from you."

Emma sees Candy Princess smile.

"Instead I'm taking you from him," the smile widens.

The girl finally breathes. She's going to scream.

Only bile comes out. Bile and blood.

At the sight of the blood, Candy Princess licks her lips.

"It is a shame I can't eat you. You look absolutely scrumptious. Even now! Oh but look at me, always thinking about food. I want you to know, Emma, that I never eat my friends. That's unladylike. And I want you to know that this isn't just because of him. No, your death will mean something! These dancers, these filthy things, they have a very special song. It's going to help me make the universe into such a magical place. That's why I needed this amulet too. I just need to figure out where Mr. Valiant is hiding the power source and I'll be able to fulfill all my dreams. I wish you'd be able to see it, I really do! And Victor, he'll rule alongside me. I'll take such good care of him."

Emma starts to cry, and Candy Princess gently wipes each tear away.

"I promise," says Candy Princess.

Emma struggles to stand.

To crawl.

To scream.

To breath.

But she can't. So she does the only thing she can.

"Shh, just relax and it will all be over soon."

She listens.

The girl takes one last breath and, while she wants nothing more than for this to be over, she holds it for as long as she can.

It's not long enough.

Satisfied, the Thing brushes away the last of the girl's tears, unable to resist licking them off her fingers. She shudders at the taste of the girl.

The Thing stands and straightens her own party dress, checking for any unwanted vomit.

The Thing breathes deeply, crinkling her nose at the smell of the place.

And the Thing screams for help.

After all, she still has work to do.

ACT 4

## Characters you should know:

Victor

Emma

Jimmy

Valiant

Sera

Candy Princess

The Roboracle

The Robot with No Name

Chalk

Ickby

The Dread Space Pirate Robots

Manbot

Donna Natrios aka The Donnanatrix

Hamlet and pretty much any character already in the public domain

One of those random characters from page 86 that were just sort of mentioned in passing but are totally going to play a major roll in things to come, probably...


**...MAYBE YOU SHOULD JUST REREAD THE PREVIOUS 3 ACTS!**

# Act IV, Scene 1

*Chalk sits atop my shoulders pumping his fists to an unfamiliar tune that won't be produced for another 300 years. We raise our trophy high to the simultaneous sound of cheers, boos, and indifference.*

*We are winners.*

*We are champions.*

*We are valiant shining stars.*

*We are Victors, for we are dancers.*

*Feedback pierces the mysterious futuretronics; a scream. My ears bleed this time as the world melts into a single sound. The rhythm of a heartbeat. I watch the line of her life. I live and die with every peak and valley. Closing my eyes, I hear her song fill the room.*

*I wait.*

*Eventually she opens her eyes, just like always.*

*"What are you doing here?" she asks.*

*"Waiting for you to wake up," I reply.*

*She frowns.*

*Just then Captain Valiant bursts in, "Victor you must come quickly!"*

*"Another adventure?" I ask.*

*"An adventure like we've never faced before!"*

*"What is it tonight?"*

*"The Lieutenant has discovered an entity among us that is sucking all the adventure from the universe. If it succeeds, life as we know it will be a bureaucratic nightmare. We'll be forced to become telemarketers."*

*"Emma, I have to go," I say*

*She grabs me by the wrist and spins me around. She's wearing the first dress I ever saw her in, a white sundress that burns in the dying day.*

*"Adventure can wait," she says. "Kiss me."*

*I do.*

*She pulls away with a smile, then turns her head and throws up.*

*She's still smiling when she's done.*

*"Are you okay?" I ask.*

*"It's just a little puke, sweetie. Kiss me more."*

*She vomits again.*

*"I'm gonna go get you some help," I say.*

*The whites of her eyes have transformed bright red; she laughs, "It's a little late for that. Now c'mere and lets make out."*

*I hesitate.*

*A phone rings and Emma answers.*

*"It's for you," she says, so I take the phone.*

*"Hesitation is poison to a hero," says Valiant.*

*"Why are you on the phone?" I ask.*

*"I told you about the threat, Victor. You hesitated and now we're all telemarketers. And it's a good thing too, because have I got the product for you! Has your little* Valiant *ever let you* down, *perhaps even been killed in action? Then you need REZERECTION, a revolutionary new product from Candy Pharmaceuticals."*

*"Candy Pharmaceuticals?" I say.*

*"Correct, as it turns out the Princess has quite the business savvy. Mark my words, we'll all be working for her some day. Now Leiutenant, tell Victor why REZERECTION is the product for him."*

*"As a woman," Sera says with no inflection whatsoever, "REZERECTION makes me quiver in all the right places and even some of the wrong ones."*

*"You already make me quiver," says Emma as she heaves*

220

*again.*

*"I still need to help you," I say.*

*"Haven't you read any fairy tales? All it takes is a kiss," she pounces on me, takes her kiss and...she's perfect all over again*

*"I saved you," I say.*

*"You always do," she says and snuggles up against me and*

"Rise and shine, sleepyhead!"

I open my eyes, turning my head to see one of the most beautiful faces I'm likely ever to see, and my heart breaks because it's not the one I wanted. It never will be. Candy Princess smiles at me and I grimace, a gesture that doesn't go unnoticed.

"Another nightmare?" she asks.

"Only after I woke up," I say under my breath, but loud enough for her to hear. It doesn't faze her. Nothing ever does.

"I think I might have something to cheer you up," she removes the covers to reveal her naked body. It's perfect, every inch of it. The only problem being that I can't figure out why I'm waking up every morning with her naked in my bed. I'm nauseous.

"I've had my fill of candy," I say.

"Okay, Mr. Crankypants!" she smiles. She never stops smiling, "We'll try it when you're not so sour!"

I get up and head to the bathroom of the Valiant Suite at the Brothel of Infinite Sadness to begin my daily routine. A routine that started I don't know how many weeks ago. All I do is stare at myself in the mirror.

(and talk to yourself.) Not because I want to. (you really shouldn't be so hard on her, you know.) Mind your own business. (that's exactly what I'm doing. She's only trying to cheer you up.) And she seems happy enough! (I just think that—) Shut up, before I do it for you. (don't do that.)

221

I close my eyes and imagine my mind.

(please.)

I search for the fissure and, upon finding it, force it closed with all my might. My body shakes and my head feels like it's in a vise, there's a wetness on my upper lip as I taste copper. It's done, albeit only temporarily. But for now it's quiet.

"I heard you talking to yourself again," I open my eyes to her voice for the second time today. Once again I turn to her, "are you—oh my! You're bleeding again." She takes my face gently in her hands and wipes the blood from my nose with her fingers.

I turn back to the mirror and do my best to ignore her, something I'm very good at, but something catches the corner of my eye.

"Did you just lick your fingers?" I ask.

Candy Princess looks at me and smiles wide, "You're silly!" She glides back to bed, naked and flawless as ever. Maybe I should follow up on all of this. But I just don't care. I shut the door again.

"Are you going to be in there long?" she asks. "Do you want your keyboard?"

"No," I answer as I splash water on my face. After a few minutes I leave the bathroom behind, trying to avoid looking at Candy Princess as I reenter the bedroom. I wish she'd put some damn clothes on.

"You look thirsty," she says, shoving a drink in my face. It smells delectable. "You should drink."

"Why is it you always have some crazy treat waiting for me?" I ask.

"I want to make you feel good," she beams. It makes me uncomfortable. I'd refuse just on principle alone, but I am incredibly parched so I take it from her and gulp it down.

Candy's smile widens, turning inside-out as her pupils dilate. An ever expanding universe grows within her eyes. Countless lives gasp between the freckles in her irises, and all are snuffed out in the blink of an eye. I get lost and set out to be found.

If ever I'd imagined the perfect moment between us…it would never have tasted as sweet. The anticipation of our rendezvous makes me push my foot down. I don't worry that the road is a trap of loose granite; I've an appointment to make and one stop along the way.

I hear a nut shear off a wheel bolt and my car rattles a new rhythm. I don't let up. No matter how fast I tear down this trail, I don't seem to move. I'm craving her.

My passenger lacking a face catches sight of the community center out here in the middle of somewhere that's nowhere and unbraces himself, trying to stand upright, and points towards his destination. Impossibly I push the peddle through the floor. The world moves faster.

Something deep within me rumbles.

With the adoration of her love I hunger.

I starve.

My friend hands me an orange that tells me to let go of the wheel. The car promises to crash and I know it's a lie. Taking the orange, I pop the small stem and peel the upper rind. The soft hollow where each slice lay into the other presents itself brazenly. An orange that wants to be eaten is a curious thing. It speaks to my fingers with telepathic precision.

Each slice should be removed delicately.

I bite in instead.

Juice dribbles down my chin as my taste buds explode in a burst of obdurate sweetness. It's rotten and it knows it.

I have to find her.

223

I have to finish.

The brakes bake a disconcerting dish. It burns, throwing us into the crowed center.

I test the air with my skin making sure it's safe to breathe.

It's wet.

Humid.

My friend stands erect as I greet his dead father with a familiar smile and handshake, counting the times I've never met him. Weighing the probabilities of the outcome of their reunion of bitter vs. sweet I conclude the answer is chocolate. I can't watch. I return to the car, now frozen by millennia of weathering. Rust and vegetation are a lover's procrastination. They mock me, so I smile. Iron and vegetables feed on weakness. This is a disputable fact that should never be in doubt. But they only prolong my journey.

I will get to her.

I can't do without her.

I come to her.

The thousand foot face of Nest Mountain laughs at my plight. Not to be mean but to show me that joy can exist in any situation where no happiness can be found. We challenge each other to climb up the other. I do my best to lose, but the mountain refuses to move. No matter how hard I try I always end up a victor. The peak is in reach, a taut cavern that plunges deep within the mountain. Still moist from a rain that never came; I try not to slip as I find my footing. My faceless friend is already before the entrance. He smiles and dives in. Spelunking is a baseless, heartless passion that offers no loyalty to the caves.

I won't follow.

But I'm craving her.

A pebble has other designs, however, and so we fight. I win.

Shortly after, I slip on the defeated pebble's rigid corpse. Rigor mortis sets in quickly with pebbles. I smack against the granite surface. It's more colorful than my eyes can see. Glittering like a candy shop it begs me to lick it.

I resist.

My tongue does not.

The ground quakes, pushing me closer to my friend who was lost long ago in the warmth of the fissure. A volcano, surely, and no longer dormant. My breaths become labored as I struggle. I'm close to falling.

Within I feel her presence in an inverted lie I concoct to make falling safe. Propaganda is my most comforting gift.

Blindly I bask in her loving radiance.

Closing my eyes, I let go.

The mountain erupts.

It's finished.

The wind thumps against my chest, trying its best to be incorporeal, but I see right through it even without my eyes. It blows warm against my chest.

And I open my eyes.

The wind lies naked against me.

*Emma* I whisper.

*No* the wind replies.

Of course no, that was never really her name. I grasp to find it, but the wind doesn't let me.

The wind whispers, *It's Candy Princess, silly.*

And I'm left to wonder how the fuck I keep getting here.

# Act IV, Scene 2

Morning again. I think. I feel like I've lost a day. Or maybe a few. Not that I care. Except for me, the bed is empty. A rarity. I stretch out, relishing it until the vacant space reminds me of what I've lost. I force myself from bed, dress, grab my keyboard and get set to find Chalk. We've got to get some work done today. A knock at the door tries to cut short my search.

"Whatever you're offering, I'm not interested," I say.

"Victor," a strong, commandeering voice speaks, "it's Captain Valiant. I think we should talk."

Of course he does.

"And in case you're thinking about not opening the door, do remember that this is my suite and I always have a spare key."

Damn it. I open the door.

"Talk," I say.

"To get straight to the point, it's time you came back to the Galley. *Adventure* awaits."

"No thanks."

"Victor, I've allowed you time to grieve here, but this place isn't called the Brothel of Infinite Sadness for nothing. It does naught but profit from your heartache. It lavishes in it."

"I've got no problem with that."

"It's no way to live."

"And?"

"And The Brothel of Infinite Sadness is what much of the universe knows as the third stage in Valiant's Six Stages of Loss. I conceived them shortly after the death of my dearest Lollipop."

"You're comparing *her* to your goddamn cat?!"

Valiant's eyes flare furiously as he cocks his head ever-so-

226

slightly and his muscles grow noticeably tense. But I don't back down.

"Victor, do you know what happened to the last person who spoke of Lollipop that way?"

"You lectured him on the 101 ways to scrapbook a family pet?"

A cold smirk form on his lips, "I broke his neck and fed him to some of the more…savage slaves."

"Oh," I say. "Sorry."

"I'll accept your apology on one condition. You must leave this place with the rest of us."

"I'm not sure—"

"Victor," he interrupts, "eventually everyone runs out of *time*. It's one of life's simplest lessons, but also it's cruelest. Those of us who chose this path of *adventure* face it more often than most, and we sometimes lose more than we can bear, but the only way to honor that loss is to bear it anyway."

I stand silently, partially because I've nothing to say, but also because I can't figure out if I imagined the added emphasis on the word time. So I ask him.

"Captain, are you hinting at something?"

"I'm simply saying that it's *time* to move on. Wouldn't she have wanted that?" Either Valiant has added a new word to his emphasized lexicon or I'm having an idea that I should have had weeks ago. I practically sprint my way to the Adventure Galley, paying no mind to whether or not Valiant is keeping up. I barrel into the docking bay and barely avoid running into Jimmy and Sera.

"Vic!" Jimmy yips excitedly. "Does this mean you're coming back with us?"

"Sure, Jimmy, whatever."

"That's really great, because there's something I've been wanting to talk with you about. See I've got this id—"

"Not now, Jimmy! Sera, where's the time machine?"

"Huh?" she replies in a half daze.

"That little doohickey that can travel through time, where is it?!"

"In the Captain's trophy room, but—"

"Thanks!" This time there's no practically about it, I sprint through the maze of corridors to the universally renowned—or at least that's what I've been told—trophy room of Captain Valiant.

I start rifling through it in a meticulous frenzy when Sera startles me, "Victor, what are you doing?"

"Looking for the time machine, I told you that. Could you help me look, I'm not really sure where to st—oh nevermind! I found it. This is it right?"

"Yeah, but what exactly do you think you're going to do with it? I told you—"

"I remember. You said the Chronotastic Dance Party exists outside of time and whatnot so I can't travel back and forth or something. But I was too overwhelmed at the time to think straight."

Sera bites her lower lip sheepishly, a worried look spreads across her face. She must not grasp my intentions. Before I can explain, Jimmy finally catches up, out of breath.

"Wha—hhhh—what's going on?" he pants.

"I'm glad you asked. I'm going to save her."

"Who her? Sera?" He asks, confused. "Not Sera? Oh OH!" Now he gets it. "Emma! Great because that's what I wanted to talk to you about."

"No need, Jimmy. I've got it all figured out."

"Really?"

"Of course, I'm just going to use the time machine."

"But I thought you couldn't—"

"Use it at the dance. Right, but there's the rest of time! I mean, come on! How stupid are we to not figure out that we have all the time in all of time to save her?"

Jimmy goes silent. Clearly he knows I'm right.

"Look, Victor," Sera starts, "I don't think you should—"

"You don't think Victor should what, Lieutenant?" Captain Valiant enters the room effortlessly.

"Time travel, sir," she replies.

"Ah," he looks directly at me, "sorry if I kept you waiting, by the way, but I ran across the Princess and her Heart on the way here. I told them you'd decided to rejoin us so they're gathering your things and should be here shortly."

"Oh, thanks," I say.

"Now tell me, Victor, do believe time-travel to be your best course of action?"

"Yeah, I do. It just makes sense, right?"

"It does have a certain logic to it, yes," he furrows his brow, as if in deep thought. "Well then it's settled. Time-travel it will be!"

"Sir?" Sera stares at the captain intently. She looks…sad. He stares right back, never flinching. Finally she nods, "Of course, sir."

"So," he flashes me that sparkling, manly smile of his, "where shall we begin?"

# Act IV, Scene 3

"Here," I say. "We can start right here. I'll be able to show up just in time to stop those robots from taking her."

"I'm not sure that's such a good idea," says Sera. "The brothel isn't stationary for very long."

"So," I say, "neither is Earth, but I managed well enough there."

"It's not that it move that's the problem exactly, it's—look there are a couple of things you have to be concerned about when dealing with time-travel. First is your location's gravitational pull. The greater the gravity where you are, the more likely you'll hold to the object while unstuck from time. There's always a risk, but the risk decreases exponentially as gravity increases. And in that respect, this asteroid is most likely massive enough to be safe, but that's not taking into account it's movement. And we aren't talking something like planetary movement which is constant and predictable. We're talking about a place that semi-regularly teleports to completely random points across the universe. I can't guess how compatible that will or won't be to time-travel. You could end up fine or you could end up in the void of space frozen solid with burst lungs."

"Um, so I'm gonna do it though," I say.

"Captain Valiant," Sera protests.

"Victor, the Lieutenant has made a valid point," says Valiant.

"Fine, I've got a solution to put you at ease. Hey Roboracle," I say.

"I AM THE ROBORACLE."

"Yeah, yeah. Is it safe?"

"THE FATES DEEM IT SO."

"There you go! No problems. Now let's do this."

I make my way off the Galley, everyone following me. Stopping at the docking terminal I ask, "Did you get the time?"

Sera sighs, "Yes. According to the records, the Adventure Galley departed at 17:23 on the date in question."

"Thanks! You won't even know that I'm gone," I close my eyes, hold my breath and tap the trinket on my wrist.

*ZAAAP*

I take a moment to collect myself before making a single movement. If this is what freezing to death feels like then it's oddly like living. Finally allowing myself to breath, I open my eyes. Yep, this is the docking station. I look around and the Adventure Galley isn't where I left it just moments ago—but I suppose that's because moments ago won't happen for several weeks—it is, however, in a very familiar place. I'm here.

I start to move.

Fast.

I shove past countless oddities that have all ceased to be odd over the last month or more. I burst into the brothel and somehow manage to pick up my pace. I can almost feel her. And I know I'm going to make it!

That's when something waddles out from behind the illuminated fountain. I'm going too fast to stop. I only have time to process that I recognize it somehow, before stumbling over it and into a patron or worker whom shoves me towards the nearest arch. I fall through.

And then keep falling.

No, scratch that! I'm drowning now! Thankfully I'm an part amphibious so all I have to do is frantically claw my way to the water's surface. I hope I manage to look manly doing it too, just in case someone's watching. Completing my task, I gasp for air. On most sides I'm surrounded by calm sapphire waters, but I notice a small island not too far away. Before I can swim to it, however, a voice flutters to me.

"I was hoping he was wrong and you wouldn't show up," I look all around before finally glancing up to see Donna, in full Donnanatrix attire, floating about my head. "But he's never wrong is he. Mwaha. Ha."

"Donna, I have no idea what that means and I really don't care. Can you just help me out of here?"

"I'm sorry, Victor," she says.

"What ar—" There's no time to finish my sentence, or even the thought of that sentence, really, because suddenly the world is a song. And not just any song, but *the* song. The only song there ever needs to be. It surrounds me. It becomes me. And I become it. It's beautiful. So I am beautiful. Being beautiful is nice. Is there a reason I came here? I feel like there was. Yes, of course! I came here for this song. How could I have come for anything else?

I let myself sink into the sound as my lungs fill with its music.


My eyes snap open and I start to flail about because there's water…nowhere? Huh. I blink and let my eyes adjust. What I'm surrounded by are four walls and bed sheet.

And Candy Princess.

"You're awake again!" She claps.

It's my room on the Galley. Holy crap, I'm confused.

"What time is it?" I ask with my head still foggy.

"Oh, I'm not sure," says Candy Princess, "I think around lunch time!"

"No, not the time time, the date time," I almost yell.

"You're back in the future, Victor," says Valiant, just entering

232

the room. The man has the most impeccable timing! "Or rather it's the present."

"How did I get here?"

"Chalk and I—I'm calling him Chalk now because he told me today that he prefers it, it's just so adorable the way you two have bonded—we were headed from the suite back to the ship when we came across you near that pretty fountain. You were all wet and salty and absolutely scrumptious! But also I was worried because I didn't know why you were wet and salty. So I sent Chalk to get the captain while I waited with you, and he brought you back here!"

"You were lying near the gateway to the Sound of the Sirens," says Valiant. "Why would you go in there?"

"I tripped on something and got knocked in there, I guess."

"Hey," Sera says, peeking in the door, "I heard some excited squeals and thought—yep, you're awake. So can't we get going now?"

"That's up to Victor, Lieutenant," says Valiant. "Are you planning to go back again?"

"Yes," I say.

Sera groans.

"But not here," I say. "It's too crowded. Too many variables to deal with. I want to go back to some time earlier."

"Well you sure as hell aren't doing it on the ship!" Sera warns. "I don't care what The Roboracle says either. It's too dangerous. If not for you, whom I don't really care about, then for the ship, which I do care about."

"Relax, I don't want to do it on the ship. She wasn't too happy with me most of the time we were aboard."

"Then where would you like to go?" asks the captain.

"I know exactly where to go," I say. "Sera, set a course for Earth! You know, uh, again. If it's alright with the captain."

Captain Valiant nods.

"Alright!" I exclaim and Chalk hops on the bed and offers up a high five.

"Whatever," Sera says.

"What was that, Lieutenant?" asks Valiant.

"Whatever, sir," she corrects herself.

"Thank you," he smiles.


"You're sure this is the place?" Captain Valiant asks.

"Yeah, this is it," I respond. The trip back to Earth had been agonizing and then the shuttle ride down here with Valiant was nearly as bad. I only had the vaguest idea of where this place was when I was last here. Luckily Jimmy was able to help out a bit.

"And you've set the time accordingly?"

"Yep, but hey…can you patch me through to the others for a second."

"We've been over this, Victor," Sera's voice buzzes in my ear. "Your comlink is always active because you keep forgetting how to turn it off."

"Right, well since I have your attention I just wanted to say that it was a pleasure knowing you all and I'm very sorry that my success here will most likely mean you'll no longer remember me."

"Noooooooooooooooooooooo!!" a shrill, girlish voice shrieks.

"Jesus, Jimmy," I say, "you'll still remember me. Get a grip."

"What?" Jimmy replies. "That wasn't me. It was Candy."

"Oh. In that case, just comfort her until she forgets about me. Shouldn't be too long. So as I was saying I, um…crap! I lost my train of thought. It's a good thing none of you will remember this. What a terrible farewell speech. Anyway, see ya!" I activate the time machine.

*ZAAAAP!*

Time-traveling is kind of like a sneeze, in that you can never keep your eyes open during it. Or at least I can't. But whatever. I blink a few times to let my eyes adjust. It was dusk when I left Valiant, but it's the afternoon now. That, as well as the absence of Valiant and the shuttle, is the only noticeable difference in this tiny suburban neighborhood. I turn toward the house that she and I—along with Jimmy, The Roboracle and Donna, against my vehement protests—shared. Albeit only briefly.

The walk to the front door seems even longer than any of the trans-universal trips I've taken, but eventually I'm there. Before I can open the door, however, the door opens for me. A minute displacement of air, as the heat of the day tries its best to ransack the cooler interior, steals my breath. And the face behind the door crushes me. Unable to breath, and thinking it's quite possible every organ in my body might fail simultaneously, one thing is certain: I couldn't possibly feel better.

"I knew I heard something out here," she speaks and proves me wrong. She always finds a way to make things better. She's wearing a faded pink and blue tank-top and very tiny navy blue shorts. She's beaming at me. I can't stop staring. Her demeanor slowly alters. She brings her left hand to her cheek, chewing on the knuckle of her pinky before tucking her hair behind her ear. It's what she does when she's self-conscious. "What?" She laughs timidly. "I look terrible don't I? I knew you were lying this morning," she pouts. "It's my hair, isn't it? It's getting all dreadlocked. I should just cut it all off." I smile for the first time in weeks. "Are you just…are you not going to say anything? Goddamn it, are we having a staring contest? Why do you like these things, they're boring! And starting one without telling me is cheating." She purses her lips and squints, trying to stare through me. It's her faux serious face. She gives it up quickly. "Ahhhh, you win.

Just say something!"

I inhale sharply and exhale deeply.

"I missed you," I say.

She shakes her head and scoffs, "You can be so weird, you know that. It's been like 10 minutes since I saw you. And speaking of which, weren't you supposed to be on your way to the store. You know, so we can have food and hygiene products and not feel so disgusting all the time."

"I did leave," I say, "but I had to come back. I need to tell you something."

"Hold that thought, sweetie, cause I really have to pee!" Pushing herself onto the balls of her feet, she kisses my nose and runs off, not bothering to close the door, and yelling "be right back" as she goes.

"I'll be here," I say in almost a whisper.

"THE FATES DISAGREE."

"What?" I turn around.

"I AM THE ROBORACLE."

"Great! But what do you mean?" Before I can get an answer, Donnanatrix zooms in front of me.

"Didn't I just see you walking down the road towards town?" she asks.

"Yes, but look! I'm from the future!"

"Again?"

The Roboracle starts to vibrate.

My muscles lock.

"ACTIVATING TIME-BREAKER SEQUENCE."

The world starts to buzz.

zzzzzzzzzzzzzz

Through clenched teeth I plead, "Donna, tell her not to come

236

after me!"

"What?" she says.

*zzzzzzžžžžžžž*

"If she comes after me she'll die!"

"Who's going to die? Emma?!"

*žžžžžžžžžžž*

I can only manage a garbled yes.

"Don't worry," Donna's voice grows distant, "we'll protect her."

"NEGATIVE," says the Roboracle.

"Negative?!" Donna screeches. I can barely hear her. "What do you mean negative? We wou—"

That's when the past implodes in one painful

*ŽΑΑΑΑΡ!*

I collapse in a cold sweat.

"Victor, are you alright?" Valiant asks, offering a helping hand. I decline.

"Jimmy!" I bellow. "I know you can hear me!"

"Yeah, of course I can," he says in my ear.

"I want you to tell The Roboracle that as soon as I get back to the ship I'm going to kill him!"

"Um," he says.

"Do IT!"

"Uh, well he was listening and just said 'NO YOU WON'T'…What's this all about?"

"The little bastard just kept me from warning her, that's what this is about! And I'm pretty sure he was also the thing that tripped me in the brothel."

"I don't mean to interrupt," says the captain, "but are we done here?"

"Damn right we are," I answer.

"To the *Adventure* Galley then?" he says.

"No, I just need to go back to a time and place before that stupid omniscient fuck came into our lives."

"And where might that be?"

"Um, let me think. Oh I know! Jimmy?"

"Yeah," he says.

"Transmit Valiant the location of your house."

"Uh, okay. No problem."

"And Jimmy!"

"Huh?"

"Do you happen to remember the date of the day we were all there? You know, when you built that crazy car."

"I think so, yeah."

"Awesome! Let's do this!"


We get to Jimmy's old place in no time. Space shuttle really is the only way to fly. I step out and don't say a word, I just

*ZAAAAP!*

But not 5 seconds go by before I hear the voice that makes my blood boil.

"THE ROBORACLE KNOWS YOU DON'T BELONG HERE."

I turn to kick him, but he's too far away.

And then the vibrations start, freezing me in place once again.

"SCANNING FOR TIME CODE. PROCESSING... PROCESSING."

"You're scrap metal in the future, buddy!" I try to say, but unable to open my lips it comes out as mush.

"SCANNING COMPLETE. TIME BREAKER SEQUENCE

ACTIVATED. TIME FOR STYX."

The air around me starts to ionize and tingle.

"THE ROBORACLE WILL MEET YOU SOON. BRING AIR-CONDITIONING. THE FATES DEMAND IT."

And then...

*ZAAAAP!*

"Gaaaaaah!! FUCK!!!!" I scream.

"Victor," Valiant tries to reassure.

"He was there again, damn it! But you know what, screw it! I know a when and where before that rusty fuck even existed."


We travel in silence. I don't want to talk and Captain Valiant seems okay with that. When we arrive I step out into what used to be a nice neighborhood. Now it's little more than ash. I'm not going to be able to find the place until I go back. I set the time machine back one day from my last attempt...

*ZAAAAP!*

The neighborhood is instantly transformed to the way I remember it. Valiant landed us only a couple dozen yards from the house I'm looking for. My house. Or it was before the world ended and my life finally took off. I walk around the side to a small tool shed. It's open. I never locked it because I rarely kept anything in there. Just a few worthless projects I worked on but knew I'd never finish along with the one thing I was here for. A gas can.

(aw, jeez! What are you going to do with that?) You're back? (well, you're kind of cracking up a bit...so yeah.) Whatever, you won't be for long. I'm going to burn my house down. It's Sunday so I know I'm in there. (why are you always doing these things?!) I have to save her somehow.

I take off the cap.

239

Huh? (what?) The reason I remember the gas can being in the shed is because I'd just used it a couple days before the craziness to siphon gas from a friends car. (why?) He owed me money, I think. Who really cares, the point is that the can was full afterwards, but it's almost empty now. Weird…oh well! Plenty to get the job done.

I douse as much of my house in gasoline as possible then pull out my lighter—I always keep one because you never know when arson might be necessary—and I light away. Now the only thing left to do is watch and wait to fade away. The flames spread even faster than I expect. A few even hop over to neighboring houses.

(should we maybe warn the neighbors, at least?) Nah, they're all most likely at church or whatever. (but what if they're not.) Then they've clearly pissed off God for not going to church, because right now their houses are on fire. (I notice we're still here despite our house being fully engulfed in flames…) I must be difficult to kill, but no worries I've got nowhere else to be.

"Oh my god my house!" A familiar voice cries out. I turn my head. No way, it can't be! "MY COMICS!!!!!" God damn it! It's me! What the hell?

(you must have gotten the date wrong.) No way, I went back to the day before I was at Jimmy's house, which is the day before the whole apocalypse started. (but we *were* at Jimmy's house the day after it all started too.) He gave me the wrong date?! (technically, not really.) Screw technically! I just burned all my comics because he gave me the wrong date! (you were going to burn the house anyway.) Only with the understanding that I'd cease to exist! But fine, I'm going to fix this.

*ZAAAAP!*

I return to the present, quickly change the date on the machine back one more day and

*ZAAAAP!*

240

Unlike tomorrow, today is overcast and windy. No bother, I storm back over to the shed and yank out the gas can again. It's a lot heavier this time; full, like it should have been tomorrow. I start splashing it everywhere. Laughing as I go along. OH YOU'RE GONNA GET IT NOW, ME!!!!!

I pull out my lighter yet again. That's when it starts to rain. But I can still make this work. I get down on the ground and try to strike a spark near a tiny puddle of gas.

Then it's starts to pour.

I can see the gas washing away.

"No NO NOOOOOOOOOOOOOOOOOOOOOO!" I scream.

(relax, man.) Fuck relaxing, I have to save her! (so what are you going to do?) What I'm going to do is break down my fucking door and kill myself with my own two hands, that's what!

I kick the front door as hard as I can.

"OWWWWWW, MY FOOT!"

Ow

(ow)

ow

(ow)!

I slump down on my front porch and try to pretend the tears running down my face are just rain.

(so now what?) Now? Now we go home, I guess.

I get up and limp back to the shed, putting the gas container back. I might have needed it later today. I can't remember. I push the button on the time machine and

*ZAAAAP!*

I'm back where I belong.

# Act IV, Scene 4

"**W**here shall we go now?" Captain Valiant asks, already boarding the shuttle.

"The Galley," I say.

"The Lieutenant has already advised against time-travel there," he reminds me unnecessarily.

"I know," I say.

"Ah," is all he needs to say. "Lieutenant?"

"I heard, sir." I hear her say. "The docking bay hatch is open and waiting."

I don't say anything until we take off, "I can't change it, can I?" It's not really meant as a question, but he answers anyway.

"No."

"Then why not just tell me that?"

"Because it's all part of <u>Valiant's Six Stages of Loss</u>. Denial, Anger, The Brothel of Infinite Sadness, Time-Travel, Acceptance."

"But that's only five," I say.

"Yes."

"So what's the sixth?"

He smirks, "*Adventure*, of course."

The rest of the trip back is silent, but after we've safely docked Captain Valiant turns to me, "May I ask you a question?"

"Sure," I say.

"You don't have to answer if you don't wish, but…did you see her?"

I nod.

"I saw Lollipop again, too," I look at him quizzically, not really surprised, but curious. "She was just a kitten and it was mere hours before I would rescue her from the Kitty-Kat Kavalkade—don't let the name fool you, they were monsters of the highest order—after which we would form our legendary partnership. I hadn't even travelled back to find her. I was looking for myself, to warn me not to form any sort of partnership with a kitten I might rescue. Of course my greatest nemesis at the time was an alien known as Tran Es Frm. Tran Es Frm could take the shape of anyone or thing. Once he kidnapped Lollipop and posed as her for 3 days before I realized something was amiss. So naturally my past-self was not too trusting of my future-self. Had my mind been clear at the time I would have remembered that this was the very conversation that convinced me to keep Lolli in the first place. Time-travel is an ironic bitch, Victor."

Again, I nod.

"Instead of traveling back to my present, however, I wondered the streets, disgusted at the realization that I was just playing out some twisted time paradox and I could change nothing. And that's when I saw her. She looked up at me from an alleyway and mewed before running back into the darkness. It broke me all over again."

"Yeah," I mostly whisper.

"But it was also wonderful," he grins.

"Yeah," this time I say it louder. We head off toward the bridge to join the others.

"So," Valiant says, and now he's full of gusto. "We have a lot of *adventuring* to make up for. Do you have any ideas of where to start?"

"Actually," I start, "before we get back to saving galaxies and all that, there's one other thing I'd like to do. But first I'm going to need my keyboard!"

# Act IV, Scene 5

"This is a song I've been writing for the last few weeks," I say. We're all gathered in Valiant's room, my keyboard set up near the door. "Chalk's been helping me out," Chalk waves, his chest reading THAT'S ME, "and he'll be accompanying me on his ukulele. The title of the song is 'I'm So Sad Right Now'. I hope you like it."

"I'll LOVE it!" exclaims Candy Princess.

"Uh, cool," I say and then I begin.

The first notes are sublime, just like I planned them. The notes that follow are even better. I'm a keyboard god! Chalk joins in right on cue. The happy twang of his ukulele the perfect juxtaposition to the majestic soul crushing I'm about to hand out. The first verse approaches. My voice sings out, an Apollonian breeze that soothes as it destroys.

> *I'm so sad right now*
> *Cause you're gone, baby*
> *And I'm missin' you*
> *Wonderin' where you've gone*
> *Now that I've buried you*
> *Metaphorically*
> *In the ground*

My fingers set the keys ablaze in the bridge to the second verse.

> *You used to come to me*
> *When I called your name*
> *Metaphorically*
> *But in reality*

*And now you don't no more*
*Because you're dead to me*
*And everyone else TOOOOOOOO!*

I slow my keyboard work to a dull throb, an ache that won't relent, as Chalk begins his solo. He nails every note. Surely there won't be a dry eye in the house

*So I'm sad right now*
*Cause you're gone, honey*
*Can't stop missin' you*
*Gooooobye Happy DAAAAAYS!!!!*
*Metaphorically*
*And not the TV show*
*Yeah I can still watch that*
*Anytime I WAAAAANT!*

We achieve the pinnacle of musical divinity. Chalk's ukulele is a music box of splendor transcending the very possibilities of sound. I lower my voice to a velvety baritone, almost speaking the final verse.

*I'm crying tears for you, baby*
*Tears of sadness*
*Metaphorically, baby*
*They're streaming down my face*
*Straight from my tear ducts, baby*
*I'm so sad right now*
*And it's all because you're gone*

And so it ends and I await my praise. Candy Princess is

practically jumping up and down with amazement.

"Thatwasthemostwonderfulsongever!" she blurts out.

"It was kind of supposed to be sad," I say.

"And it was *so* sad," she beams.

"Uh, okay…anyone else?" I look around. "Sera?"

"Well, um," she stutters, I must have really moved her, "it's just that…I don't think metaphorically means what you think it means."

"Oh Sera," I chuckle, "it's poetry!"

"Even then…" she trails off, allowing Jimmy to interrupt.

"No, but you see what Vic did was he basically gave us a meta-textual commentary on metaphors themselves!"

"Jimmy, what the hell?!" I exclaim. "You totally just nailed it! I owe you an apology for all those things I've said about you and probably will continue to say about you in the future."

"Wow, thanks man! Hey, now that you're all done with this can I tell you about my plan to get Emma back?"

"Jimmy, weren't you paying attention?" I say. "Time-travel doesn't work. It's time to accept that she's gone. Maybe you could write your own song to help with the grief. Not that it could ever be as awesome as mine, so it would definitely be a waste of time."

"But that wasn't my idea," he says.

"What? Writing a song? I know. It was mine. I *just* suggested it. Jeez, Jimmy."

"No, Vic! Time travel!"

"Doesn't work. It's like you aren't even listening to me."

"That's not my idea, though!"

"The way you can't stop bringing up makes it seem like it must have been…but hey, if you have another idea then let her rip. Although if it's as spectacular a failure as your time travel one…"

"I, um…okay look, I started thinking about it a couple weeks

246

back, but Candy Princess didn't think I should get your hopes up yet, and you weren't really making yourself available so I—"

"Are you telling me you've had this for weeks and didn't tell me?" He nods. "Jimmy—and I completely mean this—I hate you!" I storm out of Valiant's room to make my point, but I can't think of anywhere to go so I just rejoin everyone. "Hey Jimmy," I say. "You remember that time I said I hated you? I didn't really mean it. So what's this idea you had? Something about time travel?"

"Well, no," he says. "Do you remember that time that I died?"

"Not really," I say.

"Seriously?"

"Lot's of people die, Jimmy. I can't remember them all."

"Okay, never mind. The point is that I died and ever since— and especially since Emma's death—I've been having these, I don't know, flashbacks to what happened when I was dead. I'm pretty sure I went to Hell. And if I could go there and come back, well there must be a way to get in there, right?"

"Yes," Captain Valiant interjects, "I have heard a few tales of voyages into Hell. It's been something of a dream of mine to conquer the trials of hellfire, but the entrance is a complete mystery. Do you happen to remember where it is, Jimmy?"

"Um, no," he frowns.

"Whatever, she'd never be in Hell anyway," I say.

"But I went there, and Emma killed way more people than I ever did. Isn't it worth finding out?"

"It would be an unparalleled adventure, Victor," Valiant persuades.

"Sure," I say, "but if we don't know how to get there then it doesn't matter."

"Actually," Sera chimes in, "I—god I can't believe I'm about to do this—I think I can find out."

"Really?!" I start to get excited. "How?"

"The Old Star," she sighs, "Seraphim. He's kind of my dad."

# Act IV, Scene 6

"**W**ait," I start, "let me get this straight...you're half *star*?"

Sera sighs and nods sullenly.

"So," I think out loud, "then Sera is short for—"

"Seraphim, yeah. My name is Seraphim Cole."

"Huh," I say, "but wait! Didn't Captain Valiant introduce you as Lieutenant *T*.S Cole? What's the T stand for?"

"I can't believe you remember that," she says.

"Me not remember something? Yeah right! My brain is like, um…what's that animal they say never forgets things? Ah, who cares. So what's the T stand for?"

Sera takes a deep breath, "<sub>Twinkle.</sub>"

"Was I the only one who couldn't hear that?" I say.

"Twinkle, alright! My name is Twinkle," Sera blushes. And I do the only thing appropriate in this situation. I laugh hysterically. So Sera socks me in the stomach. But she's really not that strong, I'm only gasping for breath because of all the laughing. Honestly.

When I finally regain my composure I can hear Candy Princess elegantly humming a familiar song, "Twinkle, Twinkle Little Star". It's almost enough to crack me up again, but then I see Sera's angry face and...well it's still pretty hilarious but I'm worried Sera might start punching everyone. The men could handle it, but Candy Princess and Jimmy would probably start crying, so I hold my composure.

"I don't think she likes that," I whisper to Candy.

"But it's what she is," she says back with a grin so serene it's kind of creeping me out.

Sera just rolls her eyes, "Look, can we just move on, seeing my dad is pretty much the last thing I want to do so I'd rather get this over with as soon as possible."

"Sure, yeah," I say, "but I just have a couple questions."

Sera looks at me incredulously.

"First, can you do any cool star things?"

Relief washes over her, "Oh, well I can manipulate the light spectrum, which you've probably noticed," she gestures to her hair as it begins flashing a plethora of blinding colors. And there are some other things, I guess."

"Like being the energy source!" exclaims Candy Princess, giddily.

We all turn to look at her.

"Um, of the ship I mean...maybe?" She finishes shyly, refusing to make eye contact with anyone.

Sera eyes Candy in a way I can't quite place, "Sometimes I power the ship, yeah."

"Whoa, really?" I'm impressed.

"I don't do it that often, it's just that—"

"It's that *adventure* rarely pays the bill," Valiant interjects, "and the lieutenant is kind enough to keep the Galley afloat in tough economic times or when our quests afford us no time to find a port with fuel."

"Right," Sera continues, "but it's really exhausting. You probably noticed I was pretty out of it when we first met."

Jimmy nods while I say nope.

"Of course you didn't," she says in my direction.

"Aardvark!" I yell.

Everyone stares at me like I'm insane. Clearly they require enlightenment.

"It's the animal that never forgets things," I explain.

"Um Vic," Jimmy says, "that's not right, man."

"JimmyJimJimJimmy, one of us here is an aardvark and the

other one is, well…is you. So I think I know what I'm talking about. But we're getting off topic; I've got another question for Sera. Just one more," I say and Sera seems less apprehensive about this one. "So your dad is a star, but your mom isn't. So um...how'd they do it?" I make certain universal hand gestures to make my question clearer.

Sera's eyes grow wide. "Ewwwww!"

She storms off to the cockpit.

Everyone is staring at me again.

"What?"


I assumed that we'd have to travel some great distance to speak with the Star, but Sera informs us that he can be contacted anywhere that he's visible, although it could take a bit longer from this far away. For the last day and a half she's sequestered herself in a life pod, several miles from the Galley, attempting to phone home or something. Apparently she needed to distance herself from the rest of us to cut back on psychic feedback, whatever that means.

Valiant gets on the com, "Lieutenant, it's been over 36 hours. Perhaps it's time for you to return."

"Sir, we are pretty far away, and my dad has never been the most attentive, but trust me he will talk to me. Just a few more hours and I—" Static cuts through the com system. Everything switches off.

Silence transforms into a high-pitched whine as a voice like an old photograph speaks images to my memories. I see the world enveloped by nature and nothing more. I feel a picture of thunder beneath me. I hear the memory of a great beast roar and jump as the shadow of a pterodactyl swoops overhead. I remember a sky millions of years older than me grow ever brighter and louder and explode. I remember dead beasts I never knew and the figure of an almost man too luminous to look at and I remember—

251

Anger flashes red in my mind followed by broken images that I can't comprehend, only knowing they fill me with a deepening sadness that I can't escape. Mercifully, and painfully, the images clarify and show me the only thing I care to see. They show me her, just as Sera knew her. Smiling. And I smile. But without even the blink of an eye I see her lying on a bathroom floor. Dead. I see myself holding her. As a reflex, I close my eyes to escape the scene. Of course it does no good. I'm trapped in this image. The weight of my sadness embraces Sera's and crushes me. The images blur yet again and I'm acutely aware of my own shortness of breath along with a growing fever. I'm shown a marsh to which the response is hesitance. Then there's a ring which is refused. But the ring is insistent, it's connection to the marsh vague, but undeniable somehow. Finally, acquiescence. Terrible things are forced upon my mind. A goblet of wine spills like a gaping wound onto a barren field. I feel fire and taste sulphur and translucent people pass through me in a shiver. Everything speeds up, the whine in the back of my head grows to an unbearable pitch, and then...nothing.

I finally open my eyes. I'm lying on the floor, my face damp. I look around just enough to notice everyone else in a similar state. No one speaks.

Eventually the radio crackles to life.

"Hey," Sera says, "so I got Hell's address."

Awesome. If only I could stop shaking.


By the time Sera boards the ship, we've all regained our composure. Mostly, at least.

"That was a fascinating experience, Lieutenant," offers Valiant.

"Sorry about that," Sera says, looking at me. "I guess I should have known that a couple hundred miles wouldn't be enough with a voice that spans light-years."

"No worries," I force a smile, "you got what we needed, after all. So where is it, how far do we have to go?"

"Not far. I don't know how much you caught, or were able to understand, but apparently there are a lot of entrances to Hell. Basically you can expect to find a gate or two anyplace that spawns life, and since we're already right above Earth..."

"Cool," I say, "I'm sick of space travel anyway. Let's do this, what are the coordinates?"

"Thirty seven point eight seven eight three eight five degrees latitude, and minus one hundred twenty two point zero nine four seven zero seven degrees longitude," she says as Valiant punches them into the Galley's universal mapping system, but since we're talking about Earth I guess it's just slightly fancier GPS. It'll only take us a few minutes to get to the location.

"Perhaps we should rest first," the Captain offers. "Hell is likely to be a trying journey."

"Fuck all that!" I return. "If she's down there then she could be suffering and I won't allow that for one second longer than can be helped."

"Very well," Valiant nods, but Sera pauses. "What is it, Lieutenant?"

"It's just that," she sighs, "in order to get the location I had to promise my dad I wouldn't go in there with you guys."

"Oh thank goodness!" exclaims Candy Princess, causing all our heads to turn. "I just mean that Hell sounds so scary and I was frightened that I'd have to choose between going or staying all alone. Now I can stay behind and have company! We will have the best time ever, Sera!"

Sera frowns.

"Don't fret, Lieutenant," reassures Valiant, "the rest of us can more than handle whatever Hell has to offer. It's probably safer to have someone stay behind and watch after the Galley anyway."

"I guess," Sera concedes before punching some buttons, causing us to descend rapidly towards Earth.

Soon, green and golden rolling hills pass underneath us. Houses seemingly unaffected by the apocalypse dot large acreage of overgrown farm-like plots. The land recedes into a parasitic suburban sprawl of humanity. Large houses with algae infested pools. Hedges no longer straight. The street signs in the area all seem to be spray painted with the same symbol, a triangle with a circle inside it.

We fly over a small dense grouping of houses burnt either to their foundations or close to it when an indicator light starts flashing on the ships console. We are closing in on our target.

One house stands on the opposite side of a main thoroughfare, which marks the boundary of the urban developments. Such that it makes this one house seem...different.

"That one," I point the house out to my friends.

"I feel it too," Valiant chimes in. "There's plenty of room around it to set down, Sera."

And just as smoothly as she brought us up and over she brings us down.

Everyone is armed to the teeth when we exit the ship. Earth has become just an all-around dangerous place to live, but add to that our current location and the hypnotic draw this gateway emanates to whatever beasties and ghouls are around and you understand that we have to be at our best.

It appears that the locals at one point understood what was within the house and did all they could to seal the place up. Boards and other found materials are nailed over every door and window. Aged significantly, but still in place.

"At least we know no one should be inside," I try and lighten the mood.

"It's a gateway, dumbass," Sera says. "Anything or anyone could be inside."

"Listen Twink, why don't you run back on board and get us an axe?" I muster all the vile sarcasm possible for that delivery. She doesn't argue.

Valiant offers up a plan, "Everyone stays here with the ship until Victor and I give an all-clear."

It sounds good so I follow.

We walk around the house trying to find a broken board or loose plate covering entryways, but find none. Quietly we sneak to a ground floor doorway underneath an exterior staircase to the second floor. This one looks like the easiest way to enter. Valiant presses his head as close to the door as possible listening for signs of life, or even death, but hears nothing. He motions to Sera, who has reappeared at the ship entrance with an axe. Valiant waves her to stand back as he takes it from her, and I aim my pistol at the space where he will soon break through.

Only a few swings are needed to break the boards nailed across the door's face and Valiant plants a running flat-footed kick near the handle to rip the door open. I jump into the open cavity and prepare to shoot.

Nothing.

A staircase along the back wall goes up, but there's only a few small piles of rubbish along the walls and propped against support beams of this first floor expanse. No gateway. No zombies. No demons. No ghosts.

Valiant and Sera push in behind me and stand ready, letting their eyes adjust from the outdoor light. I whisper for them to follow

255

and we creep to the stairs. Floorboards creak loudly with every step so I decide to make a run for it. Our element of surprise was lost the second we landed anyway. I attempt to take the stairs two at a time but my foot goes right through one of them and I slam down against the others. I motion Valiant and Sera to keep going while my paralyzed body recovers from the pain.

Upstairs is a hallway where my friends have already kicked in and cleared half the rooms. I boot down the last door, but find nothing. Sera and Valiant turn to me from their doorways with a similar look of unmet expectations.

"Did either of you see a gateway?" I have to ask.

They both shake their heads.

"But," Sera says, "my dad did mention an offering had to be made."

"And you're only bringing this up now?" I chide.

"Look, I thought I'd wait until we actually found a gateway before I brought it up! Now I'm thinking maybe we need to make the offering to make the gate appear."

"So what is this offering we're meant to make, Lieutenant?" asks Valiant.

Sera frowns, "I, um, I don't actually know."

"What?!" I start to freak out.

"I'm sorry, but all my dad could come up with were some vague thoughts about pouring goblets full of something in a field."

"So wine, then," I perk up.

"Maybe," Sera offers.

"Great! You two go get the others, and I'll run across the street and raid some liquor cabinets. We need to turn this place inside out and then paint it with booze!" I don't wait for their reactions, I just run off to the neighboring houses.

After a bit I return with an armful of wine bottles, along with some whiskey, vodka, and even a bottle of absinthe. Whomever we're offering to might prefer the hard stuff, after all. In my absence everyone seems to have searched the place pretty thoroughly, unfortunately all they've come up with are some old mice chewed comic books titled 'Steel Canyon' and broken pieces of furniture. Still no sign of a gateway.

Jimmy sits mournfully at the base of the stairs while flipping through one of the comics. Valiant stands heroically stationary, gazing at the ceiling with one hand to his chin and the other planted in a fist at his hip, while Sera seems a wreck over her inability to find anything relevant about the gateway. She's probably contemplating the possibility that her father was just being a jerk and sent us on a fool's errand as she sits up against one of the vertical building supports. The Roboracle is doing absolutely nothing. The damnable contraption may be recharging. The Robot With No Name is next to Valiant, reciting a familiar poem. Chalk is the only one in motion. He digs through the pieces of furniture, laying them out as if he were reconstructing a crime scene. I can't be sure, but I think he's studying their breaking points.

Candy Princess emerges from the upstairs, presumably she was doing a final sweep of the rooms above.

"Worry not, friends!" I proclaim. "I come bearing alcohol!"

We proceed to splash every square inch with wine.

Nothing happens.

We repeat the process with the vodka.

Still nothing.

By the time we get to the whiskey, I'm the only one even trying and after half the bottle even I give up. There's really nothing here.

I lean back heavily on one of the support columns and take a swig from the whiskey bottle. Dejected, I slide down to a sitting position when I feel a sharp pain in my back. I reach back and find wetness. I'm bleeding. I take another shot before getting up to see what cut me. Turning to look at the beam, I'm shocked. My blood is streaked down from a rather large splinter. And it's glowing a light red that's fading rapidly.

"Hey!" I scream. Everyone gathers beside me just in time to see the glowing markings fade away from sight.

"What did you do, Victor?" Valiant questions.

I touch my back again and smear fresh blood across the beam. The glowing returns, and this time foreign markings can be seen extending even further up and down its length. After only a few moments, the markings fade away again.

"We're gonna need lots of blood," I say. "So Jimmy, it's time to take one for the team."

"What?" Jimmy says.

"I'd rather be able to use one of the robots, but they don't bleed and *someone* has to be sacrificed so..."

"No way! I already died once!"

"So you've clearly got the most experience with dying. Face it Jimmy, this is what you were born to do!"

"You're not sacrificing me, Vic!"

"Honestly, I don't see what the big deal is. You die, you go to Hell, the gate to Hell opens, we come down and rescue you while we're doing our thing. I'd do it myself, but Valiant and I are clearly the saviors and I don't see how you can save people with one of your saviors dead. That's just stupid, Jimmy, and I'm personally offended that you would even suggest it."

"I didn't!"

"Well great! Then we're in agreement. Anyone know the best way to bleed a man?" Candy Princess' hand shoots up. "Huh, that's unexpected...but okay let's do this!" Candy skips over to me, reaches down her dress and pulls out dagger. "Whoa! Where'd that come from?"

She scrunches her nose, "From my dress, silly!"

Before we can grab hold of Jimmy, however, Captain Valiant steps in, "While I certainly appreciate your gung-ho attitude, I'm quite certain we can solve this dilemma without murdering our friends. Tell them, Lieutenant."

"We have a med bay on the Galley," Sera says.

"So?" I respond.

"So we've got blood stored there."

"Really?" Candy Princess and I say simultaneously. Although hers was much more enthusiastic.

"Uh, of course. Sometimes there are accidents in deep space and, as archaic as it may sound, sometimes we have to perform blood transfusions."

"What are we waiting for then?" I ask. "To the med bay!"

# Act IV, Scene 7

We're back with the blood in no more than 10 minutes. Everyone is here and ready, except for Sera and Candy Princess. Valiant instructed them to stay onboard the Adventure Galley in case some really terrible things exit while we're entering.

Valiant hands me the first pint of blood, "I'll leave the honors to you."

We brought a total of six. Not quite the equivalent to a human sacrifice, but we didn't want to completely deplete the Galley's supply unless absolutely necessary. Hopefully it'll be enough.

I drain the bag onto the support beam and the glowing starts all over again, but this time it's brighter and the strange symbols are much clearer. Still, nothing else happens. By the time the second pint is expended I can feel heat radiating off the beam. No Hell, though. As I'm using the fourth I'm starting to worry. Yet all I can do is watch the blood pour down

down

down

the pillar. It's not until I reach back for the fifth pint that I realize we're all mimicking the blood.

Down

Down

Down

My head spins a vertigo line of discomfort that dissipates as I exhale. The broken down house has disappeared into a dank, misty swamp. Moisture seeps into my socks. We're here.

I guess.

Looking back I can see a door leading into the shack, which is weird considering the distinct falling sensation I just experienced. But

I'm not going to concern myself with it. Instead I try to survey our surroundings, except the mist is so thick I can hardly see more than ten feet in front of me.

"So, what now?" I ask.

"IF THE ROBORACLE STAYS HERE THE ROBORACLE WILL RUST."

"I, too, am rather concerned about rust, sir," says No Name.

"THE ROBORACLE DOES NOT LIKE THE OTHER ROBOT. THE OTHER ROBOT IS UNNECESSARY. THE ROBORACLE WILL SEARCH THE FATES DATABASE FOR ITS DEMISE. THE ROBORACLE WILL LAUGH AND PLAY STYX."

"First," I say, "I don't like either of you and can't wait for you to rust. Second, you're not even metal, Roboracle, so shut up. Third, seriously shut up, unless you know where we're supposed to go. So back to my question. What now?"

"Victor, my friend," Valiant pats me on the back, "I think your answer is on its way." He points out into the fog. At first I see nothing, but eventually my eye catches a distant light moving towards us. Slowly the light begins to take shape, a small river boat with a tall murky figure at its helm. We wait. And draw our weapons, of course. When the boat finally reaches us, the figure guiding it doesn't say a word. Instead he merely reaches his hand out, palm up.

I think he might want a high five? (or a low one.) Either one would be kind of weird.

"Actually, Vic," Jimmy says, "I think he wants us to pay him. You know, for passage to the other side."

"Oh, he should really speak up then," I say.

Holstering my gun, I ruffle through my pockets. Luckily, I find a decent amount of loose change and hand it to him.

He shakes his head.

"You know what? I don't have time to barter," I draw my gun again and shoot the boat driver square in the chest. His body slumps down in the back of the boat. And then he looks up at me.

"Owww!" he cries at me, accusingly.

"Sorry?" I say.

"You shot me!"

"Only once."

"Only o—do you know how many times I've been shot in the millenia that I've been working here?"

"Um, 27?"

"Once! Just now!"

"That's way less than 27. You should be grateful."

"I should be grateful that you just shot me? How would you have felt if I came into your work and shot you in the chest?"

"Surprised?"

"What? Surprised?! I take it you've never been shot."

"I don't know," I shrug. "I've been given shots by doctors."

"You're comparing a bullet to a needle? Bullets are incredibly painful."

"Needles hurt too," I try to explain.

He glares at me.

"Jeez, I didn't mean to hurt you," I finally say.

"Oh, really?!"

"Yeah, I expected you to be dead so I could take your boat."

"I don't need this! I only took this job because I like boats and meeting new people, but you took that away from me. So you know what? Take it!" He throws down his oar and jumps out of the boat.

"Awesome!" I hop in the boat and everyone else follows suit. Picking up the oar, I hand it to No Name. "Row."

"Certainly, sir!"

As the boat drifts away from the shore, Chalk waves back at the former oarsman. His chest reading NICE 2 MEET U

We sail on into the mist.

Getting across the swamp doesn't take all that long. Really we could have just swam. Then I wouldn't have had to waste that bullet. That's just one less thing I can kill in my life. I feel...empty. Stepping off the boat, I let it wash over me.

Maybe I should just stop here; it's not like anything I do ever works out right. (that's true.) Yeah, this is where I should be. (we are worthless.) It's where I deserve to be. (might as well just wait to die.) Yep, that's what I was thinking...Wait! Since when do you think what I think? (I am you.) So? You always try and talk me out of this stuff. (but we're worthless and deserve to die.) Maybe you are worthless, but I'm awesome. I'm practically a superhero. I resent having to call you me! What would Captain Valiant think of this?!

That thought snaps me out of it. Valiant must be looking at me with such disappointment now. I turn to my left expecting to find him chiding me with his glorious eyes, but instead I only find the robots. Panicked, I search behind me. Valiant stands a few paces back, looking lost and forlorn. Jimmy is even farther back, barely out of the boat. His mask is off, exposing the badass portion of his face. He's holding the mask, staring into it. I think he might be crying, but I don't care. Not really sure what to do or even what's going on, I look around aimlessly for a bit and notice Chalk on my right, sprawled out with I SUCK plastered on his chest.

"What the hell is going on?" I say to no one in particular.

"THE ROBORACLE KNOWS."

It's the only response I get.

"And?" I finally ask, against my better judgment.

"HELL," he says. "THE FATES DEMAND WE ALL

263

LAUGH. THE COMEDY IS DIVINE. HA. HA."

I consider kicking him into the swamp, but I'm sure he'd just float and find some way back to us. Instead I turn to the other one.

"You speak cryptic, obnoxious robot, right?"

"Certainly sir," No Name responds.

"What the hell is he going on about then?"

"I believe, sir, that The Roboracle is making reference to the Italian poet Dante and his Divine Comedy. Written in the early 14th Century, it provides the origin of the phrase 'all hope abandon ye who enter here'. It appears that our compatriots have been drained of their hope. An unfortunate price for admission, I must admit."

"I seem to be doing fine," I say.

"Yes, you seem to have an unusually high amount of self-confidence juxtaposed with mild dissociative identity disorder and self-loathing."

"I'm well aware of how fascinating and amazing I am, but what I need to know right now is how to get everyone else to start moving again."

"Perhaps you could try regaling them with past exploits in order to boost their spirits?"

I'm pretty skeptical of No Names idea since he's such a general disappointment, but I can't think of anything else to do.

"Hey Captain, remember that time you…uh," I pause, realizing I've never gotten around to reading any of his blistering manifestos about all his adventures. So I do what I do best. Improvise. "That time you were out in space and you did that thing that made you famous?"

"Of course I remember that," he says, "it was one of the defining moments of my life. That's the problem. I've peaked. In fact I've probably peaked well over a six dozen times. How many do I have left? One dozen, maybe two? That's not enough peaks! Why even bother."

Okay, new plan: "Maybe we could look for Lollipop while we're down here."

"Her soul was completely destroyed Soul Destroyer: The Destroyer of Souls. There is no hope."

He starts to weep.

Crap.

"Alright, here's the deal," I address everyone, "you're all going to follow me because this is Hell and I'll probably get us all killed. Sound good?"

Valiant frowns, "A *valiant* plan, indeed."

Jimmy shrugs and slowly makes his way to join us.

"Well done, sir," says No Name.

"Shut up," I turn to get a move on, and then the strangest thing...

Blue jays line the path ahead.

No one except for the robots and I seem to notice them at first, but as everyone slowly pulls to a stop behind me, they too take an interest in the odd, pseudo-Hitchcockian wannabe nightmare. There are far too many to shoot, but they should scare easily.

I run screaming and waving at the birds. They flutter backward and land soundlessly at a modest distance.

I yell.

They do nothing.

I make a fake-out jerking motion toward them. Only one slightly shuffles it feet. These jays are watching me smartly with a thousand black eyes behind which a uniform consciousness emanates hatred. Hatred for me.

They are not going to go away.

I motion for the rest of my group to follow me inland through the mist.

The jays follow.

It isn't long before we break through the mist and discover an ancient stone and mortar city. Walls stretch upward and disappear into mist. Further down the alley, people. Or ghosts.

We keep going.

I don't worry about drawing my pistol, these dead don't seem to care or notice that a foreign living-element is passing through their realm. They merely despair, much like my lagging friends, and wander listlessly through this maze of streets. Speaking of mazes...I need directions.

"Where are we going?" I ask no one.

No Name replies, "I've been tracing the radar impacts of our footfalls to graph the streets beyond human visibility in this fog, and I've noticed that both streets on either side are parallel to us, but keeping a constant arc, as if we're walking the circumference of a circle."

"First science and now math?" I can't stand his uselessness, "You're supposed to be a kill-bot, not a teach-me-useless-shit-bot! Geometry can go to hell! But, you know, metaphorically because I don't want it anywhere near me. And for your information, I know exactly where we're going. Using my extensive knowledge of circles and all that shit," I pause for everyone's attention and for the dramatic effect, "we're going to the center of this city. Robot, direct us to the middle of the circle city."

"Sir, you wouldn't have known about the circle or where we were go—"

"Don't interrupt me, Robot. I'm in charge of this pleasure cruise. Which way?"

It isn't long before we start to notice the flies. For a minute there's only one or two to swat at, but rapidly their attacks become more frequent. And not long after the flies start, we hear a low buzz of screams—now turning frightfully loud as we advance.

I look back to my comrades for their support and find them satisfyingly not lagging and tightly grouped behind me. Screams and shadows of pain play tricks on our eyes through the mists.

I swat a fly off my arm. Jimmy spits out one he's caught in his mouth.

I catch a whiff of rotting meat and gag.

Valiant pushes to the front at a light pace and then jogs onward. We follow and eventually are sprinting through the ghosts in pain.

Jimmy is running slowly behind, hindered by the Roboracle he carries in his arms.

"Toss that scrap aside and save yourself, Jimmy!" I yell behind me.

Flies pelt my face as I run. They are definitely getting thicker.

And suddenly, nothing, like we've passed a barrier that the noise, flies, smell and danger can't penetrate. So naturally, I sense tremendous peril ahead.

We proceed carefully before eventually being able to see, hazily, each of the adjacent streets converging upon us. We are nearing the center.

We see more corporeal forms of dead here. Their population seems keener to our presence, and they watch as we walk on. It's then that I see them again. The jays flying shrouded above in the fog. Still following us.

"My word!" a familiar voice startles our skyward gaze. A small angular paper floats quickly on the air to meet us.

267

"Victor!" the piece of paper cries out. "It is I, Entheus. Inspiration made flesh. Champion of Anexia and traveler of 29 galaxies."

I sigh. Can't I go anywhere without running into people I know? Not that I've got anything against Entheus, he's pretty heroic. Or at least he was until he became confetti. But still, I never know what to say in these situations. So awkward.

"My heart warms in this black place at the sight of you here, and *alive*!" Entheus exclaims before he allows his gaze to shoot behind me. His voice lowers suddenly. "But soft! There is a villain on your tail, comrade."

"Huh?!" I turn back wildly ready to gun down all kinds of shootable things, but I only see Valiant and Jimmy.

"Fear not, friend! I will handle this fiend!" Entheus flashes over to Jimmy and punches him. A tiny paper cut opens on Jimmy's jaw. Entheus stares at his fist, flabbergasted. "Blast this infernal place! I've failed you again, for even my great Motivator is powerless here in Hell!"

"Uh, why are you punching Jimmy?"

Entheus flitters back over to me, concern dripping from his face, "Victor, I fear this place is corrupting your mind! Do you not remember that he is the one who slew me?!"

"Oh hey, yeah! You must be pissed! But seriously, man, that was all just a big misunderstanding. Jimmy apologized and everything, so it's cool."

"An apology makes my murder forgivable?!"

"All I'm saying is that these things happen and sometimes you just have to let them slide. Besides, this place isn't all that bad. I mean it totally sucks, but everyone so far seems like a pushover so you could take this place over in no time, with like moral goodness or something."

"Ha!" Entheus barks coldly. "I see what this is. You come here with your winning words of death. You're nothing but another trick. A demon in hero's clothing."

"Nah, I'm just me. And actually I think maybe you *could* help me out. See, my friends here are having a case of the mopes since getting here, and with you being Mr. Inspiration I was thinking maybe you could, you know, inspire them."

"As if I would be such a fool! Now be gone with you, you foul apparition!"

"Entheus, you know something? You're kind of a dick. And FYI, where I come from fictional heroes don't just stay dead, so you're also kind of a pussy. I guess what I'm trying to say, is go fuck yourself because I don't have time for your whining."

I don't bother waiting around to see his reaction.

"Enough of a break. Lets go," I order my weary and pathetic pack of fellows. I sincerely hope that I don't run into any other old acquaintances.

"What happened to him," Jimmy asks most stupidly.

No one but distant screams reply.

Because seriously, pay attention, Jimmy.


Valiant is first to break our silent death-march, "Is it getting colder?"

I hadn't noticed, so I breathe out heavily and see the faint wisp of a vapor trail, "What's that they always say about Hell freezing over?"

"That it's terrifically good luck for us?" Valiant replies with a spark of hope in this forsaken place.

Light frost covers the ground. Like blades of grass on a cold morning, the crunching sounds of our footfalls get louder and louder as we trudge on. It isn't long before our shoes are sinking deeply into snow.

I know. Snow in hell. What next, right?

Something snaps under my boot. I don't remember branches ever making such a crisp sound back up in the land of the living. Whatever. Places to go, people to see. We exhaust ourselves trekking through this hellish terrain.

One of us trips every few minutes on uneven obstacles under the snow, but we push ourselves onward.

I make the mistake of thinking about the return trip and moan silently to myself. Hiking is so much worse than even the torment of space travel in cramped quarters with Jimmy. Blisters start pushing needles through my feet and my thigh muscles tighten like car springs.

I focus on Her instead. A renewed strength ushers me forward.

I do my best to disconnect myself from the physicality of the journey, so it's not for several minutes that the yelling behind me registers as Valiant and Jimmy. I turn to find they've simply fallen behind in the awkward terrain, and are digging on their hands and knees to catch up.

A false alarm. Thanks guys.

"Alright, we'll wait a moment here, but we gotta get moving soon," I say.

Hoping to distract myself while I wait for them, I pound my feet around in the snow. Still waiting, I stomp a wider circle and hear another snapping branch. It leaves an uneven hazard in my stomp-paved stage.

Jimmy is the first to reach me; "Hey…" he gathers his breath. "Do you see any trees?" The Roboracle hangs motionless off his back in a make-shift pack.

"Jimmy, are you high?"

Valiant finally joins us.

"Jimmy is pointing out the spectacular scenery around this circle of Hell," I inform him, "I really hope I can count on you not to be so easily distracted."

Valiant stoops to pick up the broken limb, "Victor, relax. He's merely pointing out the uneven surface content we are walking on."

He shakes the branch free of snow.

It's an arm-with-hand shaped branch. A human branch.

"Ooookay, frozen bodies! As I'd prefer not to end up like them, I declare this break over," I push my crew forward. "Make yourself useful Jimmy and wake up that boom box on your back to give us some walking music."

What feels like an hour of marching brings us to a ridge where the fog and snow fade away into a small valley. Below us lies a city saturated in lights, flashing in near epileptic fury. It's sort of hypnotic, yet something about it feels off. I mean aside from this being Hell and the fact that in the very center, surround by high walls—and what looks like hedges?—stands a spiraling tower that defies physical logic and appears to have no end. I'm not sure how we didn't see it before.

"Anyone else think that looks like a decent pad for the king of Hell?" I ask just for the sake of talking. No one bothers answering.

We work our way down into the city and set off for the tower, and that's when it hits me. Despite the pulse of the city lights, there's not a single sound outside of our group. The place is completely dead. Once we're deep in the shadow of this metropolitan wasteland that changes.

The blue jays are back, perched on building tops near the tower walls. I'm so sick of these things.

When we're close enough, I pick up a loose piece of asphalt.

271

And throw.

I surprise myself with my own extraordinary ability as the rock brings down the jay closest to me. Sprinting over, I catch the dazed bird. A small tuft of undercoat feathers ruffles the bird's smooth exterior from which flows a ribbon of blood. Like a bullet hole. Did I do that?

"Yes, you did," the blue jay opens one eye and speaks, as if reading the question in my mind.

I freak the hell out. And, unfortunately for the bird, I crush him in my hands on impulse.

"KRAW!" The jay spits for air.

"Oooh, sorry," I say.

"W—wait 'til you try," it breaths deeply, "to navigate the labyrinth."

"Uh-huh, I'm pretty good at those. Can we go now?"

"We should consider questioning the thing," Valiant suggests, "it could have useful information."

"If you say so."

He looks stern and squints his eyes at me.

"Okay! Fine," I shrug my shoulders and relax. "Talk, bird."

"KRAW! KRAW!" The jay starts. "If you do that again..."

"Jeez, I said sorry. I was startled!"

"Just don't do it again," says the bird.

"Anymore guff from you, bird, and that's exactly what I'll do," even though I don't remember what I did in the first place.

"Ahem," Valiant clears his throat in valiant protest.

"Captain, this thing is giving me guff," I try to explain, "and I've had it up to here with his guff!" I motion to about the middle of my chest, because if I'm being honest I'm not that irritated. I just like saying guff a lot.

Valiant shakes his head, so I give in and toss the bird to the ground.

Having still not fully recovered from the accidental crushing, it takes a full minute for the bird to expand back to its normal state. Then it takes another minute before it opens its eye and, spying freedom, flies immediately to a safe distance.

"KraW! KRaw!" It cries brokenly. "You bastard! What the hell did I ever do to you?! One day I'm alive and happy with my flock, perched on the loveliest oak branch filled with the most luscious grubs living in the moss, and BAM! Done! One shot right to the chest! I saw the entire aftermath. Even in death." He's frantic. "I hovered above my corpse and watched my many wives stare stupidly at my motionless body until BAM! Another shot; directed at my ladies! Naturally they took off, and I with them. I was playing at life and flew as far as the next tree when my enemy swoops in and takes over my flock."

He stops.

"Get to the part where you tell me something I care about," I say

His voice turns cold, "In despair I returned to my corpse only to find *you*! YOU SHOT ME AND THEN YOU PICKED ME UP TO PARADE AROUND! You took pictures holding in one hand, your rifle, and in the other, your target."

"Yeah...so that doesn't sound like me."

"Y-you are," the jay stutters, "Devin Kelly, right?"

"Um, actually I'm—" but before I can finish my thought, Jimmy elbows me in the stomach. "What the hell, dick?!"

"Sorry," Jimmy whispers, "but these birds, their souls belong to you. Well, actually they belong to whoever killed them, but as long as they think that's you then they'll do whatever you say."

273

"Let me get this straight," I say, "people who kill a bunch of shit get to come down to hell and have a bunch of slave souls."

"Sort of."

"That is goddamn ridiculous."

"Victor, please!" Jimmy begs. "I know about this stuff."

"Alright. But I don't really want them." I direct myself to the jay. "So anyway, as I was saying, I am absolutely that guy you think I am. Killing you is a memory I definitely have. In my brain. Now be a good slave and do something helpful."

The bird nods and takes flight, rejoining the other jays. We follow them further down the solid high walls. It doesn't take long before we come to a small hole large enough to squeeze through. I duck into it. Just like the bird said, on the other side is a labyrinth of Bowie-like proportions.

I wait for my companions to come through. I don't want to be the first one down one of these paths. I've seen way too many movies where the guy up front walks into some sort of booby trap, so naturally the robots and/or Jimmy will lead the way.

The jays perch on top of the walls and, when everyone is through, guide us down a specific route they've mapped from above. I'm surprised when we start to come out of the maze and upon a man tending a garden in an open courtyard just outside the tower. Before we get too close, I call down one of the birds.

"You guys can go now," I tell it.

"No," it replies, "we are bound to you forever."

"Aw, come on guys! I'm not even the dude who killed you."

"You aren't?"

"Nope," I pull out my wallet, briefly reminiscing over the one I lost, and show it my fancy new Adventure Galley crew card.

"Oh," the bird says, "you used us."

"It was his idea!" I point to Jimmy. I steel myself to watch Jimmy's face get pecked off. Or at least what's left of his face. I hope it's not too gross.

"I can't believe this keeps happening," says the bird. "You know what I think it is? All you humans look the same to me."

Well that was kind of racist.

"Come on, guys," he says to the rest of the birds, "let's go. It was the wrong one again." They let out a collective sigh and disappear into the black sky. With them gone we continue on towards the tower and the man in its courtyard.

"Excuse me, friend," Valiant approaches the man, "might you be able to direct us to the master of this estate?"

He doesn't bother looking up, "I don't mean to be rude, but I really must finish tending my garden. You see this flower," he motions the blossom he's hovering over, "I created it myself. It's called the Lily-liver. It's a hybrid of white lilies and human liver. I use it to inspire cowardice and indecision in the most heroic of souls. It's my very favorite. Don't you just love gardening?"

"Look," I say, "of course we love gardening. It's great. But we're looking for the Devil. We've got business to discuss with him."

"That's funny," says the gardener, "I don't remember having an appointment today. Or ever, for that matter."

"Wait," Jimmy chimes in, "*you* are the Devil?"

"Of course," says the Devil, still without looking away from his flowers, "who else would I be?"

"The, uh, the Devil's gardener," Jimmy says.

"Why would I need a gardener when we've all just agreed that gardening is wonderful?"

"Devil's got a point, Jimmy," I say. "You really need to start thinking before you speak."

"So what can I help you with?" The Devil asks, finally looking up. Something immediately catches his eye. "Oh dear God! This is not happening!"

"Um, maybe we should get ready to start shooting things," I whisper to Valiant and Jimmy.

"I can't believe this!" The Devil screams. I tighten my grip on my gun. "Droids! You have droids!!"

"Uh," is all I can manage as my grip loosens.

"You guys have to come with me," the Devil insists. "We've got so much work to do!"

# Act IV, Scene 8

"Greeetings, exalted one," I read. "Allow me to introduce myself. I am..." I pause. I can't do this.

"What's wrong, why'd you stop?" The Devil asks.

"I'm just not feeling it," I tell him.

"That's why we have rehearsals," he tries to reassure, but that's not it.

"I just don't think this is the right fit for me."

"That's why it's called acting!" The Devil is way too into this.

"I'm just not much of an actor and I'm no good with scripts. I think Captain Valiant would be better. He oozes thespian."

"But he's Han!"

I can't argue with that.

"You know," Jimmy interjects, "I was in drama club."

I shake my head. "Of course you were, Jimmy."

"What's that supposed to mean?"

"It means you can take my part."

"Fine!" The Devil concedes. "But you have to be Lando."

I shrug in acquiescence.

"Now back to rehearsal!"

The rest of rehearsal goes pretty well. Mostly due to me not having to pay attention anymore. Still, it feels like an eternity before the Devil finally says it's time for the real thing.

"Everyone take your places," he says, "I'm just going to get our Leia."

Having absolutely no idea where my place is, I just stand around and wait. I can't believe I'm even putting up with this nonsense, but Valiant told me that even for a great adventurer, sometimes diplomacy is the best course of action. At least it doesn't take long for the Devil to return.

"Okay, this is where you'll be sitting," he says, and I look up to what poor soul has been suckered into this round of role-playing. I lose my senses. It's Her.

"What kind of game are you playing?!" I exclaim.

"Whoa," the Devil looks me over, "Lando isn't in this scene, man. But hey, whatever, just stay in the background and it's no big deal."

I can't seem to do anything other than watch her. And she watches me watching her, confusion painted on her face. Time stands still. Or…wait, no. Scratch that, time is moving as usual. Must have just been me who stopped, because right now the robots are in the middle of delivering some dialog. I only catch the end, but they're pretty into it.

"…the message," says No Name. "I'm sorry, was my inflection correct on that line? I've never play acted before. It's quite charming fun, don't you think?"

"THE FATES DEMAND YOUR SILENCE. THIS IS THE ROBORACLE'S LINE."

The Devil looks to actually be enjoying their squabbling, and I kind of have to admit The Roboracle is surprisingly good.

"I AM THE ROBORACLE. BEEP. BWOOP. BEEP."

Still, there's no way I can just stand here watching this with her sitting mere steps away, so I make my move. Walking towards the Devil, I pull out my gun.

"Hello, my name is Lando and this is my gun," I say.

"What?!" The Devil asks, startled. "That's not in the script!"

I place the gun square on his temple, "I told you I'm not very good with scripts. Now hand over the girl."

"Who, her?" He motions to his slave-Leia. "Is she who you

278

came for?"

I nod.

"That's pretty convienent! To tell you the truth, I had no idea if I'd be able to find her. It's not like I keep inventory of these things. But yeah, sure you can take her."

That was easy.

"Two conditions though."

Damn.

"First, when you leave you'll go back the way you came. She'll follow you, but you can't look back or try and talk to her."

"Why?" I ask.

"Because it's my rules, okay!"

"Fine, but they aren't very original rules."

"What are you talking about? This never happened in Star Wars."

"I take it you aren't much of a reader," I say.

"This didn't happen in any of the Star Wars books either."

"Yeah, okay never mind. What's the second condition?"

"I get to keep the big droid."

"You can keep them both," I say calmly, trying not to sound to eager.

"No thanks."

Shoot.

"Soooo," The Devil starts, "can we finish the scene we've been working on?"

"Um...I guess?"

"Excellent!"

The scene takes an excruciatingly long time, and The Devil seems to take over most of the parts. Which is fine by me, as all I want to do is grab her and take her home, but I made a deal with The Devil and it seems wise to keep it since he's giving me the only thing I came for. She's stopped watching me, for the most part. Occasionally she'll look up again, as if to reaffirm my presence. All I see is hurt. She never smiles.

Mercifully, the scene concludes and The Devil prepares to bid us farewell.

"Hey guys, that was a blast. Fuckin' Star Wars, am I right? When you come back we can get our Phantom Menace on! I do a wicked Jar Jar. Meesa da bestest character in alla da universes! Hahaha, that guy cracks me up. Anyway, you know the way back?"

We all nod.

"And you remember the terms?"

"Don't look back, don't talk to her, etcetera and so forth," I say. "Jimmy, make sure you keep The Roboracle facing forward."

"No problem," Jimmy replies, already strapping The Roboracle to his chest.

"Don't forget to leave the other one," The Devil reminds.

"Right. Later No Name," I tell him and start walking out of the castle.

"Goodbye, sirs," he responds. "It has been a pleasure serving and killing for you."

I don't look back. I wouldn't even if I could. I just say, "I know."

And it's right back into Hell.

Thank god.

# Act IV, Scene 9

The trip back is actually much better than it was coming down. For one thing, Valiant, Jimmy and Chalk are no longer moping, so I have company this time. Also, Hell is kind of fascinating when forced to look at it. Sure it's filled with dead people and random acts of torture, but it seems most of the torture victims are enjoying themselves. I guess evisceration isn't so bad after all.

There are some mild annoyances though. A little while back I think I spotted my parents. Luckily I managed to avoid them. If they'd seen me I just know they'd start asking why I'm not at work right now. They wouldn't have accepted adventuring or saving my girlfriend as acceptable excuses. To my parents those things were for off hours and weekends only. Oh, and holidays too. Except for Veterans' Day, Memorial Day, the Fourth of July and Easter. Those were for war or finding eggs, maybe. My parents didn't make much sense.

The other annoyance?

"SHE IS NOT BEHIND US."

The Roboracle, of course.

"Would you stop saying that," I demand pointlessly.

"NO."

"Maybe he's right, Vic," Jimmy says.

"I'm inclined to agree with Jimmy," Valiant adds, "the robot's prophecies have yet to prove wrong."

"I know how this works, alright," I explain. "He's probably trying to make one of us look back because those asshole Fates are telling him she's supposed to stay dead. Well screw that, I'm not falling for it. Because if there's one thing I'm good at, it's staring straight ahead."

The rest of the journey is spent regaling one another with our past exploits. Valiant tells a tale of defeating an invisible foe. It had no voice and promised to do nothing, but little did it know how much Captain Valiant loathes inaction. Jimmy tries to follow that with some story about how he and his friends went to see a dead body and then had a showdown with his asshole brother and his greaser friends…okay yeah, that's just the plot to Stand By Me. I don't actually listen to Jimmy. Chalk also attempts to tell a story, but since he can't turn to us and let us read his chest, and we're too worried about accidently looking back, all we can see are his exaggerated hand gestures. It's still better than Jimmy's story.

Finally, we re-cross the swamp and pass through the doorway back into the shack.

"Ha!" I exclaim. "We did it! Take that The Roboracle!" At last I allow myself to look back. "Aww, what the hell?!"

She's not there.

"THE ROBORACLE TOLD YOU SO."

Goddamn it.

# Act IV, Scene FINAL

"**Y**ou!" I shout as I kick down the door to The Devil's garden. He's sitting there waiting, laughing his ass off.

"Jeez, you guys were gone for a long time," he snorts between fits of laughter. "How far did you make it?"

"All the way," I sneer.

His laughter grows to a roar, "No way! That. Is. Priceless."

Valiant steps forward, "You, Mr. Devil, have broken our trust. The Book of *Valiant* Law states that when a trust is broken between two parties, the first party—that being the afflicted party—must confront the second party—that being the offending party—and break them in kind."

"Seriously?" The Devil asks. "It was a joke, guys."

"Do we look amused?" Valiant asks in return.

Worry flashes briefly across The Devil's face. "Think this through guys. I'm The Devil. This is my place of power. Do you think you can actually hurt me?"

I look him over, "Yeah, probably. But just in case, we've kind of stacked the deck a bit. The great thing about Hell? Lots of bones. Jimmy!"

Jimmy starts his creepy singing thing and the room begins to flood with all sorts of fleshy monsters.

"Aw crap," says The Devil. "Droid, help your master!"

"Certainly," No Name responds before turning to me, "sir would you wish my assistance?"

"Oh," I say, taken aback a bit, "yeah do whatever Valiant wants." As much as I'd love to stay and kick The Devil a few times, I've got to find her. Of course, she finds me instead.

"I heard the noise," she says. The sound of her voice stuns me

283

momentarily, but I manage to pull myself together.

"Can we talk?" I ask her. "Maybe somewhere a little less chaotic?"

"Sure. Come on," she says and leads me to what appears, from the outside, to just be a tiny alcove, but turns out to be a rather nice bedroom. "So it's really you, huh?" I nod. She laughs. "I thought it was just some Hell-trick or something when you were first here."

"I get that a lot down here," I say. "Is this where you've been sleeping? Do you even have to sleep?"

She shrugs, "Probably not, but yeah this is where I've been living. Or whatever."

"It's nice."

"I guess."

"Does he stay here too?"

"No."

"Has he...have you—"

"No. I don't even think he's into humans."

"Maybe he's just gay?"

She blinks hard and rubs her eyes, "Is this what you really want to talk about? The Devil's sexuality?"

"Um, I guess not?"

We stand silently for too long.

"Well," she finally gives in, "how was the trip down here?"

"Fine. I tried to sacrifice Jimmy to open some gateway, but ended up not having to."

"That's good," she says.

"And then I shot this guy in a boat and made him quit his job, apparently."

"Same old, same old then?" She smirks slightly.

"Pretty much," I try to return the smile, but my nerves won't let

284

me. "You look good," is the best I can manage. She looks herself over, reminding herself of the sex slave outfit she's wearing, and rolls her eyes. "Ugh. I'm the wet dream of 1983."

"Yeah," I say. "Wait, no!"

She looks at me, confused.

"I mean, yes but that's not what I meant…this is awkward."

"Why?"

"Because you're dead."

Her expression doesn't change, she doesn't even twitch. I guess she's gotten used to the whole being dead thing. Still, she doesn't speak, which isn't making this any easier. I try to gather my thoughts, but seeing her in front of me, actually seeing her, is more overwhelming than I ever imagined. And I've imagined it a lot.

I guess that's as good a starting point as any, "You know, I've imagined this moment over and over in my mind since I found you lying there on the floor."

Finally she reacts, simply bowing her head.

"I've imagined all the things I'd say to you, but I can't seem to remember any of them. It's just…I know that I'm crazy, okay. I don't know why, but when the world went crazy it took me with it. I have this…this fracture in my mind. I can feel it. And the thing is, I can close it. It's hard and it hurts—well it's easier when you're around— but I can fix it. And I *will* fix it. I don't want to hurt you again. Because I love you, Gisela."

"Oh, Victor," she raises her head, looking me square in the eyes, "don't be such a pussy." And she starts to laugh. That's not what I expected.

My entire body deflates and I slowly crumble onto the bed, piece by piece.

Seeing this, she immediately climbs onto the bed beside me

and tries to choke back her laughter, "Aww, look at that sad face! I didn't mean it like that, sweetie. It's just all that nervousness was just to tell me you love me? I already knew that. I mean, come on, you came to Hell for me. Now is not the time for emotions! You're supposed to sweep me up and ravish me or something."

"That would have been okay?"

She shrugs, "I don't know. It's what heroes do, right?"

"But isn't that," I lower my voice to a whisper, "isn't that necrophilia?" And the laughter resumes.

"I don't even know how to respond to that," she barks through fits of giggles.

"I just wouldn't want you to think I'm some sort of necrophiliac," I try to explain.

"For having sex with me?"

"Well you are dead, Gisela."

The laughter cuts off abruptly as she scrunches up one side of her face with incredulity, "Okay, what's that about?"

"Necrophilia? I don't know, I guess some people like the feeling of room temperature?"

"Not necrophilia, sicko—"

"So you admit that you would have been disgusted by me!"

"Let's try and stay on topic here."

"And that topic would be?"

"Why are you calling me Gisela?"

"It's your name, isn't it?"

"Technically, yes. But you've never once called me by it."

"But you've wanted me to, right?"

"What makes you think that?"

"The last thing you said to me before, you know…it was the last thing you said to me."

Understanding dawns on her.

"Oh," she says quietly. "So that's what this is all about. Victor, I was really drunk and pissed off."

"People say true things when they're drunk," I say.

"I guess sometimes, maybe," she sighs deeply, "look, what do you know about my life before we met?"

"Um, I know that you might have been a compulsive liar? But that could just be one of those memories for one of the other me's."

"Huh?"

"Yeah, I don't know either. I guess I don't really know anything. I'm sorry."

"No, you're taking this all wrong. I didn't mean that as some sort of challenge. You don't know anything because I never talk about it. And I never talk about it because Gisela, that girl you found cowering under her desk at work, was a complete disappointment."

"I doubt that," I say.

"That's because you didn't know me," she says. "You know I wanted to be a dancer?" I shake my head. "Yeah, I grew up watching, like, Footloose and Flashdance and all those other movies. And all I wanted to do was dance. Cheesy, right? But I was actually good." I think back to the last time I saw her and I believe her. "And when I was 17 I got an audition with this really great dance academy."

"Like that school in Fame?" I ask.

"Sort of," she chuckles. "I worked my ass off preparing and I went in there and I bombed *so hard*. It was like the Dresden of dancing auditions, it was that bad. So you know what I did? I finished high school, went to college, majored in communications, graduated and got a job sitting behind a desk. It wasn't so awful. Or at least I managed to convince myself it wasn't. Then everything went upside-down and you showed up and wanted to give me a new name and, I don't know, it

287

was like I could finally put all that failure behind me and do whatever I wanted. Besides, it's not as if I ever liked my name in the first place. The school kids were not kind to that name."

"Ha!" I practically bark.

"What?"

"I was just reminded of that other me from that one time."

She scrunches up her face a bit, "Okay…anyway my point is that I like being Emma more than I ever liked being Gisela."

"You do realize they're both you, right?"

"Cute," her voice is laced with sarcasm.

"So you really quit dancing, huh?"

"Totally cold turkey, whatever that means. In fact, I don't think I danced at all until…until that night on Candy Island. God I hope you nailed that bitch!"

"Which bitch?"

"Candy Princess," her tone implies this should have been obvious.

"Really? That's a huge relief, I was really worried about telling you all this. I mean, I'm not sure if I did or not but—"

"How can you not be sure?"

"It's just confusing is all. Like I'd be going about my day and then suddenly I'd start hallucinating and eventually I'd wake up all naked and sweaty and she'd be there all naked and there was this Milky Way taste and—"

"What?!"

"Huh?"

"What are you talking about?" Emma demands.

"W-what do you think I'm talking about?"

"Well, I thought you were going to tell me about how you killed her!"

"Because…?"

"Because she killed me!"

"She did?"

"YES!"

"Are you sure?"

"Am I—yeah, I'm pretty fucking sure!"

Dead silence.

"I can't believe you've been boning my murderer," she says.

"Whoa! Let's be clear, I've *maybe* been doing that."

"Right, you've just been hanging out with the thing that poisoned me and she's *probably* been date raping you for weeks. That makes me feel so much better."

"I know *I'm* relieved," I say.

"You're lucky she didn't eat you, you know."

"Sure, I guess I could say that about everyone I know?"

"No, I mean she actually eats people. She went on about it while she watched me die."

"Oh," I say, "that actually clears up a lot of things."

"How are you not more upset about all of this?" she asks.

"I'm trying to be less reactionary. Seems more suave and heroic, you know?"

"This does not seem like a time for that," she says, "but you know what, it's fine. I'm over it. I was dead, you were sad and being taken advantage of. And it's not like I didn't have that fling with one of those torture demons."

"You did?"

"No!"

"Ah," I say, "so are we cool or not?"

She groans, "Yeah, but don't think we won't be talking about this later. Right now, however, I really need to hit something." She

289

storms out of the room and I rush to follow her. Making a b-line for the Devil, Emma starts tearing apart anything in her path. Mostly that's Jimmy's flesh zombies. Jimmy doesn't take it too well.

"Why's she doing that?!" he cries.

I shrug. And before I know it, Emma is kicking the Devil straight in the face. Over and over and over. He doesn't seem to mind.

"And this is for making me wear this stupid costume," she kicks him again.

"Uh-huh," the Devil says back, "I think there's a chain around here somewhere. You think you could choke me with it a bit. We forgot to do that part of the scene earlier." That only makes Emma kick him harder.

"Victor," Valiant approaches me, "we have a slight problem. Nothing we do seems to cause any lasting damage to the creature."

"I tried to tell you that I can't be hurt in Hell," the Devil says.

"Stop eavesdropping, asshole," Emma kicks him again. Suddenly, she stops. "Hey, where's Sera?"

"She remained with the Galley," Valiant replies, "along with the Princess."

"You left her with that monster?!"

Valiant cocks his head quizzically.

"Yeah," I say, "we need to go."

"That's too bad," the Devil says, "so much for payback, huh?" He laughs far too smugly.

"Jimmy," I ask, "how fast can your zombies move?"

"As fast as I want, I guess," he says.

"Great, have them take him," I point to the Devil.

"What?!" The Devil exclaims.

"Come on guys," the Devil pleads, "you don't really want to do this, right?" We all ignore him and focus on getting back to the Adventure Galley and Sera as quick as possible. On the way, Emma fills in Valiant and Jimmy on the particulars of her murder.

"Do you really think she'd hurt Sera?" Jimmy asks.

"She did poison me and happily watch me die," Emma responds.

"And all just to get me," I gloat.

"You are so lucky I love you," Emma snaps, "but before your head gets too big, she also has some crazy Universal domination plan."

"And this involved your death?" Valiant asks

"All I really remember is her mentioning something about a song and needing a power source, I think?"

"Huh," I say.

"It sounds like you are having enlightening thoughts, Victor," Valiant observes.

"God Damn, you are wise!" I say.

He just grins.

"So what is it?" Emma prods.

"Oh, right. It's just that when Sera was telling us about being half-star, Candy Princess got pretty excited about her being an energy source."

Worry splashes over Valiant's face, "We need pick up our pace."

Having made this trek a few times already, we manage record time. Or at least it feels like record time. Valiant rushes back into the living world first, not bothering to stop in the shack at all, and disappears out the front door. Jimmy's flesh-things have created a bottleneck at the gate making it impossible for the rest of us to follow.

"Excuse me, sir," No Name says while we wait for things to clear up, "but will I be staying with the Devil or may I rejoin you?"

Emma answers before I can, "Of course you can come with us."

"Aww, what?!" The Devil exclaims. I feel his pain.

"Why thank you Miss Emma," No name replies, "and might I say that it's a pleasure to see you again."

Emma and the Robot proceed to strike up a dull conversation that is in no way about me. I start shoving to get through the doorway, and that's when Valiant returns.

He slumps against the far wall of the cabin, "The Galley is gone."

"That sucks," says the Devil as he's finally carried through the gateway, leaving it clear for the rest of us, "you guys are going to let me go now, right?"

I take Emma's hand and start to lead her through the gate; back to life.

"Victor," she cries as I feel her hand pull away from mine.

"What's wrong?" I turn to her, reaching for her hand yet again. But it's not there. Or rather it's almost not there. A phantom image that should be a hand lingers in the air beside my hand. Soon that too disappears.

"I did *not* know that would happen," the Devil says.

Emma, minus a hand, stands alone in Hell with tears threatening to flood her cheeks. The threat realizes its intent quickly.

"Fix this!" I yell at the Devil.

"I just said that I didn't know this would happen," he says back.

"Then I'm done with you," I pull out my gun and point it at his face.

"Seriously?" The Devil asks. "Because you know that if you strike me down now I will become more powerful than you can possibly imagine."

I think we all groan at that.

I cock the gun.

The Devil looks up at me earnestly, "May the Force be with you," he says. "Always."

"Yeah, sure," I say, "Live long and prosper, motherfucker." I pull the trigger.

A whirlwind tears through the shack for a fraction of a second. And then:

"Not cool!" A voice yells out from Emma's direction. I look to her and see the Devil standing just behind her. "I mean really not cool, man! Star Trek?! And also the shooting me in the face? You know what? I'll see you all in Hell…like maybe you can all come back in a couple of weeks. We could hang out. Play some Battlefront." We all just stare. "Well, I'll be here is all I'm saying." He turns to walk away. After a few steps he turns back. "You don't happen to have a map to the tower do you? I've never actually been outside of it. Nah, never mind, I think I can find it."

And then he's gone.

"What now?" Jimmy asks.

I shrug, "Nothing."

"Huh?" Jimmy says, bewildered.

"We don't have a space ship anymore. And on top of that, my girlfriend is now intangible. Don't get me wrong, she's got many intangibles that I adore, but her body should not be one of them."

"You don't get to use me as an excuse not to help Sera," Emma scowls from the other side of the gateway.

"I'm not just leaving you here," I say.

"I'll be fine!"

"Okay," I humor her, "and do you happen to have a space ship or some other kind of flying contraption over there?" She frowns.

293

"That's what I thought.  So unless someone else has a plan—and looking at the captain trying to melt into the wall, I think it's safe to say he's got nothing—I'm staying right here."

"Well," Jimmy says.

"Well what?" Emma asks.

He looks around nervously.

"Oh just spit it out," I tell him.

"It's just that I might have a sort of partial kind of plan," he starts, "but, um, you guys might not like it."

As if that's new.

# Interlude

The Thing slumps to the med-bay floor, sitting on one of many empty bags, and surveys her surroundings. She's made a real mess this time. She couldn't resist. She was caught up in the moment. At least she managed to keep herself from dining on the Little Star.

The Thing pulls herself up, blood sloshing in her stomach, and walks over to the Little Star. The Thing's special brew of Rhapsberry cream worked wonders.

The Little Star sleeps soundlessly.

The Thing lifts the Little Star and carries her to a cleaner venue for the fitting.

The Thing strips the Little Star in preparation.

The urge to eat her burns in the back of The Thing's throat once more. Just a little nibble would satisfy.

But The Thing has waited to long for this moment to give in to her baser desires. She dresses the Little Star in the ceremonial costume. A sleek, alluring dress. Hand woven from the finest spun cotton candy on Candy Island.

Finished, the Thing drapes the Amulet of Anexia around the Little Stars neck. It rests gently in the hollow of her breast, its gem pulsating in time with the Little Star's heart. Their colors change as one.

Finally the Thing turns her attention to herself. Looking in the mirror, she frowns. Her pretty dress is soaked to the skin with blood. And while the Thing loves a good blood bath, she must look her best today.

After all, the best lain plans won't amount to anything if you don't look pretty.

**<u>Characters you should know</u>**

**Who cares?  They're all going to die anyway.**

**Oops! Spoiler alert…**

**…KEEP READING ANYWAY!**

# Act V, Scene 1

(**I** don't like this.) What's that? (this plan of Jimmy's, it's…weird.) Is it? (you don't think it's weird?) Not really, it seems normal enough. And practical too. (no, it's just weird.) If you say so, either way we still need to find some form of transportation. I still don't know what to do about that.

"THE ROBORACLE DEMANDS EVERYONE LISTEN. THE ROBORACLE KNOWS WHAT TO DO." That's pleasantly convenient. "WE MUST WAIT." Although still not very helpful. But it's no use arguing.

A few minutes pass.

"Might I ask what we're waiting for?" A still sullen Valiant uselessly prods.

"HELP."

"Okay then," I look over at Jimmy and notice him hauling around the stack of comics that were in the shack. "Why do you have those?" I ask.

He shrugs, "The Roboracle said I should take them. Probably so he can have pictures of Donna."

"THE ROBORACLE MISSES DONNA NATRIOS."

"Maybe it's time for Styx," I offer.

"NO," is the reply.

I want to ask why not, but instead my head explodes. Or at least that's what it fells like. The next thing I'm aware of, I'm lying flat on my face in the field near the shack. Everything is darker than I remember it being. I push myself up into a kneeling position.

Are you okay? (huh? Oh me? Yeah I'm fine. What happened?) Not sure.

I look around. Jimmy is still face down, but he's stirring

299

slowly. The robots and Chalk seem mostly unaffected. However, it's Valiant who draws my attention. He stares at the sky, grinning from ear to ear. I follow his gaze.

"Oh," I say.

Valiant nods, "The Colossal Unity."

Shortly, Jimmy joins our upward staring. Chalk pulls some limbo move, leaning way back, in mock conformity.

WHATS THAT his chest asks.

"Our ride," I tell him, "hopefully."

A familiar voice erupts around us.

"Attention beings of whatever planet this is: Prepare to be beamed aboard the Colossal Unity. You are being abducted. Don't be afraid. Unless you fear being taken against your will. In which case feel free to run around in terror. But don't do that. The transporter is very fickle and you'll probably lose limbs. You might even if you stand still. It's also very nauseating. Vomit is likely to spew from your person; if that is a biological function your species is prone to. You will have to clean it up yourself. I want nothing to do with your potential alien germs. Disgusting. I must be healthy to experiment on you. The experiments will be mostly for scientific purposes. Hardly any for my entertainment. No more than 60%."

Without anymore warning, everything goes inside out and tingly. My eyes twirl in their sockets as the scenery shifts and we're no longer in a field, but rather back onboard the CU. I don't vomit. But Jimmy does.

"Clean that up immediately," the familiar voice, now much quieter and with a face, demands.

"Dr. Ickby?" Jimmy says between retches.

Ickby looks us over, "Oh it's you. Very disappointing." He walks out on us, and we have nothing else to do but follow. "You're following me. Don't try to deny it, I can tell. I'm a scientist. Very distracting, please go away. I've other guests to deal with. Much better guests. I'll introduce you so you can feel inadequate."

"I see you haven't changed," I mutter.

"False!" Ickby screeches, "I've changed. Always changing. That's science. You're very stupid."

"I truly wish you *had* died, Ickby," I tell him bluntly.

"I did die. Painfully. Candy people ate me. But I also ate them some. Quite delicious."

"Then, um, how are you here?" Jimmy wonders.

"Clones, obviously. Don't you have clones that you can download your mind into? Of course not! Too practical for you."

"Oh," says Jimmy.

"Ah, here is one of my guests!" exclaims Ickby.

"Robots!" Valiant and I say simultaneously.

"Yes," grins the Dread Space Pirate Robots.

"Nonononono!" yells Ickby. "I'm the host, I was introducing you. Don't be rude. Very poor manners. Now where was I? Oh yes! This is Mr. Robots. He is a pirate. I rate him as a pirate a 5. Not impressive. But as a person he is a 7. Charming and handsome. As a comparison, you are a 3, Victor."

"I thought I was 4," I say.

"As a leader," Ickby says, "yes, but as a person a 3. Because

301

you let me die twice and never apologized."

"That's hardly fair," I respond, "you only actually died one of those times."

Ickby pulls out a notepad from his front jacket pocket while drifting towards the far corner. "Note to self: Subject 17c, alias Victor, shows an inability to take responsibility for own actions. Downgrade personal rating by one. If trend continues, will have to restructure rating system."

"I think he may be a while," states Robots while pouring himself a drink. "So, fancy meeting you here. Wine?"

"Don't try to beguile us with fancy words and alcohol," I tell him. "What are you doing here?"

"Failed piracy, I'm afraid."

"And here I thought you left the looting to your robots," mocks Valiant.

"Normally, yes. But such a large and glorious bounty deserves a more hands on approach," he sips from his glass. "I can't help but notice the absence of the fairer members of your party. I take it my amulet is missing too."

"You mean the one you stole," I say.

He titters, "Look at me. Do you think I bought anything you see? Even some of my body parts are stolen. I am a cornucopia of theft. It doesn't make things any less mine."

"It kind of does," I say, ""but either way I won that from you so it's mine now."

"And yet..." he trails off. "Tell me, that woman with you at the dance party, was her name Candy Princess?" I nod and the pirate sighs. "Perhaps this should teach me a valuable lesson about excessive drug use. Then again, if you can't overindulge in mind-altering psychotropic pharmaceuticals at a party why even bother living." He takes another sip and locks eyes with me. "Do you have any idea what you may have unleashed upon the universe?"

"Not only don't I know," I tell him, "I don't even care. We're on a mission of rescue and revenge, and quite frankly you are wasting our time."

"Now there's an attitude I can get behind," Robots hoots, "but please indulge an old space-faring man in his tales."

"Dude, I just told you I don't care," I say.

"Victor," Valiant interrupts, "perhaps it would be prudent to listen to him. He may offer some valuable insight into our plight."

"I bet he won't," I mutter.

"One can never know their enemy too well," he shoots back.

"Fine," I give in.

"Good, Jimmy and I will go to the command deck and see if we can't work on tracking the Galley. No Name, you stay with Victor and record Mr. Robots' story." No Name does as told, and I turn my attention back to the pirate.

"Alright, so tell me why I've doomed us all," I say.

Robots grins, "As I was saying, if not for my inebriated state, this probably could have been avoided because I knew I recognized the young lady accompanying you. Although to be fair to myself, it had been many years since I last saw her. She was no more than 13 years old at the time.

"I had come to Candy Island mostly by accident, I was merely a petulant young man overzealous for adventure and wealth. And what better setting for a heist than a small island with a massive castle. I was not successful."

"Are you ever?" I scoff.

"Such biting words!" Robots exclaims sarcastically. "But it's true. See, success may bring me wealth, but I've found it's the failed attempts that are far more memorable. Always filled with more daring exploits, torture and sexual misconduct. Even as a young man, I knew this. And this particular failure left me at the mercy of the island's monarch, a giant sugar coated rabbit known only as the Candy King. To my surprise he spared my life almost immediately, for as fate would have it the Candy King had a bit of an affinity for humans. Something clearly evidenced by his very human looking daughter.

"I spent several weeks as an honored guest of the king and his princess. They were most gracious hosts and it wasn't long before the subject of the Candy Queen—or the lack thereof—was broached. Some number of years prior, the king told me, a large ship wrecked on the island, bringing with it at least a dozen human passengers. I say at least because even the king himself couldn't properly judge the exact number who survived just long enough to be eaten by his subjects."

He eyes me as if this is some big revelation. When I show no signs of caring he continues.

"The king always did his best to discourage his peoples' taste for human flesh because he felt it would hinder future diplomatic relations. So when the king arrived at the scene of the wreck, his subjects fell on their knees in apology, begging forgiveness. He was furious. Not only had they shown weak will, they had presumably left him no snack. But his subjects were quick to point out that one did remain, a stunningly beautiful woman. The king was instantly smitten.

"Unfortunately, she was not entirely unscathed by the candy peoples feeding frenzy. They had already eaten large portions of her hands and most of her tongue. But the king cared not. He loved her. And he said he knew she loved him too by the way she writhed during love making. After numerous stillbirths—you know what they say about rabbits and reproduction, after all—she bore him a child, his little Candy Princess.

"While she might not have looked like one of the candy people, she certainly had one thing in common with them. Her appetite. When she was 3 years old the Candy King came back from a day spent in the villages to find his little princess sitting in a pile of bloody pulp, chewing on the entrails of her mother. He said that he wanted to be angry, but when his little girl looked up with her mother's eyes between her teeth and said 'I'm sowy daddy, but mommy was just so vewy yummy!' he just melted. He could never deny her anything."

"Oh my god does this story ever end?" I complain because I'm so bored I'm actually considering talking to Ickby.

"Very well," Robots concedes, "I mentioned that the king spared me due to his attraction to humans, did I not?"

"Wait! I'm being tested on this?! Is it multiple choice?"

"It was a yes or no question—"

"Did I have to specify that? Okay, is it multiple choice, yes or no?"

"—and it was rhetorical—"

"C!"

"As I was saying," Robots continues. I must have gotten it right, "I was told that I was spared because of the king's fascination with humans, but as it turns out that was only half the truth. Indeed he did like having a human friend, but he gladly would have shipped me off if not for the lovely piece of jewelry worn round my neck."

"Right," I say, "and it was the Amulet of Anexia and Candy Princess vowed to one day take it from you before you narrowly escaped and blah blah blah!"

"Actually, no," he says back, "the Candy King was quite open about his desire to procure the amulet. But seeing as I was an aspiring master pirate, he proposed a partnership. I would help find the remaining items necessary to activate the amulet's powers and in

305

exchange I would receive whatever I desired. Of course this offer was only presented after several weeks of attempted seduction on the part of Candy Princess. She had a plan to seduce me into taking her honor, at which point her father would condemn me and take the amulet by force. And if she got to eat me afterward, well all the better. Luckily I have an enhanced inner ear and was able to overhear the princess discuss her scheme with one of her handmaidens.

"Still, I can't help but wish I'd been able to have more fun with her awkward attempts at arousal. She was a striking girl. Not that I didn't manage some fun. There are many things to do to a princess without stealing her honor, after all."

"That's disgusting!" I say. Although I don't remember wanting to say it. (sorry, that was me.) Oh, you can do that? (I guess…and you should be disgusted!)

"Yes," Robots goes on, "let us not forget I'm a pirate. Playing naked games with a teenage princess is hardly the most ghastly thing I've done. So after failing at her ultimate goal, Candy Princess suggested to her father that he utilize my skills, and our aforementioned partnership was born. He informed me of what he needed: a special song and a very unique and powerful energy source. I kept my eyes peeled during bouts of piracy and he sent scouts out to do the same, contacting me with any pertinent information. I've still yet to return to Candy Island.

"We found the song with the Chronotastic Dancers easily enough, but of course they weren't willing to part with it and wanted the same deal I was given. But the king died a few years ago, according to a brief communication informing that all further communications would be delivered through one of my robots and that the princess would ascend to the throne, only meeting me once all items had been acquired. I assumed her less than sociable attitude was down

306

to me denying her the full love of the Dread Space Pirate Robots all those years ago. But perhaps she was just looking to double-cross me at the first opportunity. Commendable, I suppose.

"Either way, things moved just as smoothly. My communications robot received word from Candy Island several years ago about a strange energy anomaly that had been consistently traced back to that ship your captain calls the Adventure Galley. I then re-outfitted one of my robots and made sure it was sold to Captain Valiant. And then we waited."

"Waited entirely too long," says a nasally voice I remember all too well.

"Manbot," I hiss.

He ignores me totally, "I was left to rot as a slave for more than a year with that self-righteous windbag, even though I'd identified the energy source after mere weeks."

"Don't mind him," Robots informs, "he just can't resist putting on a show for company."

"As if I'd waste my synapses on *him*," Manbot retorts. "You're just trying to avoid confrontation yet again."

"I've already told you that I would have arrived sooner had you just told me what the energy source was. You know I can't resist kidnapping beautiful women."

"" figured it would be nice to have leverage of some sorts. Machines have desires too, you know."

"Not that I want to get involved in your lover's spat," I interrupt, "but if you really wanted leverage why didn't you just tell Candy Princess about Sera when you were talking with her at the brothel?"

"As if I've ever met her," Manbot sneers.

"I saw you talking to her," I say.

307

"Your inferior jelly filled eyes must have been malfunctioning," he says. "I assure you I don't even know what she looks like. The only non-mechanical thing I even wasted my time on was the one that hired us to kidnap your girlfriend."

"Yeah," I say, "that was her. And you think I'm stupid…"

"Hmm," Manbot hums, "a missed opportunity then. Curious that she recognized me."

"Candy Princess," No Name says, "was very fond of Mister Valiant's scrapbooks. You are featured heavily in several of them."

"I suppose I should have realized something was amiss," says Manbot. "Oh well. At least I was able to abduct your female. I hear she died at the dance party. I get giddy just thinking about it."

(can we kill him?) I don't see why not.

"Nor do I," says Valiant as he reenters the room.

"Oh Captain, my captain," titters Manbot. "You don't think I'm intimidated by you?"

"You've met my new robot companion, have you not?" Valiant asks, motioning to No Name.

"And I suppose he's meant to kill me?"

"Don't be afraid Mister Manbot," says No Name. "I've been having the most wonderful precision robot assassination technique study parties. It won't hurt in the slightest."

"There are a dozen other robot pirates on this station," Manbot informs. "Isn't that right Robots?"

"Absolutely," Robots confirms, "all the more reason your disloyalty won't be missed."

Understanding dawns on Manbot, "I see. You realize I won't go down quietly."

"I suspect you will, actually," says No Name.

"You don't have to listen to them, you know," Manbot

propositions, "You could just as easily choose not to kill me."

"Oh, I don't plan on killing you," No Name states, causing Manbot to make an odd, quizzical sound. "No, that's for my study partner."

As if on cue, Chalk drops from some unknown location directly onto Manbot's back. He stabs something into Manbot's neck joint, and rips out a bunch of wires and junk. Manbot doesn't even have a chance to struggle.

Chalk then hops down and runs over to Captain Valiant, presenting him with the wad of wires that I guess were previously Manbot's brainstem.

His chest reads A TROPHY!

Valiant takes the wires with a smile and a thank you nod before addressing the rest of us. "Unfortunately, Jimmy and I were unable to locate any residual trace of the Adventure Galley so we've set a course for Candy Island."

"What good will that do?" I ask. "We all remember it exploding, don't we?"

Chalk tugs on my pant leg. His chest reads I DO!

"Exactly," I say, "it exploded so hard that Chalk was launched nearly into orbit. I doubt there's anything left."

"Perhaps," says Valiant, "but it's our only lead. We should be there momentarily."

Jimmy peeks his head into the room, "Actually we're there now. Or we would be if there was anything left. And there's no sign of the Galley's heat signal."

"There is a way to track that Lieutenant of yours," says the space pirate.

Jimmy perks up, "Do you think you could help me do that?"

"Alas," says Robots, "that piece of information died with

Manbot over there."

"Why'd you even mention it then?" Jimmy sulks.

"I happen to find the sound of my voice very soothing," Robots smirks.

"Speaking of which," I say, "and by which I mean both the sound of your voice and your innate uselessness, that story you told me about Candy Princess was completely worthless. Once we're done rescuing Sera I plan on making it my mission to find a way to steal a few minutes from your life and give them to mine. Even if I waste years doing it. On an unrelated note, I'm pretty sure I know where to go."

"And where might that be?" asks Valiant.

"New York," I say. "Obviously."

(whoa, wait. Am I missing something? Why New York?) Let's call it a hunch. (I'm not sure we should just be gallivanting around off hunches.) C'mon, we're already on Earth, it'll take like two minutes to get there.

"Victor does have a point," Valiant agrees, "We are already travelling blind, and besides, the hunch is one of the *adventurer's* greatest tools."

(fine, let's just go.)

"I'm on it!" Jimmy yells, already on his way to the command center. Since there's nothing better to do, we all follow. By the time we get there Jimmy's finishing up with all the navigation mumbo-jumbo. All that's left to do is wait. It's about 30 seconds before Jimmy barks a stunted laugh. "You guys aren't going to believe this, but I think Vic was right."

"Well, I believe it," I say.

(I'm never going to hear the end of this, am I?) Don't worry, I'll do something even more amazing soon enough and then forget all about this.

"So we're already there?" Valiant asks. "Can you see the Galley?"

"Almost there," Jimmy says, "but we're definitely picking up the Galley's signature. One way or another, we're on the right path."

"Then let us prepare ourselves for battle!" Valiant declares.

# Act V, Scene 2

"**B**eam us down, Dr. Ickby," Valiant commands. I blink into a haze of nauseating backwards vertigo and then blink again to find myself in Central Park, mere feet away from the Adventure Galley. Glancing around, I find everyone/thing I should. There's Valiant and Jimmy and the robots and Chalk. Even Robots and his robots came along for the fun. Although they only agreed when we gave them the choice between helping us rescue Sera or helping me test out the lethality of my gun. I petitioned hard for the latter, but maybe having them around will prove useful.

Valiant takes a moment to get his bearings before forcing open a side entrance of the Galley. He motions and I follow him aboard. We proceed to stalk the corridors like a pair of fucking ninjas. You know, if ninjas used guns and didn't really give a shit about being stealthy.

We don't find anyone in Sera's quarters, or Candy Princess'. The bridge is empty too. As we pass the med-bay we have a moment of panic. The door is open and blood is smattered all over the floor. But there's nobody there, only a bunch of empty blood bags. We get as far as the docking bay before abandoning our search. The transport shuttle is missing. We exit the ship and inform the others what we found.

"And what does the great Captain Valiant propose now?" the space pirate asks with more than a smidge of delight.

"We get Ickby to beam us back aboard the CU and start a broad sweep of the city," says Valiant, ignoring Robots obvious taunt. "We should, at the very least, be able to track down the shuttle. Dr. Ickby, please beam us up." We wait to be turned inside out. Only it never happens. Valiant tries a few more times to reach Ickby, but nothing

312

comes from it.

"Can't we just use the Adventure Galley to survey the city?" I ask.

"I checked the fuel reserves while on the bridge," Valiant informs, "they're completely dry."

"Oh," I say, "I guess we'll just have to walk then."

"Where?" wonders Jimmy.

"The Statue of Liberty," I say.

(oh come on!)

Jimmy tries to stifle laughter.

"Just trust me, guys," I reassure. "Now, um, which way to Liberty Island?"

"There are probably maps and brochures and stuff in some of the hotels around here," says Jimmy.

"Cool, let's get to breaking and entering," I say.

After a few minutes of vandalism we manage to acquire a Statue of Liberty brochure and a map of the subway system that seems suitable for our purposes. We start walking. A few blocks south of the park, Jimmy stops dead.

"Hey," he says, "this is Time's Square!"

"So," I say back.

"Well, Broadway's not too far from here. I've always wanted to go there."

"I don't think they're putting on shows right now, Jimmy."

"Yeah," Jimmy sighs and starts rummaging through his backpack. "Anyone want some water?"

"Sure," I say, leaning up against the building nearest me. I take a few swigs and breathe deeply. The air is light, frigid and sweet. Like a giant ice cream parlor. It's making me hungry. "What else is in your pack?" I ask, hoping for some food.

"Pretty much just the water and these comics," Jimmy says as he pulls out those stupid Steel Canyon books.

"Why do you keep bringing those everywhere?" I ask.

"I told you," he says, "The Roboracle told me too."

"I AM THE ROBORACLE," says The Roboracle.

"Whatever," I offer the water to Valiant, but as I extend to hand it to him there's a wet sucking sound as I separate from the building. I touch the spot I'd been leaning against. It's wet. Gooey.

(paint?) It doesn't smell like paint, it smells like—(ew don't taste it!)—Too late! Chocolate? (that can't be good.)

"Um, guys," Jimmy says, "did anyone else see that building move?"

"Jimmy, stop talking crazy," I reassure, "that's my thing and— HOLY CRAP THAT BUILDING JUST MOVED!"

The building in question has clearly sprouted legs now and, more worryingly, a large, sinister and very hungry looking mouth. Also, it's a fucking building and it's coming after us. So we do the only sensible thing, we run in holy terror. Buildings, by their nature, are pretty slow which allows us to safely duck down an alleyway and compose ourselves. Or maybe just to wait to be crushed to death. Both have their pluses, I guess.

"Things certainly have gotten exciting," Valiant says through fits of laughter.

"Ickby!" I scream. "I know you can hear me because I still don't know how to turn these damn com-links off. Ickby goddamnit beam us up!!"

"You should be more polite," says Ickby. His voice is far too clear.

"Ickby," I say calmly, "are you standing right next to me?"

"Of course I am. Have you gone blind? That would be

unfortunate. I would offer my condolences but make strange faces while I did. Your blindness will prevent you from seeing them so you won't know I really hate you. By the way, I hate you."

"Doctor," Valiant inquires, "what are you doing down here?"

"I heard commotion. Something about buildings moving and I wanted to see it."

"Well that's fantastic!" I yell. "Now you can die with us!"

"Die? No one mentioned dying. This does not reflect well on you. You should have made that more clear when you mentioned living buildings. You should have said 'buildings are moving, now we will all die! Don't come down here to see them Dr. Ickby!' That is what you should have said. You are the worst person in the world, Victor."

I grip my gun so hard it starts to cut into my hand.

(oh just do it.) Seriously? (yeah, do it.)

"Ickby," I say, "you have other clone bodies out there, right?"

"One clone body would be in no way practical," he says, "obviously. But I couldn't expect you to know about practicalities. You probably don't even know the definition of the word. You might not even know what a definition is. I'm trying to say that you are very stupid, but I'm not sure you can even understa—"

And then I shoot him in the face.

"Was that really necessary?" Jimmy asks.

"Yes," I say.

"But all that noise might tip-off the building to where we are."

"You worry too much, Jimmy. I doubt a whole building can fit down this alley."

"And what if," the space pirate cuts in, "the alley turns on us as well?"

"What are the odds of that happening," I say.

He points to the ground. It's no longer pavement. Looks kind of like butterscotch.

"What do we do now?!" exclaims Jimmy.

"THE FATES SAY WE LOSE," answers The Roboracle.

"I guess that takes some of the pressure off." I say.

"THE ROBORACLE SAYS FUCK THE FATES."

"A *valiant* statement indeed," says Valiant. "From here on out we shall write our own destinies!"

"I suppose now would be an appropriate time for Styx," I say.

"STYX ARE THE VOICE OF FATE. NOW IS TIME FOR THE ANTI-STYX."

"No way, that's awesome!" I say, gearing up for some new battle tunes.

"NOW IS TIME FOR ACE OF BASE."

The Sign starts to play.

Damn it.

"We need to abandon this alley," Valiant says, but as we approach the main street the building returns. We're trapped.

"At least I was right about it not fitting through the alley," I say.

"I hope one of you has a plan," says Robots.

"Just shut up and let me think for a second!" I scold.

Jimmy starts to snicker, and Valiant is clearly repressing the urge to join him.

"What?" I ask impatiently. "Are you having a nervous break down? Because I'd appreciate if you wait until we get out of this to do that. Or at least until after I've died." Jimmy simply points at me, his snickering growing into full-blown guffaws. I look down at myself.

I'm dancing. Against my will.

What the hell? (sorry! I just love this song.)

Valiant can't hold out any longer and Jimmy falls to the

316

butterscotch pavement in stitches.

"You guys just wish you could dance this well," I say indignantly. "And it's really not easy to think with all your hysterics!"

"At least I'll die laughing," Jimmy says trying to pull himself back to his feet, but he stumbles and spills the contents of his pack. And suddenly I know just what to do.

I rush over to Jimmy and pick of the stack of Steel Canyon comics and start ripping out pages, crumpling them up and throwing them on the ground.

"What are you doing?" Jimmy wonders, his laughter mostly in control.

"Littering," I say.

"Uh, why?" he asks.

"Think about it, what's the greatest blight on any city? Litter! So when dealing with a living city, littering must be like injecting garbage into its veins or shoving it down its throat or something."

"Or maybe it's just like throwing garbage in its face which will only piss it off."

"This isn't the SATs, Jimmy, we don't have time to argue about analogies. Now if you'll excuse me, I've got some littering to do." That's when the buildings to each side of us start to shake and sprout legs. Albeit slowly. Looks like Jimmy was right. At least I might die before I have to hear him say I told you so.

"I told you, Vic!" Balls. The Roboracle's music grows louder as I prepare for imminent death.

Suddenly, the remaining comics from Jimmy's pack begin having seizures and tear themselves apart. Before anyone can comment, The Donnanatrix and the Immoral Many burst from the pages.

"Mwahahahahaha!" says Donna before turning to The

317

Roboracle. "I heard your music, baby. You've finally renounced your calling!"

"THE ROBORACLE LOVES DONNA NATRIOS."

"That's beautiful," says an unfamiliar voice behind me. I turn, but there's only a giant dumpster.

"Huh," I say.

"Hello," says the dumpster, "I'm very hungry."

"Gah!" I scream and throw the remainders of the crumpled up comic pages I'm holding. It opens its lid wide.

Crap, why'd I do that! (what?) It's a garbage can! Garbage will only make it stronger!

It seems to grin at me and begins to walk, but without warning its lid completely blows off and it drops dead as a blithe figure soars from out its insides.

"I...

"Am...

"Entheus!" It declares. Without hesitation, Entheus—who's now much bigger than he used to be—swoops down and snatches me up as the surrounding buildings, having finally formed enough, begin to close in. I feel the force of the thunderclap the two buildings make as we narrowly escape. Out of the corner of my eye I can see Valiant and Jimmy being flown to safety by members of the Immoral Many. Chalk is on No Name's back as the robot rocket boosts the two of them out of danger. I assume the pirate and his robots are fine too, but I don't really care.

Entheus sets us down in a spot that seems candy free thus far, and Robots did indeed make it out safely. Although some of his robots didn't.

"Entheus," Jimmy queries, "where'd you come from?"

"I heard faint whispers of your plight through the paper veil," he says, "and earlier I had a vision of you, Victor. A vision that spoke to my very heroic soul and told me to fight death itself."

"That was actually just me," I say.

"Ah! Then I must both thank you and apologize," he says.

"That's great, but we really should stop wasting time," I say. "Anyone know how to fight a city?"

Chalk leaps off No Name and appears to communicate something to him, but with his back to me I haven't the slightest idea what that might be.

No Name's response clears it up a bit, "Oh *that* plan. How delightful that sounds." No Name pops his chest open as Chalk climbs back onto his back. No Name reaches into his chest cavity and produces a mini RPG. He hands it to Chalk.

"What are you gonna do with that?" I ask.

He points to the sky and I understand.

"You go and you do it, George," I tell him.

He turns to me.

MY NAME, reads his chest, IS CHALK.

He slaps No Name once and his rocket boosters flare.

"Wish us luck sirs and madam," says No Name. As they take flight I have just enough time to make out Chalk's chest.

YEEHAW! it reads.

"Victor," says Valiant, "I think with the arrival of Ms. Natrios and her paper brigade we have enough force to distract the city long enough for you to find and stop the princess."

"You aren't coming?" I ask.

"She's your battle," he says. "Besides, I want to fight the city." He smiles wide. "This is going to be fun."

I look to Entheus, "Can you get us where we need to go?"

He lifts me up, carrying me high above Manhattan, "Just point me in the direction, friend."

"That way," I tell him. And we're off.

(what if she's not there?) She will be. (how can you be so sure?) Stop worrying, she'll be there, we'll break her machine—(her machine?) The one she's using Sera to power and that's turning the city into candy monstrosities. (I see.) And once that's dealt with everything will be fine and we've won. (and if there's no machine?) No machine? That's ridiculous! (but if there's not?) Look, just go with me here. I saw it all in a movie once. (you can't be serious!) False. I can't be *more* serious. (well, what movie are you talking about?) X-Men. (…) Yeah, we've got this in the bag, baby!

As we close in on Liberty Island we can finally make out their small transport shuttle, along with a miniature light show atop the statue.

(you are unbelievably lucky.) I know, just imagine if I hadn't seen X-Men!

"Entheus, drop us off at the light show and then get back to the fight with Valiant and the others." He does as commanded, leaving me face to face with Candy Princess and Sera. Except that Sera is unconscious and glowing—the brightest glow coming from the amulet around her neck—and Candy Princess has her back to me so it's more like face to back. No worries, I know how to fix that.

"Hey sweet stuff," I yell. But before I can finish off my witty one-liner, Candy turns and pounces on me, covering me with kisses.

This is awkward. (no shit.)

"Victor," chides Candy Princess, "language!"

(ugh.)

# Act V, Scene 3

"**I**'m so glad you could make it!" Candy Princess squeals.

"Really?" I have to ask.

"Of course, silly! This is such a pretty song, isn't it?" she says. I hadn't even noticed any music until she mentioned it. "It's not as pretty as yours was, but I like it and I needed it for the ritual. I hope you don't mind that I borrowed your keyboard without asking!"

(what he minds is you killing his girlfriend!) Uh…yeah!

"Oh dear, did you find Emma?! I hope so, she was lovely!"

"Um," I say.

"Did she tell you how much I was doing for you? Like killing her? I do hope she understands!"

"Um."

"And did she tell you about the wonderful things I'm going to do and how you'll be my king?!"

"I-I *would* like to be king," I say without thinking.

(excuse me?)

"I mean, um, I would like to not be king now but maybe some other time if that other time happens to be more agreeable than this one?"

"But don't you like what I've done here?" pouts Candy. "I just wanted my Candy Island back."

Awww, poor thing has no home. (she's not a stray puppy, she kills and eats people!)

"Only when I'm hungry," she says. "And I'd never eat you. So won't you please let me have my island back? Or maybe a Candy Planet. I won't go bigger than a galaxy, I promise! This one already has a candy name anyway. Please," she sticks out her lower lip. How can I say no to that?

(you've got to have the shortest attention span I've ever seen, just go grab Sera.) Oh that, right! You sure this'll work? (I hope so.)

I reach out for Sera.

"You're so cute when you talk to yourself," says Candy, "but I can't just let you take her."

"I wasn't exactly planning on it," I tell her, "and I wasn't talking to myself."

I touch Sera and I feel her slip away.

(bye for now.) Good luck.

"Thanks!" says Candy, "but you don't have to leave."

"I'm not," I say, "I wasn't talking to you. I was talking to her." I point to Sera. Candy Princess looks over and Sera's body waves.

"But...but I did everything right," Candy Princess starts to tremble, "she should be unconscious until this is over."

"Don't worry," I say, "that's not Sera. Well, it is...but it's also Emma. She hitched a ride in me all the way from Hell."

Candy Princess does something a tad unexpected. She hugs Emma. Or Sera. Whatever. "I'm so glad to see you! I know that our last meeting didn't go so well. I think I might have been a little hasty with the whole poison thing. There's no reason why Victor can't be my king and yours too. We can share!"

"I'm okay with that," I blurt out. Emma/Sera shakes her head. "Except I forgot to add *not* to that last thing I said. I have this thing where sometimes I forget to say crucial words that change the dynamic of a sentence. It's a medical condition that I, uh...just made up..."

"You know, Candy Princess," Emma finally says, "I've been really looking forward to seeing you again too."

"Really?!" Candy squeaks.

"Absolutely," says Emma, "but I do have one question to ask you. Do you know what happens to a Candy Princess when she fucks

322

with a star?" Candy Princess tilts her hear quizzically, and Sera's torso erupts with a blinding light that singes my eyelashes. When the light dissipates and my sight returns, Sera's body is standing over a toasted Candy Princess. Candy's not dead, but she is crying. Sera's hand reaches out and brushes away the tears with a single finger, which she then tastes. Emma smiles with Sera's mouth. "S'mores," she kicks Candy Princess square in the face, "bitch."

Emma proceeds to rip the amulet from Sera's neck and toss it off the statue. Then she throws my keyboard off too. I kind of feel like that was unnecessary. There was a power switch, after all. She brings Sera's body over to me.

"That was awesome!" I say. "You were like this violent, sexy Care Bear."

She shrugs, "What are we going to do with her?"

I shrug back, but I notice Emma using Sera's eyes to, well, eye my gun. So I hand it to her.

And suddenly I'm blinded by a spotlight.

"Drop your weapon," says a mysterious voice from above. "You have five seconds." I try to shade my eyes enough to figure out where that spotlight is coming from while Emma slowly sets the gun down on the ground. "Thank you for your cooperation."

A terrifying lizard man materializes in front of us, and I in no way shriek like a little girl.

"Fear not, humans," says the lizard man, "I am Agent Klyzzzzt from the Inter-Galactic Legislative Omnipresent Operative. We are here for one Candy Princess, monarch of the former island nation known as Candy Island."

"That's her," Emma points to Candy's charred mass. Although she is already healing quite rapidly.

"And are you responsible for her current condition?" asks

323

Agent Wazzhizname. We both nod. "Excellent, excellent. You're both under arrest for assaulting an inter-galactic diplomat."

"What?!" Emma exclaims.

"Hmm, did my translator fail," Kleenex taps his throat and clears it, "I said you are under arrest."

"You can't do this!" Emma protests. "She's a monster."

"Two points," the lizard says. "First, not only can I do this, it's my job to do this. Second she's not just a monster; she's a royal monster with diplomatic privileges and immunities." He cuffs us. "Now if you'll give me just a moment, I've a few forms to fill out."

"Don't worry," I whisper to Emma, "Captain Valiant will rescue us."

The lizard cop stops abruptly, "Did you say Captain Valiant?"

# Act V, Scene FINAL

As it turns out Agent Scary Lizard is a huge fan of Captain Valiant and rushed us all off to go find and meet him. It doesn't take too long to track him down. We just go towards the greatest concentration of destruction. Valiant is posing on top of a fallen building alongside Chalk while No Name snaps photos for a future scrapbook. Jimmy is tinkering around with a broken pirate-bot, and Robots is nearby watching it all.

Valiant grins wide when he sees us, "Victor, Lieutenant! Wonderful to see you both."

"Actually," Sera's voice says, "it's me, Emma."

"I see," Valiant looks worried, "is the Lieutenant…dead?"

"Nah, she's just unconscious. She'll be fine. I can actually feel her coming to."

"Then it was a most *valiant* victory," Valiant says. The lizard man giggles giddily. "And who might you be?"

"Who, me?" the lizard asks. "I'm Agent Klyzzzzt of the Inter-Galactic Legislative Omnipresent Operative, captain. And I am a *huge* fan."

"It's always a pleasure to meet a fan, Mr. Klyzzzzt," Valiant flashes his most valiant smile.

"I've read all of your books, sir. This is a true honor."

"I don't doubt it. Often I fantasize about being able to be someone else just so that I could meet myself in person. But might I ask why you have two of my friends handcuffed?"

"They were caught assaulting inter-galactic royalty with the perceived intent to murder," the space cop informs.

"Ah, but did they tell you that all of this destruction is due to the princess and we were only trying to stop it?" Valiant inquires.

"Yeah, and she killed me," Emma say indignantly.

The lizard eyes her, "You look fine to me."

"It's a borrowed body, Agent," says Valiant, "I assure you. In fact the list of offences perpetrated by Candy Princess includes murder, kidnapping, conspiracy to animate a city and failure to remember to carry her toothbrush at all times."

"No!" cries the lizard. Valiant nods. "But sir, I'm sorry to say that with all the amnesty laws it would be nearly impossible to get those charges to stick. And assaulting a beloved princess is still the legislatures most frowned upon infraction. Even with your word backing these two, the counsel would be remiss to overlook the chance to try them. You know how they can be with Courtroom Theater. I'm afraid there's nothing I can do."

"Such a shame," I hear the Dread Space Pirate chuckle under his breath.

"Wait," I say, "I've got an idea. What if we turn over the Dread Space Pirate Robots?"

"You wouldn't," Robots sneers.

"He's right there," I point to him. The lizard looks to Valiant who reassures him it is indeed the infamous space pirate. Robots tries to run, but the Klyzzzzt is far too fast.

"After all that we've been through," Robots looks at me, wounded.

"Dude, you're an asshole," I say.

"Touché."

"So are we free?" I ask.

"I'm pretty sure the legislature will be happy to pin everything on the Dread Space Pirate, and I'll probably get a commendation, so yeah you're free."" He removes our cuffs. We begin to walk away when Emma stops.

"Hold on a sec," she says, turning to Candy Princess, "I just have to ask you something."

"Is it 'Can we be friends again'?" Candy says. "Because the answer is yes!"

"Yeah, no," says Emma, "I just need to know…why New York?"

"Oh that's easy! My daddy used to tell me a story about a great and powerful man of marshmallow who once came to this city only to be brutally murdered."

"You can't be serious."

"I know, isn't it just terrible to think about!"

Emma takes this as her cue to exit. Of course, I follow her.

Sera's body looks exhausted.

"Hey," I say.

"Sera's pretty much awake now," Emma tells me. "I can feel myself slipping away. I think I'll have to go soon."

"Oh," I say.

She touches my face gently and sighs, "Sera would kill me if I did this."

"Huh?"

"But what the hell, I'm already dead," she kisses me. Passionately. Then she puts Sera's lips to my ear and whispers "see you soon" before kissing me again.

A second later her lips freeze. I open my eyes to see Sera looking back at me. She breaks our lip-lock.

"Hi," I say.

She punches me, knocking me on my ass, "Never do that again!" She then kneels beside me and embraces me. "But thanks for saving me."

"No problem, buddy," I say. My face hurts.

"I'm, uh, I'm gonna go let the captain know I'm okay," she rushes off towards Valiant. I sit alone for a few minutes before Agent Klyzzzt takes the opportunity to approach me.

"Excuse me," he says, "Victor is it? Her highness would like a word with you before we head off to the embassies."

I'm too tired to argue so I just head back over Candy Princess' way. She's almost entirely healed now. If not for her burnt and tattered dress you couldn't even tell anything had happened to her.

"Are you mad at me?" she asks coyly.

"Yeah," I say.

She frowns, "I really am sorry about killing Emma and drugging you for sex. You're just so handsome!"

"I know."

"But guess what?" she perks up. "I get to go be a big important government person. It sounds like soooo much fun! I'll make it up to you by making Victor friendly laws, okay?"

"Sure," I say, "why not."

"Okay, I've got to go now," she tells me before yelling, "bye everyone! Let's keep in touch! Oh wait, Chalk!"

Chalk skips over to us.

"Would you like to come along and be my deputy ambassador?" Chalk turns his face to me, showing off only a giant question mark.

"It's up to you, pal," I say, "but it might be a good idea to have someone keeping an eye on Candy. Besides, the government could probably use *a little heart*. Ha! Anybody?!" I offer my hand up and Chalk doesn't leave me hangin', doing some wicked gymnastic move off the near by rubble in order to high five me. He runs over to Candy Princess, a big smiley face plastered on his front. He waves goodbye while I wave back, and he and Candy—along with Agent Lizard—

328

dematerialize.

I'll miss that giant tiny heart.

Since I'm not too interested in talking to anyone right now, I stand around kicking rubble for a while. Eventually, I hear some rustling nearby and I decide to investigate. When I find the culprit behind it I immediately call over Captain Valiant.

"What is it, Victor?" he asks.

"I've got someone I'd like you to meet," I hand him a presumably homeless kitten. Valiant's eyes light up.

"What's her name?"

"That's up to you," I tell him.

"I think," he starts, "I think I'll call her Gumdrop. Do you mind if I go introduce her to the Lieutenant?" I shake my head, and Valiant head off towards Sera. "Oh Gumdrop, we are going to have such amazing *adventures.*" I stroll over towards Jimmy, who's still messing around with a broken robot.

"Hey," I say.

"Hey," he says back, "Emma's gone huh?"

"Yeah. Where's everyone else?"

Jimmy looks around, trying to figure exactly who I'm talking about, "Well, Donna and The Roboracle took off for some privacy."

"Gross."

"Ha, yeah. The rest of the Immoral Many flew off after that, and Entheus said something about needing to fulfill his destiny as the champion of Anexia. But he did say to tell you thanks for your words of inspiration."

"I do like being thanked," I say. "So what are you planning to do now?"

"I was thinking I'd keep travelling with Sera and Captain Valiant, but," he looks off longingly in Valiant and Sera's direction, "I

329

don't know."

"Why?" I ask.

"It's just…do you think Sera might maybe like me?"

"Well, you aren't exactly *my* type, Jimmy."

"I knew it! It's my face isn't it? How could she ever be with someone who looks like this?"

"Jim, buddy, I say this with all sincerity. Your face is half skeleton. It's by far the coolest thing about you."

"Really?!"

"Yeah, you should totally go for it. Besides, Sera's tough. She can protect you once I'm gone. In fact, I really should get going. Do you know if there's a pharmacy around here?"

"Huh?" Jimmy wonders.

"Forget it, I think I've found the remains of one," I say. Amidst the rubble I find the mother load. Pills of every damn color of the rainbow. I scoop up two handfuls, making sure to get some of each color. I figure the more colorful they are the faster this'll work.

And I shove them all down my throat.

"Jesus!" Jimmy shrieks. "What are you doing?!"

I swallow hard and grin wide, "I'm going straight to Hell."

www.ingramcontent.com/pod-product-compliance
Lightning Source LLC
Chambersburg PA
CBHW020334180626
46812CB00001B/206